KUTIYATTAM

THE HERITAGE THEATRE OF INDIA

Margi Madhu as Ravana.

KUTIYATTAM

THE HERITAGE THEATRE OF INDIA

SUDHA GOPALAKRISHNAN

NIYOGI
BOOKS

For Gopal

Published by

NIYOGI BOOKS
D-78, Okhla Industrial Area, Phase-I
New Delhi-110 020, India

Tel: 91-11-26816301, 49327000
Fax: 91-11-26810483, 26813830

email: niyogibooks@gmail.com
www.niyogibooks.com

Editors: Navkala Roy, Ritu Khanna

Design: Write Media

ISBN: 978-81-89738-82-2

Year of Publication: 2011

Printed at: Niyogi Offset Pvt. Ltd., New Delhi, India

Contents

Introduction

This book took a long time coming. It is the result of years of conversations with Kutiyattam performers and experts, visits to repertories and watching scores of performances all over Kerala. Considered a complex, inflexible and ancient art form requiring considerable patience and time at your disposal for a fair understanding, Kutiyattam has a way of growing on you. It is addictive enough to never to let you out of its spell for life. In early 1970, a Kutiyattam performance was held in Thiruvananthapuram by a troupe consisting of Paimkulam Rama Chakyar and a few young students who were being trained by the Chakyar at Kerala Kalamandalam. The Kutiyattam School at Kerala Kalamandalam was started in 1965 under the leadership of Rama Chakyar who had trained a group of talented young students. One of them gave a spellbinding performance of 'Sikhini Salabham' to a limited group of art enthusiasts; it was an instant success with discerning audiences in Thiruvananthapuram. This became the inspiration for the establishment of Margi, an institution devoted to the revitalisation of classical arts in Kerala. Founded in 1970, by a group of art aficionados including Appukkuttan Nair, K.V. Kochaniyan and my father T.N.N. Bhattathiripad, as a Society for the revival of classical arts, Margi began with a limited agenda. It brought several classical Indian dances and music styles to perform in Thiruvananthapuram. The first Kutiyattam festival was organised by Margi in 1970 followed by several others. In 1974, a Kathakali School was started and subsequently, the mandate was enlarged to include Kutiyattam, with the establishment of the Kutiyattam School in 1981. In the initial years, with the association of Ammannur Madhava Chakyar as the first Guru along with Moozhikkulam Kochukuttan Chakyar as resident teacher, a new generation of performers began shaping up in Margi.

I discovered Kutiyattam by chance. Unlike Kathakali, Kutiyattam was not well known even in Kerala during the seventies. Those days, I was a student of Kathakali, being trained under Guru Mamkulam Vishnu Namboothiri and not willing to miss an opportunity to attend every performance I could manage to reach. My parents, given their own love for the traditional arts, actively encouraged me in my pursuit. The establishment of Margi gave me an opportunity to watch several Kutiyattam performances, opening a capacious wonderland of experience. My involvement with Kutiyattam at this stage in Margi ranged from sitting through long hours of training schedules, persisting through performance after performance and trying my hand at writing/editing articles for the *Margi*

Facing page: Traditional lamp on the stage in a Kutiyattam performance.

Journal, all of which cumulatively honed my understanding of the intricacies of Kutiyattam. Appukkuttan Nair whom I consider as my mentor fostered my interest with parental care. The topic of our daily discussions over the telephone those days would range from an appreciation of the performance of the Kutiyattam we watched the previous day, to his theoretical analysis of the subtleties of Bharata's *Natya Sastra*.

An investigation into shared themes and recurrent narrative patterns in Indian and Western theatre gave me the impetus to pursue a doctoral degree. It was a comparative study of the comic mode in Bhasa and Shakespeare under the supervision of the scholar-poet K. Ayyappa Paniker. Though admitting to important differences between the two traditions, the effort was to find common paradigms of experience in engaging with the comic aspect (*hasya rasa*) in drama, through multiple modes of laughter and adopting an affirmative approach to life, as well as through embodying a spirit of humane tolerance that could be termed 'comedic gladness'. Apart from a textual analysis of the plays, my doctoral thesis also traced similarities between classical theatres of India such as Kathakali and Kutiyattam and modern experimental theatre in the West. Professor Paniker, who guided my research, also shared his valuable insights on Kutiyattam with me.

Kutiyattam itself was going through a transformation during this time. Freed from its bondage as a temple-oriented art form, it started receiving the attention of theatre enthusiasts and scholars all over India and abroad. Margi along with Kerala Kalamandalam and subsequently Ammannur Chachu Chakyar Smaraka Gurukulam led this change. Kalamandalam, started in 1930 by the great poet Vallathol Narayana Menon and Mukunda Raja for the revival of traditional performing arts, has now become a University. Ammannur Gurukulam, established under the guidance of Ammannur Madhava Chakyar, took up the cause of training young students, who have now matured as professional actors of Kutiyattam. By this time, the understanding was getting stronger that Kutiyattam, while it represents a pan-Indian aesthetic tradition represented by the *Natya Sastra*, was also largely different and independent from that which is revealed in the postulates prescribed in the text. While the *Natya Sastra* lays more emphasis on a broadly *lokadharmi* mode of *abhinaya*, Kutiyattam with its insistence on elaboration in acting

An episode from the Ramayana story: Margi Madhu as Lakshmana addresses Sita in Mayasitankam.

and other details of theatric representation, is firmly rooted in *natyadharmi*. As a theatric tradition that is rooted in Kerala, it evolved as much from the existing aesthetic tradition with shared cultural traits, reflected in its physical aspects such as costume, make-up and stage arrangements, to the introduction of the *vidushaka* who speaks in Malayalam for the benefit of local audiences.

Kalamandalam Sivan as Ravana, the King of Lanka, in his regal glory. Ravana is an important character in Kutiyattam performance.

Kutiyattam was fast moulding to suit the new generation of viewers with keen interest but less time at hand. New experiments with existing choreographic texts led to adaptations. Long, drawn-out *abhinaya* explicating passages after passages was giving way to tightly edited, dramatically intense shorter episodes that would appeal to an eclectic viewership. Gurus got busy consulting old performance manuals to re-invent vanished plays. Nangiarkoothu, the performance exclusively by women who were marginalised for centuries, started gaining more prominence. The fact that Nangiarkoothu could be presented as distinct, self-contained units of a single narrative (revolving on the story of Krishna) made them more appealing.

Choreographers across the world and within India started realising the potential of Kutiyattam to revitalise their own theatre grammar. With the recognition that traditional theatre can be effectively used to revitalise contemporary theatre, playwrights such as Kavalam Narayana Panikkar have attempted to explore indigenous traditions of theatre. This 'going back to the roots' to draw on the indigenous theatrical heritage has, in fact, become a movement in post-colonial Indian theatre that manifested itself as a desire to reject an overarching Western theatre idiom. Kutiyattam schools started getting invitations from all over the world for conducting performances and workshops. As Paimkulam Rama Chakyar put it succinctly, 'Those days, there was no value for a Chakyar outside the temple complex; now everyone wants Kutiyattam.' These words were proving prophetic. By the nineties, Kutiyattam artists were travelling all over India and abroad seeking new opportunities and audiences. Fortuitously, Margi got an invitation through Milena Salvini of Mandapa to perform in Paris in late 1999. As Vice-President, Margi, I led the troupe and in Paris, Norika Aikawa, the Director of the newly-constituted

Ravana confronting Jatayu in anger in Jatayuvadham.

Intangible Heritage Section in UNESCO, happened to see the performance. At her suggestion, Margi compiled a nomination dossier for the inclusion of Kutiyattam for the proclamation of the newly-announced UNESCO 'Masterpiece of the Oral and Intangible Heritage of Humanity'. The dossier included a film documentation of Kutiyattam done expertly by Adoor Gopalakrishnan and a compilation of the written document by me with the support of Rama Iyer of Margi. The nomination, fielded by the Ministry of Culture, was accepted by UNESCO and, along with eighteen cultural

Bali in the throes of death in Balivadham.

expressions from other parts of the world, Kutiyattam was proclaimed by UNESCO as 'Masterpiece'. It was indeed a proud moment for the Kutiyattam community.

The impact of the UNESCO proclamation was momentous for Kutiyattam. The recognition has brought more visibility and respect for the art in its own site. Kutiyattam, which was once held as being protracted and obscure, has now become more accessible. The Government has come forward with funding support and there is considerable re-awakening of interest; new schools have mushroomed and funding opportunities have increased. New adaptations of old choreographies have served to revitalise Kutiyattam from within and a wider viewership is constantly challenging it to become more accessible.

What does the future hold for Kutiyattam? Unlike in those days, Kutiyattam is not the esoteric domain of just a few people. At this point one can only say that this immense inheritance is certain to get the attention it deserves. There may be reformulations in its format and content and new interpretations in keeping with changed values and needs. Safeguarding the art is a shared responsibility that needs the engagement of the society and government, Kutiyattam enthusiasts, theatre practitioners and academia. Above all, to keep it alive and breathing, we need young people to nurture it with commitment and passion. After the departure of the trio of Mani Madhava Chakyar, Paimkulam Rama Chakyar and Ammannur Madhava Chakyar, a new generation of younger gurus and performers have now established themselves. One has only to watch the blooming of the young Kapila, a student of Ammannur Madhava Chakyar, redefining the boundaries of the form, to feel reassured that the future of Kutiyattam is safe in the hands of the youth of India. I am happy that my own daughter Aditi is trying to combine her legal profession with her training in Kutiyattam. And many more like her from India and abroad are now taking to the study of Kutiyattam.

Tradition in Theatre

In terms of international theatre history, Kutiyattam can well claim the greatest antiquity, as it is believed to date back to about two millennia. Kutiyattam is a form of Sanskrit theatre that draws on the plays of eminent Sanskrit playwrights of India. There is a rich corpus of plays by dramatists such as Asvaghosha, Bhasa, Sudraka, Kalidasa, Harsha, Bodhayana, Mahendra-vikramavarman and others, which has come down to us from different historical periods from the first to the seventh centuries AD. However, there are no details available regarding the exact staging of these Sanskrit plays. The evidence of a live performance practice in ancient India is reconstructed from history, from references available in Sanskrit plays and from Bharata's *Natya Sastra*, the canonical text on dance and drama (dating roughly between 200 BC and AD 200). While there is no record of an unbroken performance tradition of Sanskrit plays elsewhere in India, a living tradition of theatre surviving through centuries in the southernmost tip of India is fascinating.

Kutiyattam, widely performed in Kerala, is a unique phenomenon in the history of Sanskrit theatre in India for having survived several centuries with its own codes and conventions of performance. The practice of Kutiyattam, though it broadly follows the abstract rules of aesthetics described in the *Natya Sastra*, has its own distinctive characteristics in terms of theatric conventions and method of acting. It appears that the conventions of this theatre form were crystallised as much from the existing texts on dramaturgy and rules of aesthetics, as the artistic practices of a vibrant indigenous tradition of dance and drama. Kutiyattam is an example of a mode of theatre that follows its own aesthetic and performance principles with a firm basis on the spirit of a pan-Indian dramatic tradition, represented by the theories formulated in the *Natya Sastra*. It is a form of theatre that due to the high degree of stylisation and the elaboration in acting presupposes a certain knowledge of its theatric grammar from the performer and the viewer.

In the olden days, Kutiyattam was not accessible to anyone except *brahmins* and other upper castes. Until recently, it was restricted to the temple as a sacred art, which was a major reason for its exclusivity. Another reason for the restrictive appeal of Kutiyattam is the highly complicated, long-drawn-out acting method and theatric grammar, which is understood only to the select few who are conversant with its codes and conventions. The differences of Kutiyattam from the practice described in

Facing page: Bali in a furious mood on hearing Sugriva beckoning him to a duel.

the *Natya Sastra* are so marked that it has baffled theatre enthusiasts. This is perhaps partly the reason why scholars have tended to explain it away as an anomaly, at best as a regional adaptation or variation.

What, then, are these special characteristics of this unique theatre form? Kutiyattam is traditionally performed by the community of the Chakyars, male actors, and Nangiars, women performers, as a hereditary profession. The Chakyars are assisted by the Nambiars who play on the drum called *mizhavu* in theatre houses called *koothambalams*. Kutiyattam is an inclusive term that refers to more than one art form—apart from Kutiyattam, the mode of theatre in which the Chakyars and the Nangiars take part together, it also integrates *koothu*. The word *koothu*, which in Malayalam means acting, is divided into three allied arts—Prabandhakkoothu, Nangiarkoothu and Kutiyattam. Among these, Nangiarkoothu is the theatre exclusively performed by the Nangiars, and Prabandhakkoothu or Chakyar *koothu*, as it is otherwise known, is the verbal narrative drama of the Chakyars.

The prefix *kuti* in Malayalam stands for 'combined' or 'together', and *attam* means 'acting'; therefore, the word *kutiyattam* means 'combined acting'. Simply put, it is a theatre in which several characters come together on the stage. Apart from this primary meaning, perhaps there are several other layers of meaning embedded in the term *kuti*. It is a combination of elements drawn from the local Dravidian and the pan-Indian performance traditions. It integrates the histrionic aspect of elaborate acting of the hero and the other main characters based on classical Sanskrit and the verbal narration of the *vidushaka*, the comic character, in the regional language of Malayalam. Therefore, the performance is a combination of Sanskrit and Malayalam.

The term *kuti* in Malayalam also means 'prolonged' or 'extended'. If this meaning is applied to the word 'kutiyattam', then the term refers to one of the essential features of the art form. Kutiyattam is a theatre that extends the scope of the dramatic text and enlarges the performance score through stylised acting and elaboration of action, to a range and magnitude that goes well beyond what was imagined by the playwright. In the process of creating a world of make-believe in front of the spectator, through the powers of his creative imagination and histrionic skill, the actor magnifies the action by redefining the scope as well as ascribing new meanings into the narrative and reinterpreting it. The ideal spectator is expected to be thoroughly knowledgeable about the theatre grammar of the play and there is an imaginative collaboration between the actor and the audience, to create meaning in the theatre. The relationship of mutuality between the actor and the spectator enhances the meaning of *kuti*. In its essence, Kutiyattam is a theatre that constantly redefines the roles and relationships of the playwright with the actor on the one hand and that of the actor with the spectator on the other.

The Chakyars, the traditional actors of Kutiyattam, belong to an intermediate rank in the caste hierarchy and follow a matriarchial lineage, the rights passing from the maternal uncle to the nephew. The term *chakyar* is believed to have come from the word *slakhyar* (which means the adept and, therefore, praiseworthy), indicating their proficiency in histrionic art and verbal narration. Another version relates it to *chakaiyan*, which refers to a person employed in the practice of dance and drama. In yet another version, the word has a Buddhist reference and is derived from *sakyar*, a term referring to the Buddhist mendicants in

A woman performer has a prominent position in Kutiyattam.

ancient India and reveals the popularity of the performing arts during that time.

In the early days, there were eighteen traditional families that were devoted to the practice of Kutiyattam as a vocation. Now the number has dwindled and even among existing members, only a few have taken to this art professionally. Acting rights in different temples were assigned to different Chakyar families where the performances took place through an annual calendar. The performers regarded the art both as a ritual duty and as a sacred offering. The professional artistic activity of the Chakyars and the Nangiars were organised in such a way that it fitted well with the tradition of temple worship. For the actors, the attachment to the temple took care of their daily expenses, leaving them leisure time to devote to the honing of their histrionic skills and passing them on to the next generation. The temple, through generous gifts of land and stipend for individual performances, supported them. However, with the crumbling of the feudal order and the freedom from the rigidity of the temple complex, Kutiyattam became accessible to a wider audience and motivated people from other castes to train for it.

Koothambalams are permanent theatre structures attached to some of the major temples of Kerala. In the ancient days, though folk theatre was performed on the streets, classical theatre always had a fixed venue, such as theatre houses, temples, music halls and courts. *Koothambalams* are now the only instance of the survival of permanent structures for performances anywhere in India. Until recently, the

Sugriva in Balivadham*–the battle between him and Bali is dramatically depicted in Kutiyattam performances.*

staging of Kutiyattam was strictly limited to these theatres. If the temple did not have a *koothambalam*, the performance took place in the big hall attached to the temple.

The design of a *koothambalam* is in keeping with the architectural heritage of Kerala. Its dimension and plan are perhaps based on the descriptions given in texts such as the *Tantrasamuchaya* and the *Silparatna*, which belong to Kerala. All the extant *koothambalams* have common features, though there are variations in the size and ground plan. Kutiyattam is a mode of theatre that was institutionalised in the temple, and thus became integrated with worship in the temple, with an absolute restriction from stepping outside. Naturally it incorporated rituals associated with religious worship in its domain. There are elaborate rituals associated with Kutiyattam in terms of its make-up, orchestra, stage properties, stage organisation and the performance itself. Tampering with the codes and conventions was believed to be sacrilegious. The drama symbolically represents a visual sacrifice or *chakshusha yajna* and, therefore, each component has a sacred association. For performances that were traditionally conducted inside the temple theatre, the Nambiar initiates the proceedings by lighting a lamp in the dressing room and on the stage with a wick procured from the sanctum of the temple. This act consecrates the theatre for the duration of the play. The lamp on the stage represents the presence of divine spectators on the stage. The actor, supposed to be an initiate who has completed his *upanayana* (sacred thread) ceremony, purifies himself through a ritual bath. He then takes blessings of the temple priest, accepts the ritual cloth from him, contemplates God and his masters, and ties a sacred red cloth on his forehead. This simple act of tying the cloth is a bridge that sets him apart from the domain of human action. He goes through a transformation of personality and, any event of a personal nature, even the death of a near relative, is not supposed to touch (or pollute) him till the performance is over.

At the start of the show, the Nambiar takes his seat behind the large wooden case in which the *mizhavu* is placed, and the Nangiar seats herself on the right side of the stage. The Nambiar plays a special pattern of drumming on the *mizhavu*, called *mizhavu occhappeduttal*—the sounding of the *mizhavu*—followed by another rhythmical pattern called *goshthi kottal*. The Nangiar sings propitiatory songs or *akkitta* celebrating the gods Ganapati, Saraswati and Siva. The Nambiar gets up from his seat, offers water and flowers on the stage, and ceremoniously chants a quatrain or *sloka* for invoking the deities. This ritual, known as *arangutali* or the sprinkling of holy water on the stage, has the effect of symbolically cleansing the stage and transforming it into a sacred space and time, fit for the gods. From this ritual onwards, each act is directed towards the efficacy of the performance through the transcendence of the mundane, reaching out to the cosmic powers represented in the play. Rituals pervade the action till the end of the play, when the last actor takes off his headgear, sprinkles water on himself, turns around in style, puts out the fire by extinguishing the wicks and prostrates on the stage.[1] The process, worked out carefully, resembles the rituals of Vedic sacrifice, establishing the thesis that theatre grew out of sacrificial rituals.[2]

The typology of the plays included in the Kutiyattam repertoire has the *vyayoga*, *prakarana*, *nataka* and *prahasana* varieties, which are listed among the ten forms of drama in Sanskrit texts on dramaturgy. Kutiyattam includes the plays of almost all the major playwrights in Sanskrit. However, notable exceptions are Kalidasa and Bhavabhuti. As Kutiyattam prefers minimal text with more dramatic and less descriptive potential, Kalidasa's language, with its rich poetic nuances, does not lend very easily to its choreographic treatment. The most frequently used plays in Kutiyattam have been Bhasa's *Pratijnayaugandharayana*, *Pratimanataka*, *Abhishekanataka*, *Balacharita*,

[1] Mani Madhava Chakyar in his 'Introduction' to *Natyakalpadrumam* has compared a Kutiyattam performance to a Vedic sacrifice, by bringing out the close affinity between their rituals. 1975. *Natyakalpadrumam*, pp. viii-ix. Kottyam: National Book Stall.

[2] Byrski, Christopher. 1974. *Concept of Ancient Indian Theatre*, p. 51. New Delhi: Munshiram Manoharlal.

Facing page: Margi Sathi in Nangiarkoothu, the solo-act performed exclusively by women.

Avimaraka, *Charudatta*, *Dutavakya*, *Karnabhara*, *Dutaghatotkacha*, *Urubhanga* and *Madhyama-vyayoga*; Harsha's *Nagananda*; Saktibhadra's *Ascharyachudamani*; Kulase-kharavarman's *Subhadradhananjaya* and *Tapatisamvarana*; Neelakantha's *Kalyanasaugandhika*; Bodhayana's *Bhagavadajjukiya* and Mahendravikrama-varman's *Mattavilasa*.

A striking feature of Kutiyattam is that it bases its performance not on the full text of a Sanskrit play, but on the individual acts. These acts in their treatment become full-fledged plays complete in themselves, with their own names and performance score, stretching for several days. For example, 'Mantrankam' is the third act of Bhasa's *Pratijnayaugandharayana* and 'Anguliyankam' is the sixth act of Saktibhadra's *Ascharyachudamani*.

Among the corpus of Kutiyattam plays based on Sanskrit texts only a few exist today and the enactment details of some are not available any more. For example, only the First Act of *Subhadradhananjaya* was active on the stage until recently. In *Pratijnayaugandharayana*, only the third act, 'Mantrankam', is enacted. One of the most popular plays on the Kutiyattam stage noted for its aesthetic appeal and histrionic potential is Saktibhadra's *Ascharyachudamani*, in seven acts. Acts such as 'Surpanakhankam', 'Asokavanikankam' and 'Anguliyankam' are still favourites with the audience. Bhasa's plays have also survived down the centuries in the live performance of Kutiyattam. At a time when his plays were not available to the rest of the world, the Chakyars had them in their possession, though they were known by the individual acts of the plays, rather than in their full form as complete plays. The retrieval of Bhasa's plays by Ganapati Sastri in 1912 from Kerala and the popularity of the plays on the Kerala stage have made some scholars surmise that Bhasa belonged to Kerala. It is surprising that some other great playwrights such as Kalidasa and Bhavabhuti do not appear in Kutiyattam. The brevity of the dialogue, open-ended language and the scope for the actor to deliver an elaborate presentation may be the reason for Bhasa's popularity in Kutiyattam, as against the elegant poetic richness of Kalidasa.[3]

Even *Mrcchakatika* and *Ratnavali*, which were popular elsewhere in the country, do not belong to the Kutiyattam repertoire, perhaps for the same reasons. *Mattavilasa* has now become confined to the status of a ritual, a votive offering to the deity, with only the ritualistic portions in current use. There is evidence of the enactment of the one-act plays of *Dutavakya* and *Dutaghatotkacha* till recent times in temples.

The play in Kutiyattam provides only the bare minimal text for the actor, to elaborate into multiple meanings and imaginative improvisation. The text is only 'pre-text' and the production of the play depends on 'subtext' provided by the stage manual. The performance of Kutiyattam was codified in ancient times through elaborate manuals of performance called *attaprakarams* and *kramadeepikas*, which have been preserved in Chakyar families and handed down from generation to generation through a master-disciple tradition. The

[3] In a telling image, D. Appukkuttan Nair compares Kalidasa's plays to a bouquet of fully blossomed flowers, which spread their sweet fragrance but have to wither because they have reached the pinnacle of beauty. In contrast, Bhasa's plays are like the seeds of the flower, which the actor has to sow and nurture for the flowers to come out! 'Kutiyattam and Bhasa', *Sangeet Natak Special Issue on Kutiyattam*, Nos. 111-114, pp. 190-194.

The dramatic entry of Surpanakha as Lalita in Surpanakhankam.

theatric action in Kutiyattam is based on these choreographic texts that detail every nuance of action and interpretation of the text. In fact, these are the real performance texts in Kutiyattam, for the words in the play are only a springboard for the actor to take a leap into the world of imagined reality. These stage manuals, of uncertain dates and in all probability belonging to divergent periods in history, were jealously guarded by the Chakyar community and kept as secret documents until recently. These manuals contain all the logistic, organisational and theatric aspects of Kutiyattam and it is from these that one can reconstruct the history and method of acting in Kutiyattam in the olden days. While a *kramadeepika* is an account of practical matters such as stage organisation, stage production, use of costumes and payment of the artists, an *attaprakaram* vividly describes the method of action, movement, recitative mode, gesture, elaboration and every other detail of a Kutiyattam performance.

Kutiyattam is also the art of elaboration of action through extending the performance score to unbelievable heights of imaginative fancy. In this method of action, the poetic quality of a Sanskrit play, with multiple layers of meaning, figures of speech and oblique or obscure expression, receives complete justification. Situations of poetic richness and dramatic potential are elaborated in Kutiyattam to unravel the layers of meaning embedded in the text of the play. The richness of poetry slows down the pace of action. The focus of a Kutiyattam play is to enlarge a movement, an idea and an emotion, by exploring the full potential of the situation and bringing its *rasa* (divine nectar) to ripeness. The extension of the performance text in Kutiyattam is so elaborate that a play, depending on the need of the occasion, can stretch up to forty nights or more to complete the action. 'Anguliyankam', with Hanuman as the only character on the stage, takes about forty-one days to complete. The context of this performance is Hanuman's crossing of the ocean and discovery of Sita in the Asoka Garden in Lanka. It takes place in the form of Hanuman reporting to Sita the events that occurred in Rama's life after his parting with her, to Hanuman crossing the ocean to find her. In the process, Hanuman describes several related incidents, such as Ravana's conquest of *svarga* (heaven), the descent of the divine River Ganga to the earth and the birth of Hanuman. The performance text, replete with interpolated verses from other sources and from previous acts of the play, becomes the real play-text, providing the actor with immense possibilities of displaying his histrionic talent.

Another instance of the elaborate depiction of verbal skills could be seen in 'Mantrankam'. A speech-oriented play with the *vidushaka* as the only character on the stage, with detailed narration of the story and potential to outsource related material from a wide variety of other texts, 'Mantrankam' takes about forty nights to complete its narration. The performance of the Ramayana is another example of this elaborate presentation. The entire story of the Ramayana is in the Kutiyattam artist's reportoire by integrating three plays—Saktibhadra's *Ascharyachudamani* and Bhasa's *Pratimanataka* and *Abhishekanataka*.

A scene from Balivadham. *In Kutiyattam, the movements of the body and the hand gestures are highly codified.*

This cycle of plays, confined to the temples of Kerala, has twenty-one acts and takes a full year in its enactment, perhaps one of the longest performances in the history of world theatre!

Kutiyattam, Nangiarkoothu and Prabandhakkoothu are primarily theatres of the actor in the sense that he has complete freedom to go ahead and creatively interpret his role. In Prabandhakkoothu, theatric communication depends on the verbal skill or *vachikabhinaya* of the actor. The actor in the guise of the *vidushaka* holds the stage for days by narrating stories and anecdotes, interpreting events, making fun of the audience and the characters and, above all, imparting information on a wide range of topics through the medium of humour.

In Kutiyattam and Nangiarkoothu, the theatric communication happens primarily with the aid of body kinetics or *angikabhinaya*, assisted by orchestral support. The kinetic patterns in Kutiyattam involve dance movements, a codified language of gestures and an extremely refined pattern of facial expressions. While the movements of the body and the hand gestures are highly codified, the face, with its delicately wrought eye, cheek, brow and lip movements, and the elasticity of all its muscles, is the main field of action in the theatric communication of Kutiyattam.

The actor in Kutiyattam perfects the art of facial expression to reach unimaginable heights. The movements are so subtly worked out that it can convey any emotion to the spectator. The stylised acting through *netrabhinaya* or the manipulation of the eyes is of vital significance. Perhaps the eyes are the most important element in theatric action in Kutiyattam, for their movements and power of expression are so refined, pervasive and wide-ranging that they can portray any situation, activity, thought or feeling.

A 'good' actor is backed by a lifetime of dedicated pursuit of the art, the capacity to draw upon this proficiency or experience at will, and the special gift to go beyond it when the situation demands. Rather than a mere performer of the role assigned to him, the actor has the status of a *vyakhata*, an interpreter who unravels the layers of meaning accrued in the text. For explicating an idea to its fullest capacity, the actor slows down the pace of acting by using different devices. Acting involves not a straightforward enactment, but a circumlocution as well as a deliberate extension of the action. This includes going back and forth in time sequence, giving different (sometimes contrary) interpretations, indulging in long digressions and recreating stories that are not part of the main story. It also means repeating the narration in different acting modes, visualising different situations and so on. This method of convoluted acting is perhaps in keeping with the Indian oral tradition of cyclical narration, where events are narrated not in a linear manner, but through a process of spreading/extending in all directions, like the branches of a tree (*sakhachankramanam*). While interspersing different stories and events, the core of the narrative is not affected nor does it register any change in the axis of time. With the barest outline of the text and the guidelines given by the performance text, the actor can approach the action in his own manner. He draws upon each nuance, each line of the text and each situation to explore its full potential, building on the main text with the power of his imagination. He amplifies action through skilful improvisation during the high points of the drama.

Facing page: The hero in a virulent mood, eloquently expressed by facial and hand movements.

Sita, Lakshmana, Rama and Surpanakha in Surpanakhankam.

The theatric improvisation is effected through several methods in Kutiyattam—rituals and conventions, stylisation in speech and movement, use of orchestra to enhance histrionic action, multi-layering of the text with detailed references from other sources, non-linear sequencing of dramatic action and the deliberate amplification of events and sequences through the theatric technique called *pakarnnattam* (the actor assuming the role of another or more than one character consecutively and/or shifting roles without any change in costume). *Pakarnnattam* is a unique meta-theatric device perfected in Kutiyattam, which gives immense scope for the actor to call upon his histrionic and imaginative faculties. The actor steps out of his role and, through the stream of consciousness of the protagonist, assumes the roles, or rather projects his dramatic persona to all the other characters imagined. According to the skill and imagination of the actor, these roles get embellished and elaborated in the context or scene represented. There are no set boundaries for the actor and the action can be stretched to any limits, provided the sense of immediacy is sustained for the audience. The actor has no dramatic empathy with the role/roles presented, for it is only a 'performance', with the actor narrating the events and projecting the roles played on the stage. Thus drama assumes an unparalleled elasticity here and acting establishes the illusory nature of play—drama is pretence; to see it is to recognise and accept the pretence. The action is not addressed to dramatic credibility or logical reason, but to a world of fantasy and meta-theatric imagination.

The degree of formalism that characterises the classical theatre of Kutiyattam is higher than any other art in Kerala. Kutiyattam appeals to people who have prerequisite knowledge of this art form. The interest of these spectators in watching a play is not to unravel the story or the unfolding of the action, for the spectator is familiar with the story, the poetic text, the course of action and even the performance score. They look out for how each context, verse and word is elaborated by the actor through the manipulation of the body, facial expressions and gesture patterns. The experience is new each time, because every single performance is a recreation and no performance happens twice. The knowledgeable spectator is a creative participant of the action, for the creation of this world of make-believe is a collaborate activity between the actor and the spectator. The ideal spectators of Kutiyattam are cultivated theatregoers who usually occupy the front rows, concentrating on each nuance and expression on the face of the actor. The play does not call for total empathy either from the actor or the spectator, for they are both aware that what is presented is the representation of imagined action. The critical distance, closer to the concept of 'alienation effect'[4] in Bertolt Brecht's Epic Theatre, is in any case inevitable in this mode of theatre, where the actor takes on different roles while retaining the guise of only a single character.

The success of a Kutiyattam performance is in the creation of reciprocity between the actor and the spectator. The high level of awareness expected from the spectator in Kutiyattam is perhaps the reason why it has had a limited appreciation base. Ideally, there should be an audience of not more than a hundred people and only those seated in front can grasp the subtleties of action. However, in the past, a balance was maintained by introducing more popular elements such as the *vidushaka*. Unlike the other characters in the play who base their histrionic action on the Sanskrit passages,

Actors manipulate the body, facial expressions and gesture patterns–a scene from Balivadham.

the *vidushaka* has his own Prakrit speech and the freedom to speak in the regional language, Malayalam. By his witticisms and jibes at the hero and the audience, he evokes laughter on the stage and subjects himself, the characters in the story and the world around him to ridicule. This makes him a popular stock figure on the Kutiyattam stage, with access to the spectators. He has the unique capacity to improvise on any topic and elaborate the situation through the power of his expression. In some cases, the *vidushaka*, while using his speech in the play as an anchor, actually spins a world of narrative magic through verses, stories, anecdotes and a discussion of ideas and ideologies, all through the medium of humour.

Early Days

Dance and drama across the world are part of the web of social existence. In India, many streams of dance and drama have existed from ancient times, fulfilling different tastes and needs. Early dance had a strong community base and these were participatory acts in which everyone, irrespective of rank, gender and age, took part. There were also performances that ritualistically invoked deities and offered prayers for the collective good of the community. These dances were part of celebrations connected with seasonal cycles in agrarian communities and were intimately associated with the worship of the forces of nature, ancestors, spirits of death and disease and other guardian deities. In the course of time, some dances lost their collective character to become a source of entertainment and appreciation for a select few, with a strict division between the dancer and the spectator. Dances that were attached to courts and temples flourished with royal patronage and reached a high state of refinement. They began to be performed for an exclusive audience.

There are evidences through history that Sanskrit drama was a live mode of theatre in ancient times. Historians such as Hiuen Tsang and I-Tsing have referred to the enactment of plays by Asvghosha and Harsha. Scholars have traced the origin of theatre in India to a distant past, from the dialogue hymns of the *Rig Veda*, *Nata Sutras* mentioned by Panini, the references in early scriptural and canonical writings, the stage directions and other references regarding enactment provided in the major Sanskrit plays to the *Natya Sastra*. The fact that there is a canonical text such as the *Natya Sastra* codifying the rules of theatre in minute detail is evidence that dance and drama were highly well developed during the time when the text was written. Unfortunately, though the *Natya Sastra* is a veritable encyclopaedia of information relating to music, dance, theatre and aesthetic theory, no information regarding any actual surviving theatrical practice based on the text is available now. The only direct reference to an actual performance is the account given in the text to the first dramatic performance during Indra's banner festival.[5] Apart from this description, which establishes the divine origin of drama, the *Natya Sastra* has an elaborate chapter on *purvaranga* (the preliminaries of a play) and another on

Facing page: A typical Kerala temple; Kutiyattam is a form of theatre that started in the temple and therefore became a part of temple worship.

[5] According to the *Natya Sastra*, drama has a divine origin. The first play was enacted on the day of Indra's banner festival through the 'revealed' wisdom of Bharata as exemplified in the *Natya Sastra*.

theatre houses, which suggest that active stage performances were in vogue during the time.

Exploration into the origins of Kutiyattam takes us to the beginnings of dance and drama in ancient Kerala. Till about the tenth century Kerala was part of the larger Tamil land. The information regarding this period is available from the literature of the Sangam Age. There are differences opinion among scholars regarding the date of Sangam literature, with the time span ranging from 200 BC to AD 500. Sangam poetry has vivid descriptions of the social life during the time. According to *Patittuppattu*, an early Sangam work composed in praise of the kings of the Chera kingdom, the regions known as Kerala today were under the Chera rule. The performing arts seem to have flourished to a great extent during the age. The Chera kings were patrons of art, as is evident from the name Attukottupattu Cheralathan (the Chera king who loved dance, drumming and singing) that was given to one of the kings. There are several references to the performing art form called *koothu* in *Patittuppattu* as well as descriptions of musicians called Panars and dancers called Viralis. Details regarding the costumes worn by the dancers, the musical instruments and other aspects of dance are recorded in Sangam works.

Preliminary rituals in Kutiyattam: the Nambiar on the mizhavu *and the* sutradhara *on the stage.*

Kutiyattam claims an antiquity of about two thousand years, but its origin and early days are shrouded in mystery. There are no clear evidences for reconstructing the history of the art form for the first thousand years and therefore only conjectures are possible. Dance seemed to have been popular with all sections of society right from the early times. The word *koothu*, which was used as a generic term for dance, appears for the first time in Sangam literature. There are references to Tunankaikkoothu, Kuravaikkoothu, Vallikkoothu and Alliyamkoothu, that were popular dances of the time in which men and women took part together. A song in *Patittuppattu* mentions a performance of dancers and musicians in crowded streets in the cities. Female dancers decked in elaborate make-up and beautiful costumes displayed their talent and skill in courts, in front of kings and royal dignitaries. In ancient Kerala, girls from high-ranking families received training in dance, which was held in great esteem. In royal courts, dances were also held as part of festivities

during occasions such as victory in battle. There is a mention of dancers bidding a ceremonious welcome to King Chenkuttuvan when he returned from a trip to the north. Thus there existed two clear streams of dance in early Kerala—one, the popular, participatory dance of the community and the other, formalised, spectacular dance meant for aesthetic enjoyment, which flourished through royal patronage in the courts.

The existence of a mature dance tradition in South India during ancient times is testified by the references in Ilango Adigal's *Silappatikaram*, composed around AD 500. It seems that the codes and conventions of dance and drama were already established during the time of *Silappatikaram*, for it contains detailed descriptions and classifications of the different varieties of songs and dance performed during the time. In *Silappatikaram*, Madhavi, one of the main characters of the story, is a celebrated dancer, and there are references to the various forms of dances prevalent in the Chera kingdom. Apart from the reference to the eleven varieties of dance performed in connection with a festival dedicated to Indra, there are eight kinds of *nadippus* (dramatic actions) associated with *nataka mahilas* (actresses) mentioned in the text. However, there is no exact evidence regarding the staging of drama.

The reference in *Silappatikaram* to Parayur Koothachakkaiyan, who enacted the story of *Tripuradahanam* (Tripura consigned to flames) before the king, has become an evidence for many scholars to ascertain

A *Kutiyattam performance sometimes has several characters on the stage; there are also occasions where a single actor takes on the roles of many characters.*

the antiquity of Kutiyattam. The text mentions that, with his rare skill, the actor depicted simultaneously the vigorous and powerful dance of Siva, 'with the clanging of his anklets, clamouring of the drum on his hands, movement of his eyes and shaking of his matted locks of hair' and the graceful and delicate dance performed by Parvati, 'with the anklets, tiara, ear ornament and waistband remaining silent, the breasts not heaving in excitement or hair in disarray'. From this description, scholars have surmised that Parayur Koothachakkaiyan was from Paravur in Kerala, that he belonged to the Chakyar community and that there was an already well-established tradition of theatre in Kerala by the time of *Silappatikaram*.

Till the seventh century, apart from the local Dravidian culture, Kerala had Buddhist and Jain influences as well. The land was under the rule of several dynasties. The worship of *naga*[6] and *yakshi*[7] prevalent in Kerala right from the early days may have Buddhist and Jain influences. The local inhabitants, consisting of the Kadars, Ullatans, Paniyans and Malayans, depended on nature for their survival. They worshipped the Mother Goddess in her several manifestations, ancestors and other spirits of nature. The songs and dances of Kerala that still survive from the early days reveal some of these customs, habits and community traits. The language of the people was Kodumtamil, a localised variety of the more elite Chentamil. There seemed to have been a strong tradition of art prevalent right from the ancient times, with community dances, the martial arts and ritualistic songs performed on certain occasions in village shrines and households. In fact, some of the dances associated with different communities and other ritualistic performances such as Teyyam, Tira, Padayani, Velakali and Kuthiyottam, which survive

[6] Serpent worship was prevalent in Kerala from ancient times. There are temples dedicated exclusively to serpents, and many households have earmarked land dedicated to the serpent. Some specific rites and rituals for serpent worship are still in practice in Kerala.
[7] According to folk belief in Kerala, *yakshis* are malevolent vamps who in the guise of beautiful women entice unsuspecting men and drink their blood. They are worshipped as a way of appeasement.

today, can be traced to an ancient past. There are dramatic performances such as Vellarinatakam, Kakkarissinatakam and Porattunatakam, which also claim a very ancient origin.

The period from the seventh to the eleventh centuries was an age of great social, political and cultural transformation in Kerala. In fact, right from the very early times, Kerala came in contact with other cultures and adopted a process of assimilation. It seems that in the early phases of its history up to the fifth and sixth centuries, different dynasties and rulers, including the great Chera kings, claimed Kerala. The *brahmins* came to Kerala and settled there, bringing with them an elitist *brahminic* culture. This caused great transformation in its political and social life. They mixed with the local people and, while deftly adapting to the local practices, introduced their customs and knowledge systems and established themselves as culturally predominant in the region. The *brahmins* also introduced Sanskrit learning and established Hindu temples throughout the land. As a result, apart from Christians, Muslims and Jews, several intermediary Hindu communities, mostly encoded with fixed societal roles, mushroomed in Kerala. The Malayalam language gradually began to take shape, as a blend of the native Tamil and the elite Sanskrit. The *brahmins* slowly edged out Buddhist and Jain culture by introducing Vedic Hinduism and establishing academies teaching Sanskrit and Vedic lore. Dandi, a writer of the Pallava court during the seventh century, has recorded considerable information on Kerala in his chronicle *Avantisundarikatha*. The contribution of Sankara to philosophy and Bhaskara to mathematics and astrology established the place of Kerala in the field of Sanskrit learning in the country.

Sanskrit plays composed by the eminent dramatists Asvaghosha, Bhasa, Kalidasa, Harsha, Sudraka, Mahendravikramavarman, Bhavabhuti, Visakhadatta and Bodhayana range roughly from the first to the seventh centuries. There is evidence available that their plays were popular on the stage and were performed in many parts of India. The fact that the plays were meant to be staged is also evident from features such as benediction, prologue, stage directions and asides, provided in the plays that have a performance-based rather than a literary-based significance. The *sutradhara* (stage manager) presents the prologue of a typical Sanskrit play as an introduction. Set in the format of a conversation between him and the main actress, the *sutradhara* announces the features of the play, introduces the playwright and the context and appeals for its successful staging.

By the end of the eighth century, there are descriptions on the stage enactment of Sanskrit plays available in other texts. The most significant among these is the elaborate description of the staging of *Ratnavali* presented in Damodaragupta's *Kuttanimata*. From the account of the performance given there, it is possible to surmise that it was a blend of music, dance and improvised elaborate acting. There are also references to actors and acting in Sudraka's *Padmaprabhrtaka*, Vararuchi's *Ubhayabhisarika* and several other texts.

A highbrow theatre tradition seems to have evolved in Kerala by this time. The *brahmins* were aware of the theatre practices in North India. However, instead of transplanting them directly, they made innovations to the classical theatre in Kerala, by adapting elements from the local culture. On the Sanskritic acculturation of Kerala, Sreedhara Menon remarks that it was a

two-way process, in which Kerala also contributed to this rich legacy, transforming it as a common Indian heritage from a specifically northern bequest,[8] a contribution which, according to him, outweighed that made by any other region of similar size. They seem to have recast the local dance form of *koothu* by divesting its participatory character, elevating its status and codifying its conventions to suit their tastes. Even now, many elements of the indigenous tradition of performance are discernible in Kutiyattam, for the aesthetic principles that govern the art form have been culled out as much from the artistic practices of the popular tradition as from the texts on dramaturgy such as the *Natya Sastra*.

The adaptation of Sanskrit plays to the Kerala stage may have been initiated by these aristocratic *brahmins* equipped with Sanskrit learning, with leisure and refinement in taste. Well-versed in aesthetics, dramaturgy and dramatic literature, they played a critical role in the choreography of Kutiyattam in its early days. By then, temples as places of worship had started coming up in Kerala, which were under their domination. They made Kutiyattam an exclusive art form by confining it to the precincts of the temples reserved only for the upper castes.

The first family of actors, which was called the Chakyars, seems to have come with the Perumals, the rulers of the second Chera Empire in Kerala, between the seventh and twelfth centuries. The Chakyars established their lineage by adopting children born from illegitimate unions in the orthodox classes, for example, the union of a *brahmin* girl with a non-*brahmin* boy, which was strictly forbidden according to societal norms. The art of the Chakyars, Nangiars and Nambiars was made hereditary, thus ensuring its sustenance and continuance.

The early references regarding the staging of performances are available in the Kolloor Madham Record of 976, about the staging of *koothu* in Thrikkodithanam in the Uthravizha festival.[9] *Koothu* was divided into three allied arts—Prabandhakkoothu, Nangiarkoothu and Kutiyattam. The play *Mattavilasa* by Mahendravikramavarman, the Pallava ruler and *Bhagavadajjukiya* by Bodhayana seem to have been popular in Kerala at that time. Neelakantha Sastri, who was from Thiruvananthapuram, discovered *Mattavilasa*, which was in active use in the Chakyar repertoire for a long time. By the tenth century, Neelakantha's *Kalyanasauganthika Vyayoga* also appeared and was adapted to the stage. The repertoire of Kutiyattam, including the plays of eminent playwrights such as Bhasa and Harsha, may have been the contribution of the early choreographers. However, Saktibhadra's *Ascharyachudamani* might have been one of the earliest plays from Kerala and it has a preeminent position on the Kutiyattam stage even today. That the practice of treating single acts taken from well-known Sanskrit plays as complete performances was prevalent in Kutiyattam from the early days is evident from historical records. One such reference is from *Thiruvalla*, which mentions 'Kaliyankam Koothu', the fourth act of Bhasa's *Balacharita*.

Facing page: A scene from Nangiarkoothu, which could be presented as distinct, self-contained units of a single narrative.

[8] Menon, A. Sreedhara. 1972. *Kerala*, p. 36. New Delhi: National Book Trust.

[9] Varier, Raghava and Rajan Gurukkal. 1996. *Kerala Charitram*, p. 149. Sukapuram: Vallathol Vidyapeetham.

Coming of Age: The Middle Period

Kutiyattam as an art form was codified and refined during the time of Kulasekhara, the ruler of Kerala from 978 to 1036. Kulasekhara remodelled Kutiyattam by introducing several changes in the existing format, even adding a few innovations and raising its power as an aesthetically satisfying event primarily directed towards the tastes of the upper classes of society. The new style that he created with the help of his friend Tolan had a skilful combination of both the local and classical elements, making it cater to a wide audience.

Kulasekhara extended the repertoire of Kutiyattam to include more Sanskrit plays. He wrote two plays, *Subhadradhananjaya* and *Tapatisamvarana*, which he choreographed for the Kutiyattam stage. The choreographic manuals, known as *Dhananjayadhvani* and *Samvaranadhvani*, describe the theatric action and explain each character and situation in great detail, from the perspective of stage enactment. The two texts, together known as *Vyangyavyakya*, also serve as performance manuals and have minute details on stage presentation, revealing not only the overt level of meaning of the two plays, but also the subtext or *dhvani*.

Facing page: A vidushaka, *the comic character, in a typical pose.*

During Kulasekhara's time, the scope of theatric action in Kutiyattam was extended manifold, to cater to high tastes. To start with, instead of full plays, single acts from plays were treated as full-fledged plays. The technique of elaboration in theatric action and the detailed enactment of situations that had theatric potential became the highlight of the plays. To achieve this, each verse from a play was put through a four-fold interpretation—first, the actor orally recited the verse; then the verse was split in terms of its grammatical sequence through gestures; the inner meanings were explored and, finally, all the possibilities of the verse were elaborated through depicting the implied meanings, to unfold its *rasa*. The convention of *nirvahanamm*, the method of enacting the previous story, also contributed to this method. The few centuries that followed Kulasekhara witnessed the golden age of this art form, with the codification of new productions and the composition of new theatre manuals. Perhaps acting also reached a new pinnacle during this time, owing to the support of the temple and encouragement from royal and *brahmin* patrons.

A teacher passing on the details of choreography to a young student.

The enactment of Kutiyattam was codified through detailed texts on choreography, called *attaprakarams* and *kramadeepikas*. The *kramadeepika* presents logistical details for stage presentation such as rituals, stage decoration and remuneration for the actors, while the method of the enactment of the plays is described in *attaprakarams*. It is a marvel of history that these written documents, which are in the form of manuscripts, have survived in the families of Chakyars. These documents became the basis for choreographers and actors of Kutiyattam to formalise the art form. They could also constantly refer to, draw upon and sustain *parampara* (tradition). *Attaprakaram* details the acting of each act of a play by presenting the situation, citing each *sloka*, the methods and conventions of acting, according to the mood, situation and character. It also elaborates the action of situations of dramatic potential.

In the rigid structure of the theatric world of Kutiyattam, the *attaprakaram* works in two ways—it lays down the principles strongly and affords the shield of accuracy to a lesser actor, and gives immense scope for an imaginative actor to go beyond it.[10] The *kramadeepika* is a guidebook for the actor and the organiser of a performance. Apart from being the sourcebook on the history of performance of a bygone era, these texts are excellent reference manuals for a Kutiyattam performer even today.

A *brahmin* friend of Kulasekhara is said to have written *attaprakarams* and *kramadeepikas* for the two plays, *Subhadradhananjaya* and

[10] Paniker, Ayyappa. P. Venugopalan, ed. 1999. 'Kutiyattavum Attaprakaravum', *Kutiyattam*, pp. 10-24. Thiruvananthapuram: Margi.

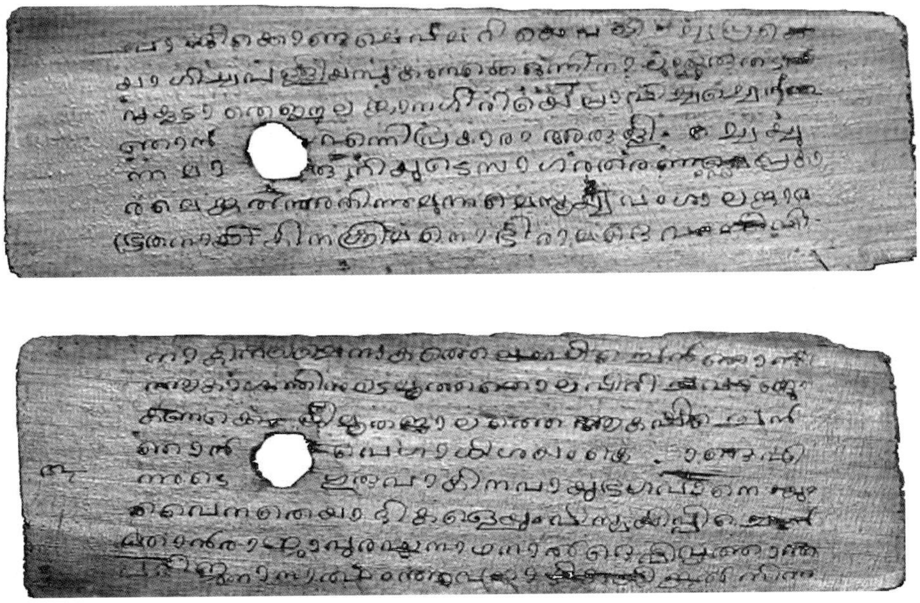

Manuscript folios of a Kutiyattam attaprakaram *that details the acting of each act of a play.*

Tapatisamvarana, which may have became a model for other plays on the Kutiyattam stage. Two commentaries of the plays, called *Dhananjayadhvani* and *Samvaranadhvani*, were compiled. According to these records, the king himself demonstrated the different roles for the benefit of the actors. In the following verse taken from *Vyangyavyakhya*, the king requests his critic-friend:

> After seeing it, if you liked it, tell me. I will myself be the actor, and you will be my spectator.
>
> Let me elaborate the acting method, And if found good, we will employ actors on the stage. Be ready, my dear friend!

Following this, the commentator (who is himself a poet) elaborately describes the action as if he has seen it in performance.

The *attaprakaram* that was established as the standard model on the Kutiyattam stage later does not follow the *Vyangyavyakhya* model of presentation.

In his pioneering study, K.G. Paulose examines the evolution of Kutiyattam as revealed from *attaprakarams* and observes that the stage manuals 'provide the clue to trace the Sanskrit theatre in Kerala'.[11] According to him, the keys to unlock the development of Kutiyattam in the middle period (post-*Vyangyavyakhya*) are the *attaprakarams* of Nilakantha's *Kalyanasaugandhikam*, Bodhayana's *Bhagavadajjukam*, 'Mantrankam' and Mahendravikramavarman's *Mattavilasam*. Several *attaprakarams* have been composed subsequently and, according to the linguistic, literary and choreographic features of the *attaprakarams* available today, their dates may be ascertained quite easily. An important stage manual that remained

[11] Paulose traces the development of stage manuals into five stages—the routine method, condemnation of non-Vedic doctrines, commentary on statecraft and polity, restructuring of texts and the introduction of the convention of *purusharthas*. Paulose, K.G. 2006. *Kutiyattam Theatre: The Earliest Living Tradition*, p. 161. Thripunithura: International Centre for Kutiyattam and DC Books.

The hero and the vidushaka. *The* vidushaka *discusses diverse topics through the medium of humour.*

as the touchstone of the choreographer's imagination and the actor's skill is that of Saktibhadra's *Ashcharyachudamani*. 'Anguliyankam' is the sixth act of this stage manual.

The fact that Bhasa's plays were unavailable till the beginning of the twentieth century and that they were an active part of the *attaprakaram* repertoire of the Chakyars became significant with the publication of thirteen plays edited by T. Ganapati Sastri from 1912 to 1915 under the Trivandrum Sanskrit Series. Eliciting common features in the plays, Ganapati Sastri ascribed their authorship to Bhasa. This argument has evoked considerable debate, which has not yet been conclusively settled. Prior to this, Ganapati Sastri also edited *Tapatisamvarana* and *Subhadradhananjaya*. Apart from these, the texts of all major plays used in the Kutiyattam repertoire are available with some of the Chakyar families even today, preserved in palm leaf manuscripts, though a great many of those manuscripts have perished. The descendants of the families of Ammannur, Kidangur and Mani still have a smaller but significant collection, and many are also in the custody of the Oriental

Ravana depicting the gesture for 'king'.

Research Institute and Manuscript Library in the University of Kerala, Thiruvananthapuram; Government Sanskrit College, Thripunithura; Calicut University, Kozhikkode and DAV College, Chandigarh.

A close study of the *attaprakarams* in terms of their content, linguistic features and the scripts employed in the manuscripts would undoubtedly reveal great insights into the history and development of Kutiyattam. Unfortunately, such a comprehensive study has not yet happened.

Realising the danger of limiting Kutiyattam to an exclusive, erudite taste, the choreographers introduced and developed the role of the *vidushaka*, the comic character, and made him a popular stock character on the stage. In Kutiyattam, the *vidushaka* has a place as important as that of the hero. Unlike the hero and all the other characters, however, the *vidushaka* has the right to verbal speech. He speaks in Sanskrit, in addition to his Prakrit and interprets the meanings of the Sanskrit words into the vernacular Malayalam. The rigid association of Kutiyattam to the temple is a characteristic feature of Kutiyattam at this stage of its history. Social relations in Kerala had, by then, been organised by

Kuttappa Chakyar (alias Kidangoor Raman Chakyar) as Vasantaka.

and large on feudal lines. Several temples had sprung up throughout the land, which established them as great centres of worship, learning and art activity. The temples had rich resources, which were under the control of the *brahmins* and rulers of the land. A record from the Moozhikkulam temple in the ninth century mentions that King Bhaskara Ravivarman contributed land to the temple. The inscriptions from the Thiruvalla temple reveal the account of the measures of rice given daily to people who were engaged in occupations connected with the temple—the priests, narrators of the puranic lore, actresses called Nangais (Nangiars), drummers, garland-weavers and so on. There was also the practice of giving land to them. The Chakyars, Nangiars and Nambiars were thus a part of the temple administration; each being given specific jobs that they had to perform. A record from the Thrikkadithanam temple mentions the arrangements made for conducting ten performances of *koothu*. The staging of Kutiyattam was strictly limited to these theatres, which were attached to the temples. If the temple did not have a *koothambalam*, the performance would take place in the big hall attached to the temple.

The development of the three art forms, namely, Prabandhakkoothu, Nangiarkoothu and Kutiyattam, during this time was phenomenal. The term *koothu* seems to have been a common term for all the forms. Records from Thiruvalla around the tenth century refer to the performance of 'Kaliyankam Koothu', the fourth act of Bhasa's *Balacharita*. These prove that by that time, the practice of enacting single acts from plays had come into vogue. Works belonging to the period, such as *Unnunilisandesa* and *Kokasandesa*, also have references to the performance of *koothu* in temples such as Tali.

The mode of narrating stories as oral recital goes back a long way in India. The art of storytelling was dovetailed into the 'high' art of Kutiyattam, probably as an ingenious method of engaging all tastes among the audience. The blending of the 'higher' art of elaborate histrionic action of the main characters of the play and the 'lower' verbal art of the *vidushaka* made it popular, though still accessible only to the people from the higher classes of society. The performance of Prabandhakkoothu has the narrator-protagonist don the guise of the *vidushaka*. He verbally elaborates different episodes and stories from the epics in Malayalam, a language that was accessible to all levels of people. The hero's elaborate action found

Left to right: Pathakam by P.K. Narayanan Nambiar; Prabhandhakkoothu by P.K.G. Nambiar, where he portrays the vidushaka.

a parody in the ludicrous actions of the *vidushaka*, who appears on the stage as a friend and advisor to the king in matters of love and sport, indulging in jokes and sometimes mildly ridiculing the king. While the theatric grammar of the elitist art of Kutiyattam remained more inaccessible to most of the people, the speech and actions of the *vidushaka* were directed towards popular tastes.

The convention of the *vidushaka* as the commentator of action gave him the sanction to directly address the audience, sometimes make personal references to them and also ridicule them when an occasion arose. It may be seen as a sort of inversion deliberately integrated into the 'high' art of Kutiyattam, perhaps understood in its collective rather than individual form. At a time when there were strict boundaries to freedom of expression, the Kutiyattam artist escaped punishment for speaking out through his subversive ways, by reducing criticism to a joke and making caricature of accepted social norms. Though the *vidushaka's* speech was couched in a metaphoric language of inter-referencing with the dramatic situation of the play, his liberties were so great that he could criticise the king during a performance. This freedom on the stage was accepted, tolerated and even appreciated by the dominant classes, as a hegemonic sanction. The venting of repressed emotions by the comic protagonist of theatre became a letting out of steam for the community at large in a collective sense through the *vidushaka* and paradoxically, a reassertion of power for the upper classes, achieved not through coercion, but through an attitude of humane tolerance.

The introduction of the character of the *vidushaka* in the plays *Subhadradhananjaya* and *Tapatisamvarana* gave a new direction to the development of Prabandhakkoothu. The practice of storytelling was in vogue in the temples of Kerala for a long time. There were professional storytellers attached to the temples who narrated stories from both, the Ramayana and the Mahabharata. Prabandhakkoothu may have been developed from this practice. It is also a take-off from the role of the *vidushaka* in the main play. The convention called *nirvahanam*, which is a recapitulation of the previous story, extended the scope of the actor for storytelling. As the hero of the play does through histrionic acting, the *vidushaka* uses the text of the play as a springboard to include different areas of scholarship and tell them in a manner that appealed to everyone. The narration of Purusharthakkoothu and the *nirvahanam* gave him immense scope to exhibit his skill and proficiency. The introduction of the *prabandhas* written by eminent poets such as Melpattur Narayana Bhattathiri also enlarged his repertoire. Corresponding to the Chakyar's presentation of Prabandhakkoothu, the Nambiars developed their own art of storytelling, which came to be known as Pathakam.

The aesthetics of Prabandhakkoothu tend to follow the same pattern as that of Kutiyattam. Essentially meant to cater to a class of people with nurtured taste, leisure and patience, it is a multi-layered, slow-moving rendition of the story, elaborating each phrase and line of the text detail by detail. The technique is that, in the process, the actor weaves new stories and anecdotes into the main plot, transforming them as the core text. There are copious references to contemporary situations and the actor directs his attention through ridicule to the members of the audience as well. Couched in the guise of textual references, connections are made to topical incidents and the immediacy of the situation becomes highly entertaining to the audience. 'Mantrankam', is a marvel of expansion of the core text to exploit the multiple shades of meaning. Though there are three characters in the play, Vasantaka, the *vidushaka*, holds the stage single-handedly for thirty-eight out of the forty-one days of the performance. In the play, Vasantaka, who is masquerading as Kazhukkoottunni, a *brahmin* beggar, plots to secure the release of the imprisoned King Vatsa with the aid of minister Yaugandharayana disguised as a madman and Rumanvan, a Buddhist

Moozhikkulam Kochukuttan Chakyar as the charioteer in Mayasitankam, *an extinct play that was revitalised by Margi.*

An archival picture of a vidushaka, *whose excessive behaviour makes him a favourite with the audience.*

monk. Through a highly-coded conversation, they conspire to release the king as well as abduct Princess Vasavadatta, whom the king in the meantime has fallen in love with. They meet in an old temple and discuss the strategy. The first sentence, 'I have placed my bowl of sweetmeats in the steps of the temple, but after I counted the coins I received as alms, I look back, to see my sweets missing!' (*bhoh devakulapitikayam mama modakamallakam nikshipya dakshinamasakan ganayitva badhva pratinivrtta idanim modakamallakam na prekshe...*) refers indirectly to King Vatsa changing the strategy of his own release since he has fallen in love with Vasavadatta. In the context of the performance of this scene in Kutiyattam, after the preliminaries (*purappadu*), the *vidushaka* recites the *sloka* and then starts a lengthy narration, in the format of *anukramam-samkshepam-nirvahanam*. In *anukramam*, the actor recites the text and narrates the story in a reverse time sequence till he reaches the beginning of the story, giving a gist of the story as *samkshepam* follows this sequence. The core text of the narration then starts in a flashback mode (*nirvahanam*).

The *vidushaka* ponders on 'two ways', leading to four, six and eight paths, hinting presumably at the ways to release Udayana. However, throughout the rendition, there is no direct reference to real-time events. These are couched in oblique and abstract language, revealing the actor-narrator's knowledge, skill and resourcefulness. With incredible mastery of detail, several stories, maxims, theories as well as philosophies are brought in for analysis and criticism in the process. The progression of the story is less important here; it does not matter that it does not lead anywhere. The narration is important, because imagination takes a flight into regions of the unknown. What is needed from the spectator is a willingness to participate by suspending disbelief and traversing the imaginary space along with the performer. This is true also in the context of the long narration of Purusharthakkoothu as well as the extended monologues in plays such as *Bhagavajjukiya* and *Mattavilasa*. In one sense, this kind of narration in Prabandhakkoothu and in the main narrative of Kutiyattam presupposes familiarity with at least the mode of narration—storyline, theatric conventions, language and the style of rendering.

The actor in between the narration also draws the attention of the spectators to himself by ridiculing their behaviour, imitating mannerisms as well as connecting the main thread of the story to a familiar and a contemporary event. These excesses make the *vidushaka* an all-time favourite with the audience.

Emergence of Women's Performance

Nangiar, the female performer, has an important position in Kutiyattam. Right from the very early days of Kutiyattam, unlike in the later dramatic forms such as Krishnattam and Kathakali (where men used to don the costume of women and enact female roles), she takes up all the female roles in a play. This is a unique feature that sets Kutiyattam apart from other performances across the world. It also meant that even in the olden days, the Nangiar had to be as proficient in acting as the Chakyar.

The beginning of Nangiarkoothu, the art of the women performers, is not clear. Historically, Nangiars, the women members of the Nambiar caste, are equally part of the temples with performance rights of their own. This is revealed in references to the practice of payment to these actresses, which goes back to the days prior to that of Kulasekhara. Archival records from Chokkoor (AD 898), Thiruvalla and Nedumburam Tali mention this class of actresses called Nangais, Nangiars or Koothachis. There is a mention of a female actor named Chiritiranangachi in the Chera inscriptions. Nangiarkoothu in its early days may have been an independent art form. With the integration of Kutiyattam into the temples of Kerala, the Nangiar started taking up the women roles, in addition to keeping the rhythm on the stage and reciting some of the verses in Kutiyattam. The enlarging of her repertoire seems to have been done during the time of Kulasekhara.

Facing page: Margi Sathi in Nangiarkoothu, a performance exclusively by the woman actor.

Legend has it that Kulasekhara married a Nangiar and when her children were ostracised from the temple performances for this reason, he wrote *Srikrishnacharitam* in two hundred and forty quatrains. This resulted in raising the social status of the Nangiars and restoring the position of Nangiarkoothu as an independent art form. That the Nangiar enjoyed special privileges in society is clear from the fact that she was given the right to strike the temple bells and pray, a sanction that was not afforded to other women. Having independent financial status, with land holdings of her own, her place in society at that time was no less than that of the Chakyar.

Srikrishnacharitam is a compilation of poems taken from different sources such as the *Bhagavata*, Jayadeva's *Gitagovinda*, Amaru's *Amarushataka*, Kalidasa's *Abhijnanasakuntala* and some original quatrains by the compiler.

Though originally the repertoire consisted of two hundred and forty verses, in the existing version, only two hundred and seventeen are available. As the title indicates, *Srikrishnacharitam* deals with the story of Krishna through episodes such as King Ugrasena's assumption to the throne, the birth of Krishna, Krishna's infancy and childhood, the killing of Putana, the subjugation of Kaliya, the *rasa* dance in Vrindavana, the killing of Kamsa and so on. It is choreographed as a digression from the main text of Kulasekhara's *Subhadra-dhananjaya* in the form of a *nirvahanam* in the second act of the play. Subhadra, the heroine of the play, tells her maid Kalpalatika to retrieve her garment, which she had lost in the confusion when she was abducted by a demon and Arjuna, the hero of the play, saves her. The performer, in the guise of Kalpalatika, recounts the story of Krishna in different episodes as a detour from the main play. During the narration, being a solo performance, she takes on the guise of other characters in the *pakarnnattam* style, typical to Kutiyattam. Some of the different episodes of the performance are: *krishnavataram* (the birth of Krishna), *putanamoksham* (the slaying of Putana, the ogress), *krishnalila* (the playful pranks of Krishna), *kaliyamardanam* (the vanquishing of Kaliya, the serpent), *vrindavanagamanam* (description of Vrindavana, the forest), *gopastrivastrapaharanam* (the teasing of the *gopis* by hiding their garments) and *rasalila* (*rasa* dance with the *gopis*).

Following the preliminary drumming and purificatory rites, the performer enters with traditional ritualistic movement and offers salutation to the stage. Assuming the character of Kalpalatika, she faces the audience and, through a language of gestures and facial expressions, relates the context of the performance to how Subhadra had sent her to retrieve her lost garment and used this as a pretext, to find out the whereabouts of Arjuna. The protagonist slips back into her role as the actor with a series of dance sequences in obeisance to different gods and goddesses, a head-to-foot (*kesadipadam*) description of Siva and Parvati, and finally salutations to all the living creatures of the celestial, terrestrial and netherworlds.

The next day, the actor begins the actual performance. At first, the narration happens in the form of a reverse chronological sequence and steadily taking the audience back to the past. The next is the depiction of the gist of the story (*samkshepam*), in the puranic mode, from the time of the creation of the world to

The different moods of the woman in a Kutiyattam performance: Usha Nangiar depicting fear and caution.

Kapila Venu and Aparna Nangiar as the heroine and her maid-in-attendance.

the circumstances that lead to Lord Vishnu's incarnation as Krishna, to the founding of the dynasty of Yadus and the establishment of the palace of Mathura. The performer then enacts the main episode of the performance as *nirvahanam*. Here, the performer once again gives the context and summarises the events from the beginning, of Ugrasena's enthronement, Krishna's birth and so on, till she comes to the current context of the episode being enacted. The Nangiar seated on the stage recites the portion of the text and the actor elaborately depicts the meaning of each verse, which cumulatively builds up the structure of the narrative.

The fact that the original choreographers intended Nangiarkoothu as a separate but allied art is evident from the departures in technique from the mainstream Kutiyattam.

In Kutiyattam, the Nangiars and the Chakyars themselves recite the portion of the play, while in Nangiarkoothu, the accompanying Nangiar recites the text. Unlike Kutiyattam, the recitation of each verse happens after its detailed enactment. While Kutiyattam strictly adheres to the use of Prakrit language for women characters and the *vidushaka*, the verses adopted in *Srikrishnacharitam* Nangiarkoothu are in Sanskrit.

Also, the fact that women actors traditionally took on the role of women characters in Kutiyattam has made an impact on the theatre grammar of Kutiyattam. It is seen

Facing page: Different moods of a woman–addressing another person in an affectionate manner. A pose by Margi Usha. Above: Depicting an aggravated temper.

that women in Kutiyattam have the same conventions of theatric performance, such as *purappatu* and *nirvahanam*. There are important scenes where women actors have the scope to elaborate theatric action, such as the role of Lalita (the disguised Surpanakha) in *Surpanakhankam*, Tapati in *Tapatisamvarana* and Subhadra in *Subhadradhananjaya*. Malayavati in *Nagananda* is another important role in which the actor could hold the stage on her own, with *nirvahanam* and together with other actors, through combined acting. The role of Katyayani in the fifth act of *Subhadradhananjaya* has immense acting potential through elaboration of action.[12] A Nangiar also took on important roles such as those of Subhadra in *Subhadradhananjaya*, Tapati in *Tapatisamvarana* or Lalita in *Supanakhankam*. Sometimes, she had to display unusual theatric feats such as committing suicide by hanging from the ceiling or drowning in a river, situations that demanded extreme control and dexterity. Another complete text based on the Ramayana story, titled 'Sriramacharitam', has been compiled by Margi Sathi with a detailed choreographic text as well as a theatre manual.

Apart from the histrionic role, the Nangiar has to be trained in recitation too, for she is also the singer in a Kutiyattam performance. She has to remain on stage during the entire performance of Kutiyattam, Nangiarkoothu or Prabandhakkoothu, sing the invocatory

[12] Usha Nangiar. 2003. *Abhinetri*, pp. 182-198. Navi Mumbai: Keli.

Performance of Nangiarkoothu inside a koothambalam.

verses, introductory songs as well as sections of the text in some cases. She also keeps the rhythm on the small cymbals and is an indispensable part of the performance.

In the case of a Nangiar, the first performance is usually conducted before she reaches puberty. The initiation performance called 'Nangyar Koothu Purappadu' lasts for two days and is fixed on an auspicious day according to the girl's horoscope. A girl who has not had an *arangettam* is not entitled to use the name 'Nangiar', and is not allowed to take part in temple performances.[13]

Apart from individual names for each actor, the members of each family also had an identification marker (such as 'Mani', 'Ammannur' or 'Pothiyil') with the family name representing a distinct acting style. This was passed on through generations. It is believed that till the nineteenth century and the earlier part of the twentieth century, there were eighteen Chakyar families in Kerala. Many of them have now become extinct and the others have merged together. The descendants of some of these families still survive in Kerala and continue the tradition of acting.

The pervasion of the *bhakti* movement across Kerala and the strengthening of the temple-

[13] Daugherty, Diane. 'The Nangyar: Female Ritual Specialist of Kerala' in *Asian Theatre Journal* Vol. 13, No. 1, Spring 1996, pp. 54-67.

Above: Kalamandalam Sailaja, Kalamandalam Girija, Margi Sathi and Usha Nangiar–teacher-performers of Nangiarkoothu in the present generation.

oriented social structure made a deep impact in Kutiyattam. By the fourteenth century, Kutiyattam was entrenched firmly into the temple complex, giving each Chakyar family the right to perform in specified temples, thus ensuring the sustenance of these families. The deep-rooted association of Kutiyattam to the temple as well as the gift of landed properties from the temple gave the Chakyar community economic stability and standing in society. This was the time when the codes and conventions associated with this theatre got fixed through the compilation of *kramadeepikas* and *attaprakarams* for all the plays. With financial security for the actor and a world of connoisseurs, the interest of the art was also protected, and Kutiyattam flourished to great heights.

Temple as Site for Performance

A distinguishing feature of Kutiyattam is that it was traditionally performed solely inside *koothambalams* attached to some of the major temples in Kerala. A *koothambalam* is a circumscribed theatre space, limiting action to the small stage and has a clearly demarcated seating area for the audience. Constructed according to the specifications prescribed in the ancient texts on architecture such as *Silparatna*, *Mayamata* and *Tantrasamucchaya*, it serves as an ideal space for Kutiyattam.

The architectural plan of the temple complex included the *koothambalam* as part of the five structures of a temple. The design of a typical *koothambalam* reveals an adherence to the basic postulates of the *Natya Sastra*, while incorporating local needs and traditions. Many of the *koothambalams* found in Kerala are exquisitely designed, with precise underlying architectural principles. A *koothambalam* has a square plan, with clear two divisions—the stage and the space for the audience. The roof, made of wooden shafts fitted into carefully constructed grooves, represents a typical feature of the architecture of the region and is usually covered by copper sheets. Inside the theatre, the downside of the roof has highly embellished sculptural motifs and designs carved into it. The central portion depicts Brahma, the creator of the universe, surrounded by *ashtadikpalas* or the eight guardian deities of Indian mythology. Sometimes, the sculptural work is rich enough to have narrative sequences from the stories of the epics carved into the wooden roof and the pillars. Supported by wooden or granite pillars, the floor has a seating capacity of not more than a hundred. The stage is a slightly raised platform with a precise layout, earmarked with two doors on both sides for the exits and entrances of the actor and the drummers, location of stage properties, position of the drummers and space for acting.

Most of the *koothambalams* in Kerala were constructed during or after the fourteenth century and many of them have since then been reconstructed. Therefore, they are not badly preserved. An inscription at the *adhisthana* (base) of the Harippad *koothambalam* dates it to 1769.[14] There are major *koothambalams* in the Vadakkumnathan

Facing page: Prabandhakkoothu inside a koothambalam, *which is a part of the temple's structure.*

[14] Panchal, Govardhan. 1984. *Kuttampalam and Kutiyattam*, p. 36. New Delhi: Sangeet Natak Akademi.

temple in Trissur, Krishna temple in Guruvayur, Kootalmanikyam temple in Irinjalakkuda, Subrahmanyan Temple in Kidangur, Mahavishnu Temple in Thrippunithura, Siva Temple in Chengannur, Lakshmana temple in Thirumoozhikkulam, Bhagavati temple in Thirumanthamkunnu and Subramanya temple in Harippad. There are several smaller *koothambalams* attached to temples across Kerala, evidently for staging plays, though it is doubtful whether some of them (such as the ones in Arppookkara, Thirumanthamkunnu as well as those in Kottappadi) are suitable for the enactment of full-fledged Kutiyattam plays. Recently, a new one was added in the premises of Kerala Kalamandalam, a major art institution devoted to the classical arts in Kerala.

The status accorded to *koothambalam* as one of the *panchprasadas* (five-fold structures in the plan of a typical Kerala temple) signifies the importance attached to the performance and also underscores the fact that at least from the fourteenth century, Kutiyattam had an inextricable connection with the temple as a place of worship.

When the temple became the sole venue for the performance of Kutiyattam plays, it was natural that it imbibed the basic ethos of spirituality and a rigid adherence to sacred rituals. Theatre began to be considered as a sacred event and the Chakyar's dramatic function in the play began to be equated with that of the priest in the temple. Deities were considered the most important spectators of the play. The viewers were the *brahmins* and other upper Hindu castes. The theatre hall, the stage, the *mizhavu*, the lamp, the actors—in short, everything—was invested with a sacred significance. The theatrical action itself was deemed as a mode of offering to the deities with its rituals bearing a close resemblance to those worshipping God inside the sanctum.

Koothambalam *attached to the Vadakkumnathan Temple, Thrissur.*

Theatrical performance inside the temple was divided into three clear categories—*atiyantarakkoothu*, the performance fixed as a matter of routine according to the annual calendar, *kazhchakkoothu*, which was meant as entertainment for the spectators and *vazhivadukoothu*, held as votive offering to the deity. Among these, *atiyantarakkoothu* was kept up in a regular manner mainly because the temple directly sustained it and each Chakyar family had the rights to perform in specific temples. It was perhaps this regularity of stage shows that honed the skills of the actors and kept Kutiyattam going for long years down the centuries. *Kazhchakkoothu* may have been special shows for specific occasions, perhaps arranged as an entertainment for the king or the *brahmin* patron. Plays such as *Mattavilasa* and *Balacharita* were held as votive offerings; prayers were directed towards the achievement of a wish. Therefore, ritualistic and devotional elements predominated in them. The element of ritual pervaded all aspects of the staging of a play, right from the decoration of the stage, make-up and costume of the actor, the purificatory rites of the stage, the recitation of the verses called *akkitha*, to the ritualistic dances called *nityakriya* and the concluding convention called *mutiyakkitha*.

The tendency for excessive as well as indiscriminate elaboration in Kutiyattam was vehemently criticised by an anonymous *brahmin* scholar of the fifteenth century. His critique, titled *Natankusa* (literally, a 'restraining hook' or leash for actors), is actually a scathing criticism of the manner in which Sanskrit plays were presented on the Kutiyattam stage. The descriptions of acting that were given in the text are also a testimony to the fact that the conventions of Kutiyattam were already established and remained more or less unchanged for several centuries after that, till perhaps the middle of the twentieth century.

The author cites the authority of former authorities on *natya* such as Bharata, Bhoja, Magha and several others to demolish the foundation on which Kutiyattam is built. The work is positioned from the perspective of an understanding of the mainstream theatre tradition as prescribed in classical texts such as the *Natya Sastra* and a stubborn refusal to admit that Kutiyattam is an independent form and a regional variation. During the course of this scathing attack on Kutiyattam, the author displays his thorough knowledge of the art form. His erudition touches all the minute details of the dramaturgy, such as the complex techniques and characteristic features of Kutiyattam, but he argues for its complete reform. Issues such as dramatic identity, imitation and representation of action, elaboration as well as repetition come in for strong criticism.

Koothambalam *in Kerala Kalamandalam, Cheruthuruthy.*

The author of *Natankusa* advises the Kutiyattam artist, 'the performance should strictly adhere to the precepts of Bharata. Keep out the interruption to the story. Remove the things unconnected. Stop your elaboration...Let everything be as it is.'[15] He criticises the convention of incorporating lengthy rituals called *kriyanrittam* while presenting the story. He also objects to the device of *pakarnnattam*, which is crucial to Kutiyattam. As examples, he chooses to cite the histrionic elaboration of Hanuman in 'Anguliyankam' and the verbal elaboration of the *vidushaka* in 'Mantrankam'. His aesthetic goals, obviously, are at variance with some of the basic acting principles of Kutiyattam and his suggestions for reform are not valid.

Though a virulent attack that is directed against the basic performance principles of Kutiyattam, *Natankusa* is historically an important record, for it gives a detailed description of the performance of Kutiyattam in the fifteenth century.

'The ability to see a performance,' writes Anuradha Kapur, 'is as culturally bound as the performance itself.'[16] The degree of formalism that characterises the temple-oriented classical theatres such as Kutiyattam is greater than the secular and folk art forms. These theatre forms retained their rigidity and tightness of structure down the centuries owing to their adherence to tradition and spirituality. However, with the dwindling of the resources of temples in the wake of a new order, Kutiyattam suffered a serious setback. The crumbling of the feudal order and the introduction of Western education brought in a different situation for traditional art forms across the country. With the deterioration of land, money and lack of encouragement, many art forms became mere rituals. In Kutiyattam, the role of the Nangiar was truncated to such an extent that it began to be replaced by the male actor himself handling the role, resorting to the convention of *kettatuka*.[17]

Without the opportunity to perform and improvise important scenes, the Nangiars lost their skill and became pale shadows of their former selves. Many of the eighteen traditional Chakyar families became extinct and the rest merged together. The stage manuals were either lost or came to be the preserves of some families, not to be shared with the outside world. Confined to temples and with a lack of proper encouragement as well as support, the performances deteriorated into mere rituals and became a duty rather than an artistic expression. The days of Kazhchakkoothu and Vazhivadukoothu were practically over, Kutiyattam survived only due to the steadfast devotion of some of the Chakyar families to somehow persevere with efforts at sustaining this art, through practising the ritualistic Atiyantarakkoothu, in spite of heavy odds.[18] The restrictive character of the complex art form of Kutiyattam may have been the indirect cause of the mushrooming of other forms such as Krishnattam and Kathakali in Kerala by the beginning of the seventeenth century.

A new stream of performance that developed, linked to religious worship and ritual, was dance-dramas, which adapted their plots from the rich corpus of Indian mythology,

---

[15] Paulose, K.G., ed. and trans. 1993. *Natankusa: A Critique on Dramaturgy*, p. 158. Tripunithura: Govt. Sanskrit College.
[16] Kapur, Anuradha. 1990. *Actors, Pilgrims, Kings and Gods: The Ramlila at Ramnagar*, p. 23. Kolkata: Seagull.
[17] The practice by which an actor pretends that he is listening to the words of the other person and commenting, 'Oh, did you say that...?'
[18] See Margi Madhu. 1999. 'Atiyantarakkoothu' *in Kutiyattam*, pp. 58-62. Trivandrum: Margi. He has extensively dealt with this issue.

A scene from Surpanakhankam.

such as the Ramayana, Mahabharata and Bhagavata. The conventions of these dances were crystallised as much from texts on dramaturgy and rules of aesthetics as from the artistic practices of the popular tradition. Krishnattam, said to have evolved in the latter part of the seventeenth century, is a ritualistic mode of theatre celebrating the legend of Krishna, the divine hero of the epic Bhagavata. In Krishnattam, the element of *bhakti* dominates its aesthetic aspects. This theatric form, usually presented as votive offering in the temple of Guruvayur in central Kerala, has a distinctive devotional and cultic character. In spite of the high refinement and codification of these performances in their aesthetics and grammar, art forms such as Krishnattam and Kathakali retain their vital connection, in some cases even in rudimentary form, to indigenous forms such as Teyyam and Patayani. These indigenous influences are more marked in the case of Kathakali. To create a world of non-illusion and make-believe, Kathakali adopted an elaborate and symbolic technique of stage presentation, involving interpretative dance movements and an evolved language of gesture and facial expressions. This highly refined and codified dance drama, integrating various elements from the folk and classical arts of Kerala, emerged as a fully evolved art form approximately towards the end of the seventeenth century. Right from the early times, the appreciation base of the classical arts such as Kutiyattam was limited to a small circle of connoisseurs and enthusiasts who, in turn, depended heavily on feudal patrons for encouragement, sustenance and sponsorship. With its persistence on exclusivity and ritualism, Kutiyattam resisted change, stubbornly stuck to tradition and was perhaps the last to submit to the call of the world.

Bali, with his characteristic red beard, in a typical pose.

Patronage in Transition

The flowering of the spirit of nationalism in India along with the rise of democracy in the early twentieth century brought about a fresh interest and lease of life to the arts with the new educated elite adopting a different approach to the study of the traditional arts. The attitude towards the arts underwent a change roughly by the middle of the nineteenth century. The transformation of India from a predominantly agrarian to a 'modernising' society with a large number of urban centres changed the economic base of the landed aristocracy.

In the early part of the twentieth century, great transformation across India in the social and political structure led to a revival of interest in the classical arts as being a vital link of our culture that connected the present with the past. Under the impact of modern education and the search for an 'Indian' identity through the spirit of patriotism, there was a renewed interest in India's glorious past. In this context, the classical arts came to be recognised across the country as the real expression of heritage and hence they once again gained force.[19] This led to the establishment of institutions dedicated to the arts in several parts of India—Rabindranath Tagore founded Viswa-Bharati in Santiniketan, Bengal, in 1901 and Rukmini Devi Arundale established Kalakshetra in Chennai in 1927.

The secularisation and 'sanctification' of the dance of *sadir* (from which Bharatanatyam as we know it now emerged), performed by temple dancers (*devadasis*) inside temples, renamed as 'Bharatanatyam', also resulted in its getting not only a new garb, but a new venue on the secular stage. In the words of Rukmini Devi, 'My intention is that dance, now abolished in the temple, should create the temple atmosphere on the stage.'[20] While the ancient *devadasi* system was condemned as degenerate and crude, in the reinvention of *sadir* as Bharatanatyam, this form was invested with fresh notions of

Facing page: Margi Madhu as Ravana contemplating on Sita's beauty in Ascharyachudamani.

[19] With reference to her study on Bengal, Tapati Guha-Thakurta sees this new resurgent nationalism as a reflection of the Orientalist discourse: 'The new nationalist ideology of Indian art and its search for traditional roots had strong roots in Orientalist debates and writing. British Orientalism produced and structured much of its notion of an Indian art tradition. While it had provided the core of historical knowledge and archaeological expertise on the subject, it would also stand at the helm of aesthetic interpretation of Indian art at the turn of the century.' *The Making of 'New' Indian Art: Artists, Aesthetics and Nationalism in Bengal, c.1850-1920*, p. 147. 1992. Cambridge: Cambridge University Press.

[20] Ramnarayan, Gowri. 'Rukmini Devi: Dancer, Reformer, A Profile', Part 2 in *Sruti* 9, July 1984, pp. 17-29.

A get-together of the Kutiyattam community in the sixties.

'purity' and 'respectability'.[21] The starting of Kalakshetra in a school format, the opening up of performances on public stages as well as the patronage by the elite classes are some of the factors that led to the revitalisation of the dance style as Bharatanatyam.

About the same time in Kerala, Vallathol Narayana Menon, the eminent poet and one of the pioneers of the new movement for the arts, along with his friend Mukunda Raja, established Kerala Kalamandalam in 1930 as a school for the revival of the classical arts. This marked a turning point in the history of the classical arts in Kerala. What was once considered the privilege of the upper classes in society now became accessible to everyone. Among the classical arts of Kerala, Kathakali was the first to receive the attention of the new patrons. The introduction of a school format in Kalamandalam was a revolutionary step. It altered the traditional mode of training in which the student was expected to learn his art, staying at his guru's house in close proximity to the teacher, through a time-tested method of imitating, imbibing and learning. Another innovation introduced by Vallathol was the establishment of 'Kathakali clubs', which sprang up all over Kerala and also in some cities outside the state.

To suit the new purpose of extending the viewership base, drastic changes were made in the format of Kathakali, such as curtailing and editing several portions of the text to suit an approximate duration of four to five hours. However, with the shifting of the venue of Kathakali to regular theatre halls, the intimate association that had existed between the spectator and the actor in earlier times was replaced by a more impersonal note. Krishnattam continued to be a one-troupe performance attached to the Guruvayur temple. Because of the basic insistence on spirituality and the limitation of its subject matter, there was no attempt

[21] In her significant study, Avanti Meduri interrogates notions of 'respectability': 'What makes dance really 'respectable'? Did dance performed on platforms before the educated and respected classes of society–and thus in an open system–acquire respectability by virtue of being presented before the public?' 'Bharatha Natyam–What are you?' *Asian Theatre Journal*, Vol. 5, No. 1, Spring 1988, pp. 1-22.

to take it outside the temple and hence the changes were rather limited.

By the 1930s, the changes that had taken place in Kerala as a result of the great upheavals in societal structure, made the practice of Kutiyattam dwindle to a mere ritual. Any change in the established norms of Kutiyattam meant that it tampered with the 'purity' of the form and none dared do it. However, modernising projects were already gaining ground. Anxieties about the deplorable state of affairs in Kutiyattam agitated the minds of those who had a stake in the art; those who had pursued it as a vocation had by the turn of the twentieth century understood that the monopolistic adherence to sacrality and narrow tradition would not sustain the art anymore.

New debates on the transformation of tradition, with a new agenda, were already in emergence. Ammaman Thampuran gave erudite lectures in the early fifties on Kutiyattam, which caught the attention of the outside world. Ammannur Chachu Chakyar, the great Kutiyattam maestro, understood the contradiction between the theatrical elegance of Kutiyattam on the one hand and the decayed state to which it had deteriorated due to a stubborn fidelity to a temple-oriented 'tradition' on the other. His starting of a Kutiyattam *Kalari* in Irinjalakkuda paved the way for not merely establishing the Ammannur School of Kutiyattam, but in sustaining the lineage through his illustrious successors, Ammannur Madhava Chakyar as well as Parameswara Chakyar. Chachu Chakyar gave intensive training to his students on different nuances of Kutiyattam and the oral rendition of *prabandhas* such as *Dutavakyam*, *Rajasuyam* and *Asanapurushartham*.[22] In fact, Paimkulam Rama Chakyar, the master performer belonging to the Koypa family and founder-teacher of Kalamandalam, was also trained under Chachu Chakyar.

However, the critical moment of emancipation from the rigid, age-old tradition in Kutiyattam happened when Paimkulam Rama Chakyar took the initiative to take the dance outside the temple. Braving severe criticism and protests from intransigent critics and even from the members of his own Chakyar community, he ventured to step out of the temple, with the first performance held in a Nambudiri household near Kottarakkara in 1949. After that historic moment, the transformation of the art was dramatic—Kutiyattam began to be performed in houses and other public places; it started receiving sanction from connoisseurs and theatre people across the region. The revolutionary step is evocatively described by Paulose:

> To realise this epoch-making obligation, he [Paimkulam Rama Chakyar] had to prepare himself for a long time. In 1943, during one of the occasions of a get-together at the grounds of Thekkinkadu, Joseph Mundassery [the litterateur] angrily said to Chakyar, 'Keeping it under the wraps, you will destroy this great art.' Paimkulam had great respect for Mundassery. He might have on that occasion decided to showcase it outside. In 1949, Pisharoti Master [K.P. Narayana Pisharoti, scholar on the classical arts and literature] gave a lecture in Guruvayur at the invitation of Guruvayur Devaswom, and it was Chakyar who revealed to him the intricacies of the art. He closed the lecture with a request that the art should be shown outside in a public space. The

[22] Venu, G. 2003. 'Introduction' in Usha Nangiar, *Abhnetri*. Navi Mumbai: Keli.

Three great masters: Paimkulam Rama Chakyar, Mani Madhava Chakyar and Ammannur Madhava Chakyar.

audience responded positively to this request and the Chakyar knew that the time has come. While he was nursing this idea, he got a chance to do it, and that was what he did...[23]

After this innovative breakthrough, transformation happened at a rapid pace. Mani Madhava Chakyar, the great maestro of Kutiyattam and a champion of change from traditional models, performed for the All India Radio in 1951 and, in 1956, the Zamorin of Calicut sponsored a performance for a radio broadcast. Still, though Vallathol Narayana Menon was keen to start a school for Kutiyattam in Kalamandalam, he could not do so during his time. The school had to wait till 1965, when K.N. Pisharoti, the Chairman of Kalamandalam, took upon himself the radical enterprise in collaboration with Paimkulam Rama Chakyar. This endeavour was fully supported by K.P. Narayana Pisharoti, the veteran scholar who compiled several *attaprakarams* and also did a pioneering translation of the *Natya Sastra* into Malayalam. By then Kutiyattam had become an irresistible attraction for an alert section of the international audience. Among the early admirers, Clifford Jones from Pennsylvania University, Christofer Byrski from University of Poland and Milena Salvini from Mandapa, Paris, deserve special mention.

With the opening of an institution for Kutiyattam in Kalamandalam and the change of the traditional format in training,

[23] Paulose, K.G., ed. 2005. *Kutiyattattinte Puthiya Mukham*, pp. 30-31. Thripunithura: International Centre for Kutiyattam.

the inevitable new phase of Kutiyattam began with the admission of students from outside the Chakyar community. Though this met with heavy opposition from the conservative sections, it proved that change from an ingrained culture built around habit and tradition was inevitable even in a traditional art form such as Kutiyattam. The school format revolutionised training through pedagogical re-orientations–for example, the older method of learning (*mudras*) through the recitation and enactment of 'Ramayana Samkshepam'[24] gave way to a course based on textual sources, through the application of *Hastalakshanadeepika*[25] formulations. To suit the tastes of a new spectator base, edited versions and stand-alone sections in condensed form were choreographed. Mani Madhava Chakyar's choreography of 'Kailasoddharanam and Parvativiraham', drawn as a segment from Bhasa's *Abhisheka Nataka* and Paimkulam Rama Chakyar's condensation of *Bhagavajjukam and Jatayuvadham* to suit a single day's evening performance are two examples.

This new orientation made Kutiyattam more easily accessible to a wider audience and, as a result, invitations for performances from all over the country and abroad started coming in. In 1962, V. Raghavan, the noted Sanskrit scholar and patron of the classical arts, invited Mani Madhava Chakyar to perform in Chennai. In 1964, Madhava Chakyar also received an invitation to perform in North India under the inspiration of Kamaladevi Chattopadyaya, and with the active support of Kapila Vatsyayan, the eminent scholar of Indian arts and performance traditions. This tour took Madhava Chakyar to New Delhi and Varanasi. The first trip of a Kutiyattam troupe abroad was in 1980, headed by Paimkulam Rama Chakyar, with thirteen artists from Kerala Kalamandalam. The school was subsequently able to produce a new generation of artists and teachers, thus ensuring the sustenance and continuation of the art.

Surpanakha and Lakshmana in Surpanakhankam.

[24] *Ramayana Samkshepam*, meaning abridgement of Ramayana, is a short narrative passage in Malayalam through which the Kutiyattam actor learns the process of correlating hand gestures and the meaning of the text.
[25] The text used by the Kerala actors which describes the twenty-four basic gesture patterns of single hands and an equal number of combined hands.

Aesthetic Tradition

Kutiyattam as a theatric art is not easily accessible to everyone. It caters to an initiated audience conversant with the story, text of the play, performance text in the form of the acting manual, acting methods and conventions; in short, its complete theatre grammar. Owing to the totality of commitment required from both, the actor and the spectator and the complexity of its theatric language, Kutiyattam still remains as a theatre catering exclusively to only those who are willing to share its intimate yet boundless experience.

The *Natya Sastra* provides a theoretical grid and offers a good model for dramatic art, but it has by no means remained the only one model of theatric practice in India. There have been several modes of performance of Sanskrit theatre across India, with different styles and regional variations. There is unfortunately no direct evidence on any of them, except textual references from earlier sources. There are numerous rudimentary evidences and references on performance practices, for example, *Nata Sutras* by Panini, a practice of plays referred to by Patanjali and the descriptions of actors in texts such as *Arthasastra* and *Kamasutra*.

Facing page: Kalamandalam Girija and Kalamandalam Sailaja in performance.

Sanskrit plays themselves tend to give ample references to stage enactment. For example, there is this account of a dramatic performance of Kalidasa's *Ratnavali* described in Damodaragupta's *Kuttanimata* (AD 900), which points to the fact that in ancient times a live mode of theatre existed in different parts of the country. There are references to the enactment of drama in the three plays of Bhavabhuti. The conceptual framework of Kutiyattam broadly follows the aesthetic formulations enunciated by Bharata in the *Natya Sastra*. However, the method of enactment in Kutiyattam, which has survived in the south of Kerala, has its own uniqueness, distinctive characteristics and conventions, which might be called a regional adaptation than a conscious deviation from the *Natya Sastra* practice. It has survived several centuries because it adapted itself to the local environment and culture, catered exclusively to the tastes of the local Kerala audience and extended its performance score over the years through internal enrichment.

Many facets of both, the social and religious practices of a given community often get reflected in its theatre. The definition of 'local flavour' in any theatre language is indeed problematic, for theatre represents the collective experience of the culture from which it emerges. To understand the creative processes inherent in Kutiyattam

Kalamandalam Sailaja striking a dramatic pose in a Nangiarkoothu performance.

as a theatric art, and explore its similarities and divergences from a pan-Indian model represented by the *Natya Sastra*, it is essential to probe the basic conceptual patterns implicit in Bharata's text on dramaturgy. A composite treatise both descriptive and prescriptive, the *Natya Sastra* is an attempt to define *natya* or dramatic art in its entirety. In the thirty-six chapters of this massive treatise, Bharata tries to explicate the meaning, purpose and practice of *natya* through the framework of a rich mesh of interrelated ideas. In an attempt to understand *natya*, Bharata discusses in minute detail the method of enactment of the plays and the different elements of a play, including the word, sound, movement, line, colour, feeling, expression and experience, which are all integral to it. In the chapter on *natyotpatti* (the origin of *natya*), Bharata dwells at length on the definition, content and manifestations of *natya*. Verses 106-124 describe *natya* as having an all-pervading significance. It is intended to convey sound advice (*hitopadesa*) through the presentation of events and actions, all directed towards the practice of *dharma*. It deals with wide-ranging subjects such as scriptures, art, moral advice, right conduct, peace and war, love and murder, retribution, humour, peace, fortitude for the valiant, knowledge for the ignorant, scholarship for the scholarly, sports for the lords—in short, everything dealing with the lives and actions of people in the three worlds. Far from being merely a specific branch of art activity, the domain of *natya* is described as being interdisciplinary—pervading the whole world, containing within itself multifarious experiences and perspectives on life. The cardinal point regarding the all-pervasive significance of *natya* is described in the verse,

nanabhavopasampannam
nanavasthantaratmakam
lokavrttanukaranam
natyametanmayakrtam[26]

(This *natya* that I have created is enriched with several moods and states, imbued with different situations and inner meanings. It is the representation of the happenings of the world.)

In this aphoristic definition, the word *bhava* means 'a state of being'. The phrase *nanabhavopasampannam* basically involves the transformation of the abstract unmanifest idea to the concrete manifest

Bheema in Kalyanasaugandhika.

that results in a state of being. The second statement, *nanavasthantaratmakam*, refers to the many situations, contexts and conditions (*avasthas*) that become the subject matter of *natya*. The third idea, *lokavrttanukaranam*, does not simply mean the imitation of the affairs of the world, but a creative transformation of the material available to the artist in his experience of life.

At a primary functional level, *natya* or dramatic performance is described as a composite art that integrates poetry, music, dance and drama. Poetry is at the core of a play and a performance has to do justice to the rich poetic nuances in the text of the play. *Natya* is derived from the root *nat*, which perhaps emerged from the Prakrit *nrtt* (meaning dance). Consequently, *natya* is both *drsya* and *sravya*, to be seen and to be heard; the essentials of performance as described in the *Natya Sastra* are propitiatory rituals,

[26] Nagar, Ravishankar, ed. 1981. *Natya Sastra of Bharata Muni*, p. 38. New Delhi: Piramal Publications.

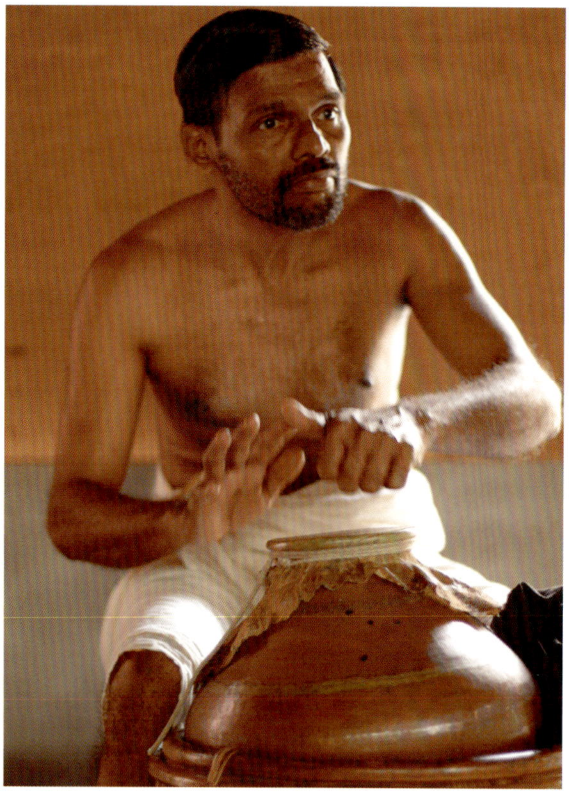

Playing on the drum called mizhavu.

elements and qualities of dance and music with their different tempos and styles of performance, use of each organ of the body, dialogue and its characteristics, delivery of speech and rhythm, stage, stage properties, musical instruments and several other details that go into the making of a theatre. The performance involves not the mere rendering of the lines of the text, but chanting (singing) those lines, dancing and dramatising them through body movements, gestures and facial expressions. The process of dramatic communication is contained in the suggestive word *abhinaya* (meaning, 'bringing [the actor] to [the spectator]'). Rather than the simplistic sense of acting, the word *abhinaya* relates to a whole range of communication strategies that the actor employs in theatre, which Bharata classifies into four categories, including *aharya*, relating to costume, make-up and stage properties; *vacika*, verbal rendering and *angika*, histrionic action. He also defines a fourth category called *sattvika*, the communication that goes beyond the limitations of ordinary dramatic action, when the supreme skills of the actor integrate with the essence of human experience and creativity.

The notion of *rasa*, perhaps the central concept in Indian aesthetic theory, which has been discussed in a number of ways and in the context of different disciplines, is crucial to the system of theatre described in the *Natya Sastra*. The discussions on *rasa* are so wide-ranging that they cover the concrete meanings such as that of a simple sap, juice or flavour to abstract ideas ranging from 'the essence of a thing', 'the aesthetic delight derived from a performance' and a philosophic quest akin to 'the attainment of the highest pinnacle of bliss' (*brahmananda sahodara*). The concept of *rasa* as a category of aesthetic theory is dealt with in the *Natya Sastra* as well as through the several commentaries of the text and also in independent critical works. It is an organising principle that governs a poetic work or a performance, akin to 'tasting' or 'savouring', which Bharata illustrated by using a culinary metaphor. Simplistically, *rasa* is the essential flavour of a work of art, which cannot be considered as an objective entity; in Indian aesthetics, it is both a process and the end of an artistic experience.

While discussing the basic nature of *rasa* in connection with drama, two perspectives have been predominant: one that emanates from the creativity of the performer and the other from the experience of the spectator, the latter referring to the experience of delight enjoyed by an involved, sensitive spectator while watching a play. Depending on the essential perspective adopted in defining *rasa*

Gesture depicting the word 'Rama'.

as expression or experience, discussions on this central concept have to fall into either of these categories.

The conceptual framework offered by the *Natya Sastra* and other prescriptive texts find their application in performance traditions spread over several modes of dance and drama across India. However, the existence of a coherent, unified theory of dramaturgy does not always constitute the unified configuration of a performance tradition, for one cannot pin these formulations down to a single mode of performance. In the process of the accommodation of these theories to the several local traditions spread across the length and breadth of India, one finds a rich diversity of regional performance styles,

Above: Paccha *(green) make-up is used for characters who have royal but gentle mannerisms. Facing page:* Facial *make-up for Sugriva.*

sometimes with distinctive and sometimes with overlapping features. In fact, many of the folk and classical styles of performance claim to have 'directly' descended from the canonical prescriptions in texts such as the *Natya Sastra*. In some cases, the collective signature of a common dramatic theory with painstakingly worked-out conventions of performance has made it easier for many regional performance styles to adapt themselves to these postulates. Consequently the temple-oriented Dasiyattam takes a new name of 'Bharatanatyam' and a whole range of performance styles including Kuchipudi, Odissi and other regional styles claim to have evolved from the *Natya Sastra*.

The age-old question whether performance pre-dates theory or otherwise is always a matter of debate, but in actual practice, both are inter-dependent. In Kutiyattam, as perhaps in any live performance tradition, the codes of performance have always gained supremacy over theoretical analysis, with great actors down the years swearing upon *gurunathante vazhi* (the way of the preceptor) as sacrosanct. Perhaps the insistence on the practical aspects is the reason why a great theatre tradition such as Kutiyattam was able to survive through centuries. Like the codified text of the *Natya Sastra*, the documents called *kramadeepikas* and *attaprakarams* contain all the practical aspects relating to the theatre of Kutiyattam, including the details on stage setting, make-up and costume of each character, special features of each character, gait, posture, movements, expressive patterns, speech and recitation, and even the remuneration for the actor.

Though the aesthetic principles that are implicit in the *Natya Sastra* provide the basis for the performance of Kutiyattam, in theatric practice, Kutiyattam has distinctive

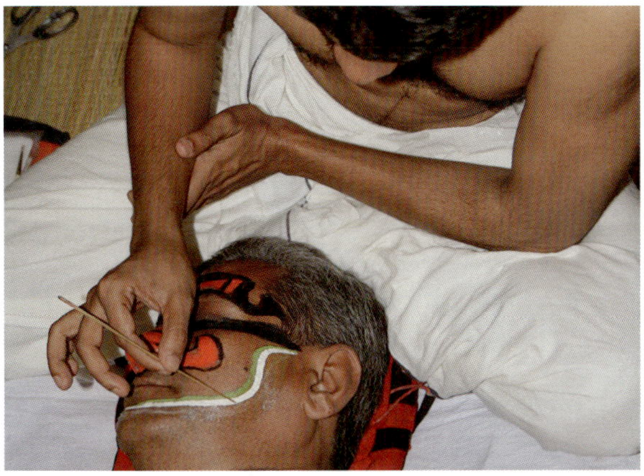

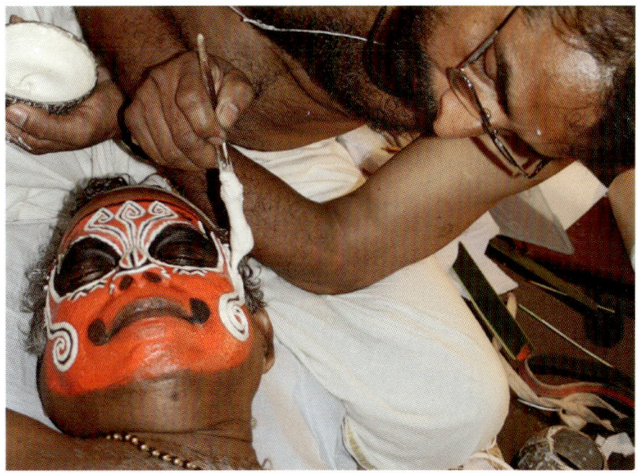

characteristics that are not solely dependent on the model of the *Natya Sastra*. The artistic activity in Kutiyattam depends on the verbal and non-verbal elements such as gesture, body movements, facial expression and stylised speech or recitation, and is aimed at providing full scope for the evocation of *rasa*.

What, then, are the differences between Kutiyattam and the *Natya Sastra* model? The communication of an abstract idea to the mind of the spectator requires transformation through performance codes shared by the actor and the spectator. The theatric conventions of Kutiyattam have their own distinctive characteristics that do not entirely depend on the rules of the *Natya Sastra*. While the *Natya Sastra* has neatly categorised even the minute aspects of dance and theatre into a wealth of details, Kutiyattam tends to be more abstract and symbolic. The difference between the two approaches may be seen with reference to the four modes of *abhinaya–aharya, vachika, angika* and *sattvika*.

The physical aspects of Kutiyattam such as stage settings, properties, costume and make-up have a firm basis on the artistic tradition of Kerala. Any art form originating in a distant past must have survived because it employed technologies appropriate to the context and time, and the case of Kutiyattam is no different. For its costume and make-up, Kutiyattam has, to a great extent, adopted elements from materials available locally, which are in tune with the environment. There is no evidence of the earliest *aharya* patterns in Kutiyattam. Though now it is difficult to conjecture the earliest form of Kutiyattam or the different stages of its development, it is possible to find some parallels between this 'elite' art and some old forms of other indigenous styles of dance and drama in Kerala.[27] The

[27] See Ammaman Thampuran. 1989 (1935). *Koothum Kutiyattavaum*. Calicut: *Matrubhumi*. It holds the view that the costume of the Chakyar is indigenous to Kerala and is derived from earlier forms.

early costumes seem to have been made for a particular event, from perishable materials of easily available things such as the spathe of an areca palm, tender leaves of the coconut tree and chrysanthus (*tecchi*) flowers. (Now this practice has changed to include more non-perishable articles such as wood, metal sheets, cloth, even paper.) The *aharya* tradition of Kerala spreads from folk and ritualistic arts such as Teyyam, Patayani and Mudiyettu, down to Kalamezhuttu (the ritualistic ground drawing), the traditional mural paintings, and extends to the comparatively 'recent' arts such as Krishnattam and Kathakali.

The costume, make-up and stage settings of Kutiyattam follow a model vastly different from those of the *Natya Sastra*. The instruments that constitute the orchestra are:

Mizhavu: A big copper pot-drum with its mouth covered by leather, the *mizhavu* is held vertically inside the frame. It makes a booming sound that reverberates through the stage with its specialised resonance. The *mizhavu* is the chief instrument, played by the Nambiar, which sets the rhythm of the performance. Generally, there are two *mizhavus* on the stage.

Kuzhitalam: A small cymbal that is used by the Nangiars to modulate the rhythm while reciting the passages of the text.

Idakka: A percussion instrument that is shaped like an hourglass; played in the background.

Timila: Another percussion instrument, again shaped like an elongated hourglass and played with the hands.

Kuzhal: A wind instrument that is used in Kutiyattam on special occasions.

Sankhu: The conch, an auspicious instrument, is used at the beginning of a performance.

In its twenty-third chapter, the *Natya Sastra* elaborately describes the different types of costumes worn by the characters and the details of stage props such as palaces, chariots, banners, statues of animals, and so on. The typology of the *aharya* in the *Natya Sastra* model represents the corporeal time, place and class of the character depicted in a play. In contrast to this, the stage setting in Kutiyattam has a ritualistic and symbolic significance, with decorations such as tender coconut leaves and shoots adorning the stage. Performed traditionally inside *koothambalams*, the stage is decorated with fruit-laden plantain trees (*vazhakkula*), tender leaves of the coconut tree (*kuruttola*) and a vessel filled with paddy (*nirapara*), considered as auspicious symbols. A huge brass lamp (*nilavilakku*) is placed at the centre of the stage, with two lighted wicks facing the actor and one facing the audience. The *mizhavu* in its wooden board is placed at the back of the stage. A stool placed at the middle of the stage (*pitha*) and a small, handheld curtain (*tirassila*) complete the stage properties in Kutiyattam. The *aharya* in Kutiyattam is designed to do justice to the 'supernatural' atmosphere of a typical Sanskrit play, inhabited by other-worldly characters such as gods, demons and celestials that interact with humans. For example, how does a play depict Rama, the god, Sita, the goddess with unsurpassed beauty, Ravana, the ten-headed demon, through mere physical representation? This can be achieved only by avoiding the emphasis on a person's physical characteristics alone and dwelling on the 'psychological traits' represented by the character.

The costume in Kutiyattam is designed not for individual characters, but for the common characteristics represented by these characters. Facial make-up gives emphasis to the depiction of expressions. It covers the physical characteristics of the face through a complicated facial make-up by accentuating

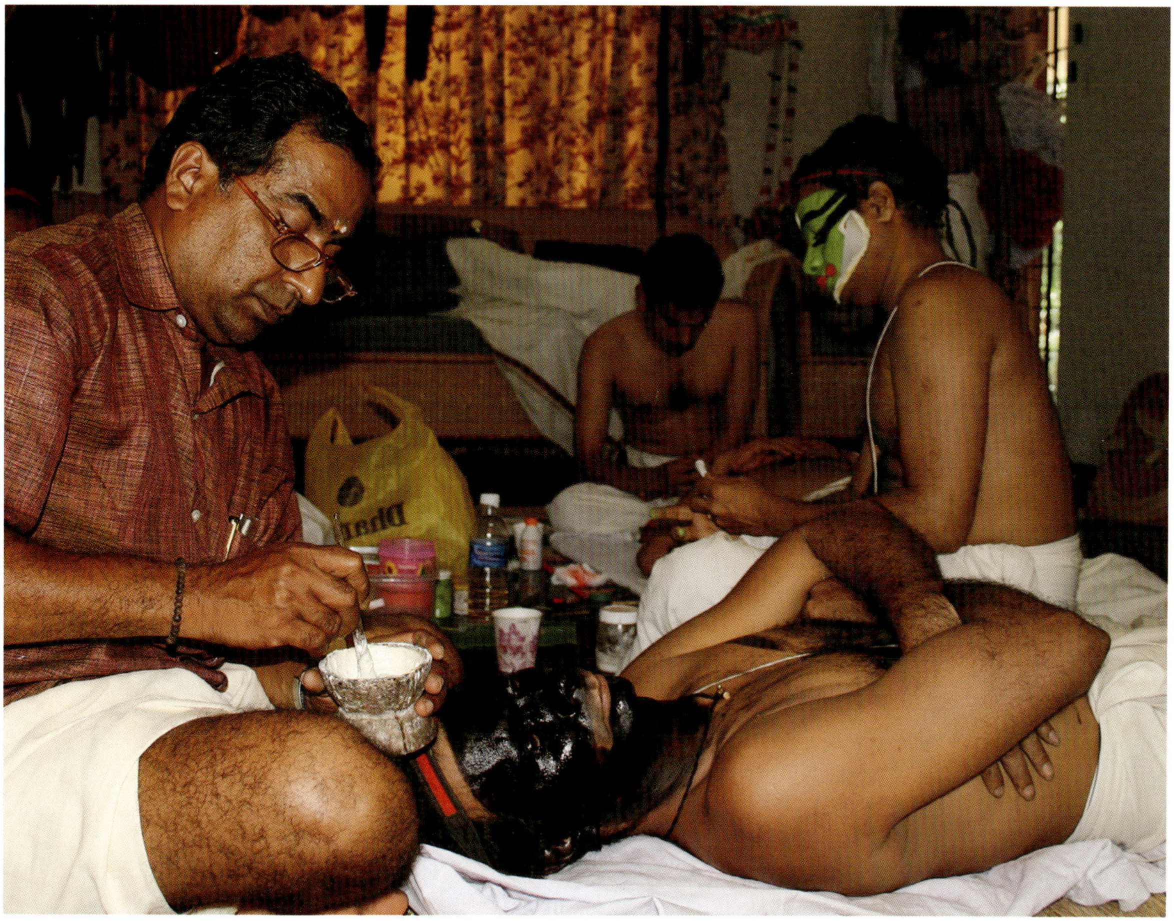

The greenroom where characters get their make-up done.

the eyes, brows or lips of the actor and conceals the ears and chin, which do not have any bearing on theatric communication. For example, Jimutavahana in *Nagananda* and Samvarana in *Tapatisamvarana* have the same make up and costume, while the facial make-up of Bhima and Arjuna are different even though they are brothers, because they are different in their basic character (*svabhava*). The *vidushaka* appears as a comic character with characteristic make-up consisting of lines on the face, chest, arms and legs, with both sides of the moustache bent in opposite directions, and adorned with flowers in one ear and a dangling ear-drop in the other.

According to the character traits, facial make-up is divided into *paccha* (green), *katti* (with a moustache resembling an inverted knife), *tadi* (beard), *pazhukka* (light red) and *kari* (black). *Paccha* is used for characters such as Arjuna, Rama, Lakshmana and Samvarana who have royal but gentle characteristics. *Katti* represents royal and haughty characters such as Ravana, while *tadi* is for demonic characters or characters representing animal traits such as Hanuman, Sugriva and Bali. *Tadi* has different colour patterns according to the character traits and quality—for example, a black beard for Sugriva, red for Bali and white for Hanuman. *Pazhukka* is used for Bhima, while an ogress such as Surpanakha uses *kari*. The facial paints consist of naturally occurring substances such as *manayola* (arsenic sulphide) and turmeric for yellow, *chayilyam* (mercury sulphide) for red, *manayola* and indigo blue (for green) and soot (for black). The eyes,

Previous page: Bali's entry in Balivadham.
Above: Margi Sathi applying her make-up as she gets ready for the performance.

headgear with a slanted top called *vasukeeyam*. In the earlier days, the *aharya* of the female character in Kutiyattam did not have much significance; for even *kramadeepikas*, which detail all the logistic aspects of Kutiyattam, are silent on the costume and make-up of the female character.[28] However, in the latter part of the twentieth century, under the initiative of Paimkulam Rama Chakyar in Kalamandalam, many innovations were brought about in the costume of the female character. For example, the conical cap (called *kootu*) worn by the Nangiar as headgear was replaced by an attractive *kireetam*, made of wood, covered with red velvet and decorated with golden and silver trinkets, with a silver head of a cobra at the top.

highlighted by black collyrium and tinted red by inserting *chunda* (solanacca) seeds, attain brightness and flexibility, to express any shade of feeling.

The costumes are not as spectacular as that of Kathakali. In spite of apparent similarities in the headgear and other adornments such *katisutra*, bangles, *tolvala*, garlands on the body, the get-up in Kutiyattam is much simpler, with more of a suggestive quality. In the skirt-like garment worn from the waist downwards, the legs are exposed till the knee at the back and painted with white rice paste. Unlike the practice described in the *Natya Sastra*, the costumes and make-up are not determined by the person's physical characteristics, but by their importance in the play in terms of theatric potential. While Arjuna and Bhima are both brothers, Arjuna being a more 'important' character in Kutiyattam has a regular headgear called *kireeta*, while the less central character represented by Bhima has a

Though Kutiyattam is generally abstract and suggestive in its theatric presentation, there are several occasions when it resorts to spectacle and a display of stage conventions for 'theatric' effect. One such occasion is the presentation of *ninam* (blood display) by the maimed Surpanakha in 'Surpanakhankam' of *Ascharyachudamani*. During the play, the demoness approaches Lakshmana in the guise of a lovely damsel and pleads with him to make her his wife. Lakshmana spurns the advances of the lady. She then shows her true colours by assuming her own form. In the tussle that follows, Lakshmana cuts off her ears, nose and breasts. In her maimed condition, displaying her blood-spangled body, she runs to her brother Ravana and pleads for revenge. The 'blood' for this scene is prepared by mixing lime, rice paste and turmeric, and the tender leaves of coconut trees immersed in 'blood' make the mangled organs. The slow approach of the red-spattered ogress wailing loudly with faltering steps, through the midst of the audience, to the accompaniment of lit torches and loud drumming, creates the impression of heavy bleeding and torturous pain,

[28] Rajagopalan, L.S. 1997. *Women's Role in Kutiyattam*, p. 16. Chennai: Kuppuswami Sastri Research Institute.

Ninam, literally, 'blood display', a gory scene depicting the blood-stained body and garments of Surpanakha in Surpanakhankam.

evoking both awe and revulsion in the mind of the spectator.

Two other spectacular scenes are *parakkum koothu* (the flying scene) and *ozhukal* (the drowning scene) in *Nagananda*. Both these scenes are required to be done with extreme care, skill and precision for any lapse could spell danger for the actor.[29] During the olden days, the *samudragrha* (ocean retreat) in 'Swapnanka' seems to have had stage properties such as the auspicious lamp, incense beds and a fountain! Kutiyattam is an art form that favours suggestive acting to such an extent that a lit lamp represented Sita's presence in 'Asokavanikankam' on the stage. This kind of extravagant display of horror and terror in the *ninam* scenes and the 'flying scenes' seems startling. Perhaps this is an instance in Kutiyattam that fascinates everyone and may have been created taking into cognisance the different tastes among the audience.

[29] To depict a flying scene, the actor, by means of a thousand strings attached to his body, is slowly brought down to the stage and this had to be done with great dexterity by the 'sutradhara' or the Nambiar who controlled the strings; otherwise it spelt danger for the performer.

The Preparation

The complexity and refinement of Kutiyattam is the result of the patient learning of the formal system through many long years of training under a teacher. It is a system that has kept itself alive by the transmission from the master to the disciple. Traditionally, Kutiyattam was sustained through a matrilineal joint family system, where the children were part of their mother's family, and consequently through *guru-shishya parampara* (master-disciple tradition) extending from the maternal uncle to the nephew. The guru, the performer-preceptor, had the unquestioned authority to mould the student through years of training and the student imbibed the skills in utter devotion and dedication. In the olden days, the art had the support of the temple and this left the actors with considerable time to hone their skills and pass them on to the next generation. In the past, Kutiyattam being a hereditary occupation, the Chakyars and the Nangiars were exposed to it from birth. Plays, play texts, acting techniques and even roles were familiar to them from early childhood. However, it is only when they start formal training that they went on to become accustomed to the complex theatrical grammar of Kutiyattam.

Facing page: Margi Madhu as Ascharyalakshmanan in an intense moment in Ezhamankam.

On ritual occasions, the Chakyars were not free to perform in all the temples. Specific Chakyar families had performance rights of the temples assigned to them through hereditary lineage and transgression was strictly forbidden. Though there were eighteen families engaged in the performance of Kutiyattam in the past, only five survive. They are Pothiyil, Ammannur, Koypa (Paimkulam), Mani (Perinjellur) and Cheriyaparisha. Of the community of Chakyars, some became adept in histrionic acting, while some others were more skilled in speech. (An old saying goes like this: 'Pothiyil has speech, Ammannur histrionic acting and Kuttanchery has humour at his command!') Now the major 'schools of acting' are divided among the lines of Mani, Paimkulam and Ammannur representing the major actors of recent times, Mani Madhava Chakyar, Paimkulam Rama Chakyar and Ammannur Madhava Chakyar.

In the Chakyar families, a child is traditionally initiated into Kutiyattam by the age of seven. Formal instruction begins for a student when he is around eight years old and continues through life. The student apprentices learn from the master, starting at around four in the morning and continuing till about eight in the evening. Training comprises learning of the text, the performance text, mode of chanting, speech patterns, code of hand gestures, body movements, facial expressions and the elaboration of dramatic situations,

Gesture depicting the word 'you' by a female performer in a cheerful mood.

which is the crux of dramatic action. Since the face is the main field of dramatic action, great importance is given to the movement of each part of the face, such as the eyes, brows, cheeks, lips and to the expression of emotions. The Nambiar who assists the actor on the *mizhavu*, also learns the rhythmic patterns and mode of drumming for different occasions. The playing of the other instruments in Kutiyattam—*timila*, *edakka*, *kurumkuzhal* and *kuzhitalam*—also requires special training, but is of secondary importance in comparison to the *mizhavu*.

The preparation to be an actor works at two levels—training for mastering the performance grammar and taking lessons in Sanskrit. The student learns the basic grammatical rules of Sanskrit and is slowly exposed to the plays. The means of transmission of the grammar of performance is primarily imbibing both, the technique and style of the master. The student evolves into a mature actor by a process of arduous learning through the daily repetition of small units of performance. The harder a student strives to practise his initial lessons, the firmer his grasp becomes, which he can put to use when he is a full-fledged actor. At the initial stage, technical mastery is what the art is about, with the result that for the performance, the seemingly different segments—the percussion, the time sequences (*tala*), the chanting mode, the gestures, dance patterns, the fully-developed facial expressions—coalesce into a single organic whole.

The next stage is the painstaking process of learning each part, situation and play, in consultation with the performance manuals. Beginning with small roles and ritualistic dance sequences, the actor gradually develops his repertoire to include more complicated roles. The actor's own capacity to draw on his training and his years of study of the texts equips him to slowly graduate to take on more complex roles. By then the actor is expected to be familiar with the epics and the text of the Sanskrit plays and also to keenly follow the performance manuals of Kutiyattam. The years of study hone his skills, familiarise him with the grammar of performance and develop his imaginative faculties to achieve a certain level of mastery. Once he attains this stage, he understands the subtle nuances of each action and character in the plays and is considered a full-fledged actor. Given the structure of the situation in a play, he can develop as well as elaborate it according to his creative and imaginative faculties. By assimilating himself into the character represented, the actor becomes an interpreter rather than a mere narrator of his role and is able to represent the action of the character objectively and analytically. In a lifetime dedicated to the continuous rendering of the same plays and characters, a 'good' actor always brings in something novel to the performance and conveys the impression to the spectator that he is seeing it for the first time.

In Kutiyattam, the body integrated with the emotions evoked by the mind is the sole canvas of theatric action. Therefore a major share of the training concentrates on preparing the body and mind to take on any part in a performance. According to the traditional method of *gurukula sampradaya,* the initial training includes getting up early in the morning to start the practice, which continues late into the night with few breaks in between.

Paimkulam Rama Chakyar records that 'there are twenty-four ragas in Kutiyattam, but only twenty-one have been identified with respect to their application to the verses'.[30] The *ragas* are: Veladhuli; Varati; Toti; Puraniru; Andhali (Artan); Paurali; Tanah (Danam); Antari; Ghattantari; Kamari; Tarkan; Viratarkan; Gandharam; Dukkhagandharam; Kuralkkuinji (korakkurinji); Vimala; Muddhan; Kaisiki; Indalam; Muralindalam; Chetipanchamam; Bhinnapanchamam; Virapanchamam and Srikanthi.

A rigorous training session.

There are prescriptive rules for the application of all these *ragas* to the verses. They are generally not taught by their names or their rules of operation, but by the practical aspect of the manner of chanting a specific verse. Regarding the musical aspect of Kutiyattam, the noted scholar L.S. Rajagopalan observes that 'this is not an ordinary recitation of the *slokas* in the typical Kerala style nor is it the singing of the *slokas* in any Karnatak or

[30] Paimkulam Rama Chakyar. 'Svaras in Kutiyattam' in *Sangeet Natak Special Issue*, No. 111-114, pp. 91-100.

Stance depicting a grand peacock spreading its plumes and dancing.

Hindusthani *ragas*. It would be more or less appropriate to classify it with the chanting of the Vedas. The Chakyars call it 'swarathil cholluka'.[31] The manner of articulation is difficult to describe, but to the connoisseur, the emotional impact of the sounds as well as the compelling intensity of the utterance communicate the meaning.

Of equal importance in Kutiyattam are the time cycle patterns (*talas*) that keep the rhythm in place. Primarily controlled by the orchestra, especially the *mizhavu* drummer, *talas* set the pattern of the performance and are to be internalised by the actor and the drummers alike. The rigidity of the code and the several inter-locking components of acting coming together in a performance lead to great coordination for a performance of Kutiyattam. The *talas* are basically eight in number. These are *dhruvatala* (with fourteen time beats); *ekatala I* (with one beat); *ekatala II* (two beats); *triputatala I* (one); *triputatala II* (two); *atantatala* (fourteen); *jhampatala* (ten half beats, leading to five full ones); *lakshmitala* (a specialised beat for depicting the flight of Jatayu, the mighty bird). In addition, there are *talas* such as *panchari* and *mallatala*, which are in use. There are prescriptions regarding the use of *talas* according to each *raga*. This facilitates the expression of different emotions. The facial muscles to be made flexible include the brows, muscles under the eyes, cheeks

[31] Rajagopalan, L.S. 'Music in Kutiyattam' in *Sangeet Natak Special Issue*, pp. 113-122.

and lips. Each of them serves a different function for the evocation of an expression; for example, the up-and-down movement of the eyebrows assists in expressing pleasure and wonder; the movement of the muscles under the eye enhances the moods of valour and rage and the downward curving of the lips indicates sorrow. The eye movements are of special significance in Kutiyattam, as they are the main field of action and expression. An actor's ability is judged by the capacity to bring 'life' to his eyes. In a discussion on the special training given for the eyes, Madhava Chakyar mentions twenty-one varieties of movement patterns.[32] When the student becomes proficient in the manipulation of the eyes and the other facial muscles, he learns to evoke *rasabhinaya*—a crucial aspect in theatric communication.

In the first act of *Subhadradhananjaya*, Arjuna's description of the hermitage illustrates the technique of elaboration by restoring to facial expression alone. The *sloka* goes like this:

sikhinisalabho jvalachakrena
vikriyate patan
pibati bahusah sardulinam stanam
mrgasabakah
sprsati kalabhah saimhim
damstram mrnaladhiya
muhurnnayati nakulam
nidratantrim lihannahipotakah

(Butterflies falling into the fire do not get burnt; instead they fly away. The tigress feeds the deer calf with milk from her udder. A baby elephant pulls at the fang of a lioness, mistaking it for a lotus stalk. The mongoose puts a baby snake to sleep, by licking it all over.)

The incidents described here, which go against the laws of nature, are brought in to emphasise the peaceful atmosphere of the hermitage and to evoke the dominant *santarasa*. The actor enacts and elaborates the meaning of the *sloka* by the use of his eyes and facial expression only, avoiding hand gestures and body movements. The flight of the butterflies, the burning fire, the falling of the butterflies into the fire and their going back unhurt are described in detail with deft eye movements. Similarly, the description of the tigress suckling the deer calf, the baby elephants pulling at the fang of the lioness and the mongoose licking the baby serpent to sleep are all depicted through facial expressions, which establish the sophistication reached by a Kutiyattam actor in expressing emotions.

There are nine basic emotions—love (*srngara*), wonder (*adbhuta*), valour (*vira*), anger (*raudra*), ridicule or the comic expression (*hasya*), grief (*karuna*), fear (*bhayanaka*), revulsion (*bibhatsa*) and tranquillity (*santa*). Though the preliminary training is a mechanical exercise by which the student learns to express each emotion by the rules of the book, in its ultimate level, *rasa* is not a static phenomenon; it can have variations in terms of intensity, depending on the context and character. In the actor's interpretation of the situation, worldly emotions such as anger, love, sadness or fear get transmuted into an idealised level represented by the play, through the use of imagination. This is why the *rasas* are not to be depicted in isolation, for they cannot be taken out of context. (The attempt to express *navarasas* in lecture-demonstrations of Kutiyattam usually falls flat because *rasa* is not a mechanical working of the facial muscles.)

[32] Mani Madhava Chakyar. 1973. *Natyakalpadrumam*, pp. 110-111. Cheruthuruthy: Kerala Kalamandalam.

Gesture depicting the word 'here'.

A performance in Kutiyattam is regarded successful only when the acting takes a slow tempo, minutely elaborating the *rasa* and allowing it to register in the spectator's mind. Only an actor who has absolute control over his technique and is capable of transcending it can excel in *rasabhinaya*, achieved by spontaneous facial expressions and by an imaginative identification of the context presented on the stage.

As the next step, the teacher gives the special instruction of 'infusing breath' (*vayu kodukkal*) into the eyes, which in Kutiyattam is a remarkable feat of 'enlivening' the expression. The principle is to learn to concentrate the 'vital energy' on certain specific channels of the body; in this case, the eyes, to 'enliven' the emotion portrayed. The manipulation of breath energy in the human body for the communication of *rasas* is more strenuous. The emphasis is not to spend all the energy in a single outburst, but to gather it and spend it through a slow, deliberate process of self-awareness and, through this, lead to self-transcendence. Ammannur Madhava Chakyar describes in a succinct manner the method of practising breath control with his teacher Kotungalloor Tampuran for the death scene (in the case of death, the five kinds of breath are *kshudrakan*, *tamakan*, *chinnan*, *mahan* and *oordhvan*) of Bali in *Balivadham*:

> I would draw a breath, and he would point out, this is not right, that is not right, etc. All the five breaths had to be executed properly. During this exercise, if your *chinnan* [a kind of breath simultaneously to be executed in the enactment of death] is blocked, you have to start again. The second and third breaths would then come out properly. Only when you reached the *mahan* [the penultimate breath] could you say, 'I have done it'.[33]

[33] Narayana Pisharoti, K.P. April-June 1996. 'The Dominant Rasa: An Interview with Ammannur Madhava Chakyar' in *Sangeet Natak* (No. 120), pp. 22-41.

The process of controlling the vital breath during training has to be done with utmost care and caution, for any slip can cause detrimental results.

The basic body posture is a *samapada* position, closer to a sitting mode though the torso is above the ground, with the front portion of the legs open, heels pushed in and knees flexed outwards. (To ensure that the knees are stretched out, a stick is placed between them during training, so that they do not come together.) This posture being the most fundamental stance of Kutiyattam, a student is expected to begin adopting it with a short duration and gradually extend his capacity to hold out for long stretches of time. While assuming this posture, the student also rotates the clenched fists and practises the chanting and recitation of the verse.

Oil is liberally applied to the body and the student lies down on a mat that is spread on the ground. The master, leaning on a bamboo pole fixed above, massages the student's body, including the organs, sub-organs and muscles. He applies pressure on specific points, lightly touches or rubs vigorously other parts of the body. The massage patterns of Kutiyattam draw on the gymnastic tradition of Kalari that is popular in Kerala. This practice, done continuously in the morning for about a month each year during the monsoon season, makes the body adaptable to the special needs of Kutiyattam.

Exercise (called *sadhakam*) of the body, with emphasis on different parts, is crucial to Kutiyattam training. The stretching exercises are called *meysadhakam*. There are several patterns of body movement through flexing, stretching and leaping in the air, stretching of the hand and rotation, which give strength and fitness to the body.

In Kutiyattam, there are basic dance steps, sequences, interpretative dances as well as movement patterns for specific characters and special occasions. The primary dance steps are the simple ones done to the beat of 'Thi Tha Tha Tha' and these progressively get more complex. Dance steps with more complicated patterns are *chari, tattu, chuvatu chavittal, arangu perumattam* and others. For example, *chuvatu chavittal* is in slow tempo, in Triputa (*tala*), with dance steps and leaps to the mnemonic beat of 'Dhakkukkukkum Dhakkukkukkum Threm Threm Thitti...' *Chari* is a dance with mincing steps, directed towards the four directions, in Triputa.

Dance sequences such as *valiyakku, chandanavalli* and *kalappurathu natakkal* are more complex. These are either representative of different characters or part of ritualistic dances. *Chandanavalli* is part of the preliminary (*nityakriya*) ritual of the Nangiar, while *kalapppurathu natakkal* is the characteristic gait of a hero who is a male character.

There are different gaits (*parikrama*) for the entry and exit of the characters. Women walk in the gait of *chollunti natakkal* while *brahmin* characters have a circular gait. A proud and pompous character such as Ravana has a circular gait and leaping steps, with the legs thrown into the air to indicate arrogance.

Kutiyattam has a complex language of hand gestures capable of expressing any idea or sentence. The interpretative gesture pattern is so versatile that it is a complete language, with nouns, verbs, plurals, prepositions and suffixes in place. Broadly based on the treatise called *Hastalakshanadipika*, the gestures of Kutiyattam have been adopted by other art forms in Kerala such as Kathakali. To start with, the twenty-four primary *hastas* or *hastamudras* (primary hand poses) of *Hastalakshanadipika* can be roughly equated with the alphabets in a language.

A combination of *samana mudras* (the same hand pose for both the hands) and *misra mudras* (those with mixed hand poses) can create any word in the gesture language of Kutiyattam. The twenty-four *hastamudras* are:

> *Pataka*; *mudrakhya*; *kataka*; *mushti*; *kartarimukha*; *sukatunda*; *kapittha*; *hamsapaksha*; *sikhara*; *hamsasya*; *anjali*; *ardhachandra*; *mukura*; *bhramara*; *suchimukha*; *pallava*; *tripataka*; *mrgasirsha*; *sarpasira*; *vardhamana*; *arala*; *urnanabha*; *mukula* and *katakamukha*.

Each of these poses makes several words—for example, *pataka* is made by bending the ring finger. From *pataka*, both the hands adopting the *hasta* and holding them straight, facing the front side can make the word *surya*. For *simha*, the hands holding the same *pataka hasta* are held one above the other (left hand down). Apart from these, *pataka hasta* can create words such as king, elephant, ox, crocodile, arch, creeper, flag, wave, chariot, netherworld, earth, seat and several others. Similarly, each of the basic *hastamudras* can generate a host of words, to constitute the complex vocabulary of Kutiyattam.

The Malayalam word '*attam*' roughly means dance or performance. There are specific dance patterns in Kutiyattam that suggest subtle mime components. Here the rhythmical pattern is more sophisticated and the dances bring out the mood or characteristic of that particular situation. The rhythm synchronises with the action to evoke a particular mood or character trait. For example, in *mayilattam* (the dance of the peacock), the imitation of the features and manners of the object represented is not a copy of the movements, but an artistic recreation of the essence of the characteristics. Rather than through the physical setting or costumes, the actor uses the technique of elaborate acting to explore every nuance and detail and interprets the idea for the benefit of the spectator. Set in rigid convention, in the dance of *mayilattam*, the actor elaborately depicts the actions of a peacock—combing the feathers with its beak, spreading the plumes, swaying happily from side to side and strutting movements orchestrated in various tempos. Here interaction between the dancer and the spectator happens not merely through empathy of the latter and understanding of the characteristics of the object represented (the peacock), but through a shared code of communication between the actor and spectator, by locating themselves within a complex structure of mutual understanding of the various nuances of the play.

Patappurappadu (the preparation for a battle), as the name indicates, is a vigorous dance sequence set to its own conventions, describing the minute details in setting out for a battle. The dance is rigidly structured with a set rhythmic cycle and synchronised movements. The actor impersonating a character, say, Ravana, describes each weapon, flaunts it and sharpens it to make it ready for use. He orders that the horse-drawn chariot be brought and deposits the weapons with great flourish. Set to a vigorous tempo indicating valour and confidence about victory, it is a stock convention in Kutiyattam.

The different components of the invocatory rituals called *nityakriya* are part of the initiation of a student of Kutiyattam. These are the preliminaries of a play and not the main story. These dance segments are non-interpretative and form part of the customary conventions of this theatre. They consist of dance steps and hand patterns set to fixed rhythm and tempo. This provides an opportunity to study

Training session for mizhavu *drumming.*

the technique and, until the student masters it thoroughly, other *kriyas* are not taught. It is a part of the daily practice of a student, however advanced he is in training.

The conventions also include the various descriptions such as *varnana*, *panchangam*, *stobham* and so on. Elaborate descriptions are part of the well-established conventions of Kutiyattam. These are not necessarily character-specific; rather they are fixed items to be performed on given contexts or situations. For example, the enactment of *panchangam* (the description of the physical beauty of the beloved, emphasising five organs—hair, eyes, face, breasts as well as feet) is set by tradition. The elaborate depiction of each organ emphasising the superior physical grace is a cultural construction, a representation of the ideal/quintessential female beauty and, therefore, there is an artistic abstraction of reality. However, in the action and communication of this convention, it is possible to show individual talent and a sensitive actor can bring in a touch of innovation by the imaginative extension of a nuance or an emotion. The situation, charged with expressive energy, is improvisational and immediate in its experience.

The *varnanas* of places such as the forest (*vanavarnana*), palace (*rajadhanivarnana*), ocean (*samudravarnana*), garden (*udyana-varnana*), heaven (*svargavarnana*) and hermitage (*asramavarnana*) are of special interest in Kutiyattam, for they are modes of performance that give rise to a range of opportunities to the artist for elaborate action. While there is a general framework of the action in each of these descriptions, their content and range are open-ended, drawing freely on the insights and skill of the artist. The description of a garden vividly portrays the flowers, plants, creepers, creeper-houses, mounds, retreats, lakes, lotuses in the lakes, bees coming to drink the nectar from the lotuses, swans playing in the lakes, swings, the soft breeze—and whatever detail the actor wants to include.

Another prescriptive item is the learning of the 'characteristic traits' or *stobham* of the stock characters. In Kutiyattam, while there is great variety and subtlety in character portrayal, many of them have stock, framing traits and a set of rules of acting. These may be considered as points where the actor 'steps into' the role. There are *stobhams* for many characters such as a bird (*pakshistobham*), monkey (*vanarasto-bham*), ogress (*rakshasistobham*), *vidhushaka* and many others with stock traits. The *stobham* of the *vidushaka* includes cleaning his sacred thread, untying and cleaning a tuft of hair, drying his vest and fanning himself vigorously with it, bulging both the cheeks and surveying the audience with a comic expression. A monkey is introduced by scratching his chin and body, shaking the branches of a tree, trying to leap from one side to the other and such other stock actions. The character represented might be a powerful and dignified Hanuman or an ordinary monkey, but irrespective of their station or importance in the play, they begin the action with the same *stobham*. Similarly, a mighty bird such as Jatayu, even if he is 'humanised' in his devotion to Lord Rama, commences his action with the depiction of *pakshistobham*. The movements of characters are also different, according to their traits. Each animal has its characteristic *stobham*, such as that of a peacock, elephant or lion.

Cholliyattam is a rehearsal involving the coordination of all the elements of theatre—the acting of the Chakyar/Nangiar is assisted by the drumming of the Nambiar, the chanting of the *slokas* and the rhythm beats by the Nangiar. *Cholliyattam* offers the student familiarity with the formal system of learning in Kutiyattam, for unless he is sufficiently familiar with the theatre grammar and his role, the student cannot control all the details and let the mind be filled with the intensity of the situation. The orchestra and the singer, or the person who chants, remains on the stage as an integral part of the performance. Through long years of training and absolute familiarity with the material, there is an unspoken communication between the performers and also between the actors and the drummers. Rather than rehearsing for individual performances, this formal system assures a shared understanding that bursts forth into powerful creativity.

In Kutiyattam, the elaboration of the text is achieved in multiple ways. Primarily, the verse from the play is elaborated by subjecting it to a four-fold interpretation. The actor first recites the verse, demonstrates its verbal meaning, analyses it according to its syntactical meaning by bringing out the implications of the text and finally elaborates the ideas implied in it.

A typical example for the augmentation of the text in Kutiyattam is the first act from Kulasekhara's *Subhadradhananyaya*. A favourite one in the theatre is the process of *koppaniyiykkal* (adorning the heroine), which is integrated into the *abhinaya* of a *sloka* from *Subhadradhananjaya*, when Arjuna dwells on Subhadra's beauty, Arjuna, already in love with Subhadra (whom he has not met in person yet), dwells at length on the beauty of the maiden (who is actually Subhadra herself), who he had saved from the clutches of a demon. Captivated by her beauty, he describes how her eyes, fluttering like the petals of water lilies and darkened with collyrium, dart with fear and bees swarm around her, hoping to take in the fragrance of her face. The water lily is described through a slow depiction of the *mudra*, accompanied by the facial expression of wonder and delight and the quivering of the petals and blooming of the flower.

> *Calakuvalayadhamnoranjanasnigdhamaksnor-*
> *Bhayacaladhrtiyugman keyamalolayanti*
> *Mukhaparimalalobhat bhrngadattanuyatra*
> *Sithilayati Subhadramudritam manasam me.*

(Who is this damsel, with darting eyes resembling dark *kuvalaya* flowers? Her eyes, with their beauty enhanced by the application of collyrium, flutter in fear. She is accompanied by swarming bees that gather around, drawn by the fragrance of her face. This girl loosens the chords of my heart, already sealed by Subhadra.)

In the enactment of this *sloka*, the actor who takes the role of Arjuna subjects it to a four-fold elaboration. First, he recites the *sloka* with appropriate *mudras* and then enacts it without the aid of recitation. He then analyses the verbal meaning and in the end elaborates on the deeper shades of its meaning. He recites '*iyam ka*'—who is she—with action and dwells elaborately on the *nayika's* race, her parents, family and other aspects of identity. Then he confesses, 'My heart is opened' and, elaborating on this, adds, 'which has been sealed by Subhadra.' He goes on to explain how Subhadra had entered his heart through the ears (by listening to the praises of her beauty narrated to him by his friend Gada) and sealed it so that nobody else could enter. Now, a sequence of questions and answers: 'How is this damsel...with darting eyes.' 'How are the eyes...bearing the beauty of dark *kuvalaya* flowers.' 'How else...swiftly darting, due to fear.' 'How again? The beauty enhanced by the application of collyrium.' At this point the actor elaborates on the application of collyrium. He takes on the role of the *nayika* asking her friends to dress her up. He plays each of the friends. The entire process—unknotting and doing up the hair, adorning it with perfume and flowers, tidying the curls, applying *sindhur* on the forehead, adorning the *nayika* with ornaments, helping her dress—is elaborately depicted according to the creative imagination of the actor. The *sakhis* are not satisfied, however, as something is missing. One of them suddenly remembers that they have forgotten to apply the collyrium and proceeds to do so.

The entire sequence is occasioned by the one phrase 'eyes made up with collyrium' (*anjanasnigdhamaksi*) in the text of the play.

The second instance relates to the *sloka* beginning with 'himakara' from 'Asokavanikankam' of Saktibhadra's *Ascharyachudamani*. Ravana is presented as pining for Sita. He indulges in a *kesadipadam* of Sita. Tormented by the arrows of Kama and revived by the cool breeze, he suddenly notices the rays of the moon adding to his discomfort. Addressing the moon, he calls out, 'Himakara' in a pleading voice, in *shadja svara*. When the moon does not hear, he calls out again, more spirited this time, 'Himakara' in *panchama*. When the moon still fails to respond, he asks, 'O moon, don't you hear me? Have you gone deaf?' and screams loudly, 'Himakara.'

> *Himakara himagarbha rasmayastavakinah*
> *mayi madana vidheye yena*
> *vahnim vamanti*
> *na tava balamanangasyapi*
> *va duhkhabhaji*
> *janakaduhituresha sarvarinatha saktih*

Now he proceeds to elaborate this verse, by splitting the text according to its meaning. A summary of this break-up and the method of enactment:

Tavakinah rasmayah vahnim vamanti—your rays pour fire down on me, like burning embers. There is no reason for that. How are your rays? *Tavakinah rasmayah himagarbhah*—they are as cool as ice. Why do they make me burn?

Madanavidheyah—I am under the spell of Kama. How is that? Kama prepares himself to fight me. Wielding his bow and arrows, he comes near me and showers arrows on me. Because of this, your rays have become unbearably hot. *Na tava balam*—However, it is not due to your greatness.

Why? Because of your power. *Anangasyapi va na*—Is it Kama's? No. *Tava balam_anangasyabalam na*—Not the power of either of you. Then whose power is it? *Esha janakaduhituh*—This is the power of that daughter of Janaka. How is she? *Duhkhabhaja*—she is the seat of misery. (Reciting it again in a sad tone.) Why? When Sita was living with Rama, suffering the cruelty of nature and eating only wild berries and fruits, I abducted and brought her here. Then she became very sad and miserable. This is the power of that despondent Sita. You know that. *Sarvarinatha*—you are the husband of the night. You know the pangs of separation when you have to remain apart from night each day.

Reciting the last two lines, the actor concludes his *abhinaya*. The enactment of this verse allows the actor to elaborate *srngara* in all its shades—expectation, yearning, passion and despair.

A distinctive feature of Kutiyattam is the freedom granted to the actor for impersonating multiple roles in a dramatic situation without any change in his make-up and costume. Through this device, called *pakarnnattam*, the actor transcends the boundaries of dramatising the character and is allowed a fluid transmutation into different roles. As a result, the performance works at several levels. This permits the actor donning the costume of Hanuman in 'Anguliyankam' to impersonate himself as Sita and also do a series of other roles. This play is the acid test for the actor who plays Hanuman for he singlehandedly manages to depict the entire narrative sequence of Hanuman crossing the ocean in search of Sita, finding her in Asokavatika and conveying Rama's message to her. The action here takes about twelve days to perform. Hanuman in the course of his elaborate narration intersperses the action with several incidents, anecdotes and stories. Through *nirvahanamm* he recounts in detail the entire story of the Ramayana. As a solo performer he takes on the different roles and shifting perspectives in each of these stories, which requires the actor to exercise his intellectual, imaginative and histrionic faculties to the fullest.

Similarly, in 'Toranayuddhanka' of Bhasa's *Abhishekanataka*, Ravana, while reflecting on how he came to acquire all his glory, indulges in a long digression of mono-acting in which he describes the lifting of Mount Kailasa as well as the subsequent quarrel between Siva and Parvati. In this scene, the actor in the guise of Ravana has to have great dexterity while changing roles in quick succession. The change to a woman's role is indicated merely by taking the end of the lower garment and fastening it on the waist, but the transformation of the facial expression and the demeanour from the masculine to the feminine is very subtle yet powerful. The effective depiction of the changes in personality, while alternating

Facing page: In an indulgent mood while depicting the gesture for 'a young girl'.

A young boy being groomed for Kutiyattam.

roles as man and woman, and the portrayal of the changing moods of Parvati, make great demands on the actor. The actor's challenge is to excel in each of these roles. This is perhaps the height of artistic impersonation achieved in Kutiyattam.

Some of the important qualities of a Chakyar who is narrating a Prabandhakkoothu or taking the part of a *vidushaka* in Kutiyattam include familiarity with the plays, theatre manuals and literary works such as *kavyas* and *prabandhas*, listening and learning from the masters in performance, skill to outsource related material while talking, sense of humour and the capacity to hold the attention of the audience for hours. More than formal training, this requires verbal skills and resourcefulness. Nangiarkoothu as an art form is a take-off from Kulasekhara's *Subhadradhananjaya*, which later got the status of a separate entity. In the *nirvahanam* mode of narrating the previous story of the play from the present moment of the action, the performer is in the role of Kalpalatika, the maid of Subhadra, the heroine of Subhadra-dhananjaya. At Subhadra's orders, Kalpalatika sets out in search of her mistress's lost bodice (*gatrika*) and on the way, recalls the story of Lord Krishna from the imprisonment of Ugrasena, Krishna's grandfather, to Krishna's building of a palace in Dwarka.

The Nambiar is the controlling element in a play and so has to be adequately trained. The preparation to become a good drummer starts each morning when he practises hand manipulation (*pathakakkayyukal*) and rhythm vocalisations (*vayttari*) in different tempos, starting with the slow, gradually reaching the fastest and coming back to the slow. With *pathakakkayyukal* under control, he graduates to the drumming patterns such as *mizhavocchappetuthal* (sounding of the *mizhavu*), drumming for invocation, rituals and dance movements. The drumming for dramatic conventions such as *patappurappad* (preparation for battle), *kailasoddharanam* (the lifting of Mount Kailasa), *koppaniyikkal* (adorning a damsel with ornaments), *mayilattam*

Training session in progress.

and *stobhams* and innumerable other rhythmic variations are highly specialised. He also needs to learn modulations of the *mizhavu* according to the mood and situation of the play. At an advanced stage, he learns to play the special pattern of drum-recital called *tayambaka*.

The other tasks of the Nambiar apart from being a drummer are to introduce the play by chanting the invocatory *arangutali sloka*, to recite the Tamil section of the text on some special occasions, to help in the greenroom (*nepathya*) with the make-up. He is also allowed to indulge in the verbal narration of stories from the epics, called Pathakam. The stories are selected from the Prabandhas, a genre of classical Sanskrit literature. Though similar to Prabandhakkoothu, Pathakam is technically much simpler and less erudite, for it is a straightforward narration of events. The costumes are also much simpler.

Communicating Meaning

Kutiyattam gives immense scope to both the dramatic and verbal skills of the actor. While the hero and the other characters of the play indulge in elaborate *angikabhinaya*, *vachika* or verbal speech is the prerogative of the *vidushaka*. The *vachikabhinaya* in Kutiyattam consists of the recitation of some sections of the play or verses by the Nangiar sitting on the side of the stage, the oral delivery of the text by the different characters in the play, the Nambiar's narration of the sequences in Tamil, the specialised speech of some characters such as Surpanakha, the *vidushaka's* oral delivery and verbal elaboration of the text.

The Nangiar's recitation of *akkitta* is an important part of the *purvaranga* rituals. The Nangiar is present on the stage throughout the play, from the arrival of the *sutradhara* to the ritualistic ending (*koothu mutiykal*) of the performance. She recites the *akkitta slokas*, *bhramari* songs, *alama* songs, *nirvahanam slokas*, *churnikas* and other verses from the play. The *alama slokas* introduce some characters by giving short descriptions. The Nangiar's musical recitation is integrated with different *ragas* and *talas*.

Kutiyattam adopts an incantatory style of rendition for the oral delivery of the text for different characters. The verbal rendering of the *slokas* does not have any resemblance to ordinary speech, nor can it claim 'musical' quality. The *Natya Sastra* divides notes in music into seven, the origin or source of sound into three, cadence into four and goes into the minute classifications of each nuance, pitch, note, style and context. Kutiyattam does not conform to this codified pattern of music, nor does it imitate the speech of everyday human utterances. As observed by the Kutiyattam maestro Paimkulam Rama Chakyar, 'the musical style of Kutiyattam enhances the *rasabhinaya* of the actor through the medium of *vachika*, with the powerful exploitation of the technique of suggestion'.[34] The mode of chanting is sometimes given the name *raga* in Kutiyattam parlance. However, the recitational pattern of Kutiyattam does not have any similarity with the *ragas* of Carnatic music; rather the term *svara* (sound) is more suitable, for it has more resemblance to Vedic chanting in the pattern of the *udatta*, *anudatta* and *svarita* modes.

The noted musicologist L.S. Rajagopalan observes that the recitation of *slokas* by the Chakyars may be assigned a place midway

Facing page: A scene from Abhijnanasakuntalam *depicting Sakuntala in an agitated mood.*

[34] Paimkulam Rama Chakyar. 1994. 'Svaras in Kutiyattam' in *Sangeet Natak Special Issue on Kutiyattam*, pp. 91-100.

between the chanting of the *Yajurveda* and the *Sama gana*.[35] According to Rama Chakyar, the identified *ragas* in Kutiyattam are twenty-one, but Mani Madhava Chakyar in his *Natyakalpadrumam* recognises only twenty. The *svaras* of Kutiyattam are chosen according to the type of character, situation in the play and the *rasa*. For example, *artan* is employed for *srngara rasa*, *muralindalam* for the *sambhoga srngara* (love-in-union) of Rama, *dukkhagandharam* for *karuna* and *tarkan* for *raudra*.[36] The actors train themselves to utter the verses in the prescribed *svaras*. Rather than going through the intricacies of a strictly codified musical pattern, the learning of this recitation is based on familiarising oneself with and mastering the chanting mode.

The role of a Nambiar is not only restricted to merely being just a part of the orchestral group, but sometimes it also includes acting as a *sutradhara* to direct the action. In the Ramayana, which extends to twenty-one acts and takes a full year, the Nambiar performs the functions of the prologue as Nandi Sutradhara and recites the *arangutali sloka*, as well as the epilogue or *bharatavakya*, the extended speech in Tamil, acting as a third party. The convention of talking in Tamil does not necessarily mean the language of Tamil, but only means that the actor talks in the regional language, to appeal to a wider audience. 'Tamil' sections are found, for example, in *Dutavakyam*, 'Anguliyankam', among others. In 'Anguliyankam', in the conversation that ensues between Hanuman and Sita, the part of Hanuman is recited by the Chakyar and Sita's by the Nangiar who sits on the stage. The Nambiar explains the meaning of these verses in Malayalam in a manner similar to a reporter who addresses a less-initiated audience. This practice, called *kuticchollal*, is a mode of combined action through the medium of *vachika*.

Another character who is privileged to speak in the regional language, although in a distorted form, is Surpanakha in 'Surpanakhankam'. Though she disguises herself as a lovely woman to entice Rama and Lakshmana, after Lakshmana's rejection she gets back to her original form of an ogress. With prancing movements and wild mannerisms, Surpanakha shrieks a high-pitched vocalisation of 'pooyi, pooyi' and erupts into a crude speech, summing up her life, travels, meeting with the brothers Rama and Lakshmana and Rama's beloved wife Sita. Her dialect is a corrupted version of Malayalam. Her blackened body, wild costume and grotesque mannerisms, interspersed with crude jokes, hoots and wild prattle, is intended to indicate her 'station' and evoke derisive laughter from the audience.

For his extended narration and interpretation in Malayalam, the mode of speech used by the *vidushaka* is sometimes compared to the parlance of the Nambuthiri *brahmins* of Kerala. The *vidushaka's* speech, while indicative of his own situation as an 'upper caste' (though impoverished, in most cases) *brahmin*, also reflects the influence of the local culture in Kutiyattam, than a mere adherence to the postulates of the *Natya Sastra*. The *vidushaka* has a vital role in Kutiyattam. The *vidushaka* has the freedom of indulging in *vachika* throughout. In addition to his Prakrit speech, the *vidushaka* speaks in Sanskrit and Malayalam, addresses the audience directly, as though referring to a situation in the play, and makes fun of the audience. Besides, he has the unique

[35] Rajagopalan, L.S. 1994. 'Music in Kutiyattam' in *Sangeet Natak Special Issue on Kutiyattam*, pp. 113-119.
[36] For a detailed discussion on *svaras* and their application see Mani Madhava Chakyar. 1973. 'Svaraprakaranam' in *Natyakalpadrumam*, pp. 61-76. Cheruthuruthy: Kerala Kalamandalam.

Drummer performing on the mizhavu, *which is placed in a large wooden case.*

advantage of being both inside the drama as a character and outside it as a commentator. Appearing in most plays as *narmasachiva* (the companion-in-sport) to the hero, he pictures himself as a foolish *brahmin* in the service of the king, providing companionship and entertainment, indulging in jokes and mildly ridiculing the king. The devices used for evoking laughter are descriptions of his impoverished state, topical references and parody, ridiculing the characters and the members of the audience and self-mockery. His other task in theatre is to interpret the meaning of the Sanskrit and Prakrit *slokas* into Malayalam, by gaining for himself access to all levels of spectators. This feature of the *vidushaka* adopting dual roles on the stage is unique to Kutiyattam.

The verbal flair of the *vidushaka* becomes apparent in the art of Prabandhakkoothu as well as in the plays in which the *vidushaka* appears, for example, *Subhadradhananjayam*, *Tapatisamvaranam*, *Naganandam* and 'Mantrankam'. The verbal elaboration at the beginning of 'Mantrankam', which takes off with *bho* (hey, you...') and lasts for thirteen days and another monologue, which lasts for thirty-eight days, are examples of this phenomenon. The actor who takes the stage for such an unbelievably long duration has to be an expert talker and communicator who can hold the attention of the audience. The oral elaboration of the *vidushaka* has freshness and spontaneity, which also reflects years of learning, practice and refinement on the part of the actor to be able to hold forth on the stage for several days. The freedom of the actor to engage in a long monologue is not just to ramble on haphazardly, but to work within an implicit, broad structure of the subtext of the play and communicate to an esoteric audience.

In an attempt to analyse the concept of *angikabhinaya*, the *Natya Sastra* minutely analyses each part of the human body by dividing it into six main organs (head, hands, chest, sides, waist and feet) and the head into six sub-organs (eyebrows, eyes, nose, lips, cheeks and chin) and gives the movement patterns for each in intricate detail. There is a neat classification of the use of the feet, hands, torso, neck, facial organs and facial muscles and elaborate descriptions of their application on the stage.

Kutiyattam has incorporated a great deal of regional influences in both its structure and format. In *angika* or histrionic acting, Kutiyattam does not follow the rules of the *Natya Sastra*, but adopts a model of acting with its own distinctive characteristics. With regard to body movements and dance patterns, Kutiyattam tends to lay more emphasis on the abstract and the symbolic, rather than on the physical features of the object represented. The *angikabhinaya* in Kutiyattam may be seen with reference to its three vital elements–the code of gestures (*mudra*), body movements and facial expressions.

The elaborate code of gestures, which roughly correspond to the alphabet, word and sentence or, in other words, its theatric language, is adopted from the text *Hastalakshanadipika*. There are considerable differences between the two practices in terms of the basic *hastas* and also the meanings made out of them. In Bharata's terminology, *hastas* are of three types. These are *asamyuta* (those used for one hand), *samyuta* (those used for both hands) and *nrtta* (those that are used for pure dance poses).

In *Hastalakshanadipika*, the classificatory system is different, with *hastamudras*, *samanamudras* and *misramudras*. The *hastamudras* are *asamyuta* as well as *samyuta*, according to the usage; while *samanamudra* refers to the hand poses being the same in both hands. In *misramudras*, they are different for each hand. The differences also pertain to the names and positioning of the *hastas*; for example, *patakahasta* in *Hastalakshanadipika* is equivalent to *tripataka* in the *Natya Sastra* and *mrgasirsha* to *hamsasya* and *kataka* to *katakamukha*. In comparison, Kutiyattam seems to have *mudras* of a more symbolic nature, sometimes with a resemblance to tantric *mudras*.

The body movements of Kutiyattam are broadly divided into three types: *irunnattam* (action while sitting on a *pitha*), *patinnattam* (a slow tempo) and *ilakiyattam* (action with appropriate movements and improvisation). While in *irunnattam* the actor is in a sitting position throughout, in *patinnattam* the actor is again in a stationary position, with the feet kept closely together and only the body moving. In *ilakiyattam*, the actor has the freedom of movement of the whole body and this is also an occasion for the actor to depict elaborate action. Regarding dance movements, the term *chari* refers to the movements from the feet to the torso and are, in fact, dance steps described in the *Natya Sastra*. The *chari* and *gati* (gait) of Kutiyattam do not correspond to those mentioned in the *Natya Sastra*. There are two varieties of *chari*, *akasa* and *bhaumika*, depending on whether the feet touch the ground or are kept above and there are many movement patterns for each of these in Kutiyattam. Some examples of *bhaumika chari* are *kalakalavadyam* (steps, with the legs in a position close to each other), *konattu* and *kettiyiriykkal*. Some examples of *akasa charis*, which integrate leaps and movements in the air, are *vattattil chadi natakkal* (gait with a

circular movement, indicative of travelling some distance), *ambarayanam* (steps indicating travel through the skies), *parikramam* (a fast movement in *triputa tala*), *nrittam* (a vigorous dance movement performed by the *sutradhara* or other characters at the conclusion of the first day's performance).

New generation of mizhavu *percussionists, playing the drum with a great deal of concentration.*

Apart from these, the movements also indicate the traits of each species, class and character. There are, however, specialised gaits, which depend on the type of the character. For instance, there are special gaits for the hero, the *vidushaka*, a woman, demon, animal and so on. These are actually signature traits for different characters, helping the actor to 'get into' the roles. For example, the gait of a monkey is a stylised imitation of its leaping movements, while an ogress such as Surpanakha has prancing steps. There is no attempt here to imitate the 'real' movements of a monkey; rather they are stylised representations of the real. The vigorous movement of Rama and Lakshmana to the three sides is called *kalappurattu natakkal*, while women characters adopt the graceful gait of *chellunti natakkal*. The *vidushaka* has his characteristic gait, stance, gestures and expressions, intended to evoke laughter in the theatre. Being a mode of theatre that employs the movements of the body and facial expressions for conveying meaning, Kutiyattam has developed histrionic acting in such a way that it can convey any idea and elaborate any shade of feeling. For example, the words 'you', 'I' or 'come' can be shown in a variety of ways, according to the mood, context or

gender of the person depicting it. Ravana, when addressing Sita as 'you', has a delicate hand movement, reinforcing the emotional essence of *srngara rasa*, with his face depicting love, longing, fear of rejection and, above all, desire. Ravana's address to Hanuman, when the latter breaks into his garden, is filled with rage and loathing at this unpardonable behaviour. To give another example, a lotus is described in great detail by the slow opening out of the hands with quivering fingers depicting the petals, full blooming of the flower by the spreading of the fingers and the face expressing the corresponding emotions of wonder and pleasure at its beauty. The 'bee' has the middle fingers of both the hands quivering, the hands themselves imitating the circular movements of the bee, with the eyes following the hands in a 'semi-circular double rotation', corresponding to a horizontal '8' movement. The signs and language of Kutiyattam have their own iconic identifying traits through an internal referencing and shared understanding and are replete with elegance and power. There are specialised acting conventions in Kutiyattam, which require the actor to call upon his histrionic capabilities to the very maximum. The descriptions or *varnanas* of palaces, mountains, oceans and forests are part of the stock conventions of Kutiyattam.

While the action in Kutiyattam can cover a great range by elaborately depicting the height of a mountain or the expanse of the ocean through *angikabhinaya*, the actual movements of the body are highly restricted. The actor occupies only a small space on the centre of the stage, facing the lamp.

Facing page: The character type of kari *(facial make-up in black)–Surpanakha in an anguished mood.*

The height and range in the action are depicted solely through the movement of the organs, limbs and muscles of the actor's body and not through spatial movement across the stage. When the actor describes a mountain—for example, Ravana's description of Mount Kailasa—he first surveys the mountain in great detail: standing in the basic posture with legs bent at the knees and hands crossed across his chest, he follows the girth and height of the mountain in great detail. To assess the width, the actor's eyes slowly move horizontally, taking in the entire range of the mountain.

To depict the height, he slowly lowers himself to the ground while retaining the same posture, with his eyes pointing upward, to reach the maximum level to which the eyeballs can reach. To look at the bottom of a pit or a cave, he raises his body as high as possible and lowers his eyes, to the maximum level that they can reach. Now he surveys each and every detail—the lofty peaks, the bulging rocks, the gaping pits and the cascading waterfalls, which begin as small rivulets and end up as mighty swelling rivers. In the dense forest, he sees elephants loitering about, breaking palm leaves and chewing them, bathing with mud and lazily dozing off. He sees wild peacocks dancing in abandon, spreading their plumes at the sight of dark clouds. There are hungry lions in search of prey. The descriptions contain multiple perspectives, with the actor here transcending the boundaries of Ravana's character to become the elephant, the lion, the snake and the peacock in quick succession, while keeping the original character of Ravana intact. The theatre here works on several levels simultaneously, with shifting points of view, flowing easily from one to another.

The *Natya Sastra* describes *sattvikabhinaya* as the highest form of acting, which emanates from the mind through an imaginative empathy with the situation of the play.

However, the exact implication of the concept is still a matter of interpretation and debate among scholars and practitioners. Bharata uses several inter-related ideas to describe the concept of stylised acting in theatre. The related ideas of *samanyabhinaya* (loosely translated sometimes as 'basic representation') and *chitrabhinaya* ('specialised' representation) come close to a method of acting using all parts of the body.[37]

Finally, there is the concept of *natyadharmi*, the style of representation that employs tacitly accepted devices and conventions for dramatic communication—*loke yadabhiyojyam cha/padamatropayujyate moortimatsaabhilaashamcha natyadharmee tu saa smrtaa.*[38] ('Though the idea exists in an abstract sense, it has to be given a concrete, artistic [stylised] form, and this is the essence of *natyadharmi.*') Kutiyattam employs the technique of *natyadharmi* to a degree, which Bharata conceptualised as 'creation of the mind' (*manasairsrshtih*) but did not perhaps enunciate as the model in his work.[39]

The performer of Kutiyattam creates art directly and not through the illusion of what is accepted as 'reality'. The drama makes sense from the wider perspective of a universal timelessness and the characters depicted are not entirely 'human'. This kind of a presentation becomes credible on this account, for the presentation is also something more than the 'real', a method of trying to transcend the boundaries.

In Kutiyattam there is an absolute transcendence of the external aspects of the stage and the character represented by an actor. The attire is no reflection of a character's personality, for the performer takes several roles in quick succession and creates the obstacle in understanding the play in 'real' terms. The classic example of Hanuman, complete with tail and monkey-like features, taking the role of Sita describing her pangs of separation from Rama, or the arrogance of Ravana while lifting Mount Kailasa, has to be understood from the unique perspective of the aesthetics of Kutiyattam.

To wonder whether an actor dressed as a monkey can effectively portray the deeper feelings of Sita would be to miss the aesthetic core of the play.[40] It extends theatric action manifold times than is imagined by the text of the play, through improvised, stylised acting. It is capable of doing justice to the rich poetry of the Sanskrit dramatic text with different layers of meaning contained in figures of speech such as *slesha* (multiple meaning), *vyangyartha* (implied meaning) and *vakrokti* (crooked expression). It adopts a non-illusionistic method of action where the acting portrays emotions through abstract movement, non-linear narrative and exaggerated delivery. Situations of theatric potential are elaborated to unravel the multiple layers of meaning embedded in the text of the play.

In an attempt to explain the highly abstract idea of *sattvikabhinaya*, Appukkuttan Nair offers the concept of the five *kosas* or 'sheaths' that surround the self that are described in the ancient texts on Indian

[37] In an analysis of Bharata's concept of *samanyabhinaya*, Kapila Vatsyayan draws attention to the body-mind relationship for the depiction of inner states of consciousness. See Kapila Vatsyayan. 1996. *Bharata: The Natya Sastra*, pp. 82-83. New Delhi: Sahitya Akademi.

[38] According to Bharata, *natyadharmi* is conventional acting with speech, activity, beings and states of an extraordinary character, requiring specific limb movements, dance enunciation and involved action.

[39] The text is, *divyanam manaseissrishtir/grhesupavanesu canaranam yatnatah karya laksanabhihita kriya* (NS. II.17) (Divinities build castles and gardens in their minds; the humans resort to physical actions according to stipulated standards)

[40] For a detailed discussion, see Paulose, K.G., ed. 1993. *Natankusa: A Critique of Dramaturgy*, Thrippunithura: Govt. Sanskrit College.

Sita and the charioteer in Mayasitankam.

philosophy.[41] Among these, *angika*, *vachika* and *aharya* are of the most *sthula* (concrete) nature, while *sattvika*, the most abstract and quintessential method of acting is *sukshma* (subtle) and is a combination of the three *kosas*, *pranamayakosa* (the sheath of life-breath), *manomayakosa* (of the mind) and *vijnanamayakosa* (the sheath of wisdom). The actor learning the art of controlling the life-breath (*prana*) achieves the application of this concept of *pranamayakosa* into the acting technique of Kutiyattam. The inhalation, exhalation and compression of breath and its concentration in different parts of the body evokes different expressions, action and speech, which the actor adapts for the stage. In Kutiyattam, this practice, called *vayu kotukkal* (infusing breath), adapted from the psycho-physical gymnastic tradition of Kalarippayattu from Kerala, makes the actor achieve unbelievable elasticity in performance. Channelling of this vital energy enlivens the performance considerably, by applying the breath to the eyes to create the different *rasas*

[41] Nair, Appukkuttan. 1994. 'Kutiyattam and Bhasa' in *Sangeet Natak Kutiyattam Special Issue*, pp. 190-194.

A percussion ensemble in performance.

(*rasavayu*), to the voice for modulating the voice (*svaravayu*) and to the other parts of the body such as the torso or the fingers.[42]

Manomayakosa, the sheath of the mind, is perhaps the essence of what Bharata calls *manaseih srishtih* (the creation of the mind). Since the setting of a play and the incidents depicted are a matter of imagination, the stage is entirely a fluid space for the actor to represent a number of locales and contexts—the idea of walking, flying, riding on the chariot are all represented by specialised gait patterns, but are imagined by the mind through a process of aesthetic identification. The play is created as a reciprocal process of mental creation between the actor and the audience. The representational element becomes more pronounced in situations of elaboration of action, enabled by the sheath of *vijnanamayakosa*, where the actor needs to call upon all his faculties of learning and experience to develop an idea right up to its fullest extent.

A typical example is 'Mantrankam', which deals with the plots and intrigues hatched by the three ministers of King Udayana to free him from the captivity of the King of Avanti. Here the *vidushaka*, in the guise of a jesting beggar, narrates his story and reflects upon the possibilities of saving his master from prison. His monologue, lasting for

[42] For a detailed discussion of the topic of *vayu*, see Gopalakrishnan, Sudha. 1993. 'Sattwikabhinaya' in *Kathakali: The Art of the Unworldly*, pp. 145-148. Mumbai: *Marg*.

many days, touches upon several subjects and is laced with stories, verse passages, anecdotes, maxims and proverbs. Behind the incongruous, ludicrous speech lurks another dimension of meaning: when the beggar says, 'Ha, I have put my bowl of sweets at the feet of the deity', what he actually means is, 'The king is safe at the hands of Princess Vasavadatta.'

The performance is intended to make the spectator aware of the two dimensions of the play, the obvious level of laughter and a deeper level of probing into the nature of reality. The most obvious example is Bodhayana's *Bhagavadajjukiya*, a play categorised as *prahasana* (which is translated as farce, a comic drama in common parlance). The title of the play is itself suggestive of humour, with the curious juxtaposition of two types of characters with seemingly contradictory character—*bhagavan* meaning a saint and *ajjuka*, a courtesan. The play has an extremely hilarious situation when their souls are exchanged, with the result that both of them adopt the mannerisms and the language of the other.

The sage's disciple, Sandilya, who has all the characteristics of a typical *vidushaka*, is another source of humour. The play cleverly interweaves both these threads to produce a comic effect. The play in its adaptation to Kutiyattam takes several days, with the *vidushaka* taking up the major share of the action. While narrating his life up to a time when he joins his guru, he touches on various topics. With his characteristic humour, he subjects several institutions to sharp ridicule and criticism. Among the subjects that he elaborates are Buddhism, philosophy and funeral rituals associated with people belonging to different sects. To do justice to this role of the *vidushaka*, apart from being a master humorist and storyteller, the actor has to be proficient in all *shastras*, *darsanas*, religious systems, rituals and many other areas of knowledge (in the true nature of *vijnanamayakosa*).

The *vidushaka* in 'Mantrankam' similarly holds forth for about thirty-eight days, with subjects as wide-ranging as *Dharma Sastra* (code of ethics) and *Artha Sastra* (economics). To be able to hold the attention of the audience for such long stretches of time, he intersperses his monologue with humorous stories, topical references, parodies and other such devices. The actor, like a magician with a wand, through elaborate verbal acting spins a world of make-believe. Words have double—sometimes multiple—layers of meaning; with each articulation, the idea gains in depth. The actor alternates between the narrative, lyrical and dramatic modes at will and the juxtaposition of these interlocking modes contribute to the enrichment of meaning of the text. The technique of multiple perspectives is not merely a mode of presentation; it becomes the core of the play.

Rituals and Conventions

Kutiyattam is a highly codified art with conventions laid down through generations and continued with unquestioned authority and precision. Arguably for reasons of sustainability, this strict adherence to tradition was perhaps a fact that helped to preserve it through the ages. From the early days of its origin till recently, Kutiyattam was invested with high aesthetic and spiritual values. The patrons of the art gave it a high-ranking status and invested it with its own principles of sacred power, right and responsibility. During the middle ages, Kutiyattam was made a part of the temple tradition with the integration of Hindu religious rituals and was considered exclusive in terms of all the three vital elements of theatre—actors, performance space and the spectators. (The actors were from the temple dwelling or *ambalavasi* community of the Chakyars, the theatre was situated inside the temple complex and the spectators were from higher castes.) While the deity was believed to be the chief patron and *rasika* (connoisseur), the spectators, with high aesthetic refinement and judgement, were the human counterparts.

The art came to be regarded as a mode of visual sacrifice or *yajna* fit for the gods, rather than as a mere performance for entertainment. The rules and regulations surrounding the ritual complex were so intricate and rigid, with prescriptions and prohibitions, that any lapse was considered an offence to the deity, requiring expiation. In the past, since the days when it was created, the performances were conducted according to the annual ritual calendar. Each Chakyar family was given rights of performance in specific temples throughout Kerala where performances were held. The financial status of the performers was, in turn, made secure by liberal gifts of land and other privileges from the temple. The actual staging of the play would happen only towards the end of the Kutiyattam performance, lasting for several days.

In the past when Kutiyattam was strictly confined to the temple, the performance inside the temple complex fell into three clear categories: Atiyantharakkoothu (ritual performances), Vazhipadukoothu (votive offerings) and Kazhchakkoothu (plays performed for entertainment). Among these, Atiyantharakkoothu plays were conducted according to fixed days of the ritual calendar and were the privileges of particular Chakyar families as a hereditary assignment. While the practice has now become defunct in many temples, there are some temples such as Vadakkunnathan, Koodalmanikyam and Guruvayur that are still continuing with Atiyantharakkoothu.

Facing page: P.K. Narayanan Nambiar performing the invocatory ritual of lighting the lamp.

The rigid attachment of the performance of Kutiyattam to a sacrosanct system that is associated with the temple had its own impact on the art form. It protected the interests of the upper castes by its exclusivity and self-ascribed superiority. The perpetration of elaborate rituals became a kind of social marker, an avenue for affording it better status. A pertinent example is Mahendravikramavarman's play *Mattavilasa*, performed as a Vazhivadukoothu in some of the temples of Kerala. The play, considered a *prahasana*, severely ridicules the degenerate religious practices of the time, including those of Buddhism. In the play, the Buddhist mendicant Nagasena, with his greed for good food and weakness for women, represents the degeneration of Buddhism. Bahrukalpa, the person from the Pasupata sect who possesses the skull, which belongs to the Kapalin, is portrayed with humour. The time of the composition of the play roughly corresponds to the edging out of the Buddhist faith in South India, especially Kerala, and the infiltration of the *brahmin* ascendency represented by the worship of Siva. The adaptation of Mahendravikramavarman's *Mattavilasa* into Kutiyattam may have had a topical and political relevance, but in theatric presentation, the drunken excesses of the character of Kapalin are imbued with a spiritual significance.

Kutiyattam has clearly made *Mattavilasa* a vehicle for the denigration of Buddhist sects and appropriated privileged status for the *brahmin*. The endorsement of *brahmin* rituals and mode of worship into the play contravened the Buddhist elements and placed the latter in an inferior position.

Facing page: Mutiyakkitha, *the concluding ritual in Kutiyattam.*

In the stage enactment of *Mattavilasa*, the *sutradhara* occupies the stage entirely for the first two days beginning with the customary benedictory rituals and invocations and hails Siva as the supreme lord of the universe. Continuing with the eulogy of Siva, the actor indulges in a long narration of Siva's story. It depicts in detail the penance of Parvati, the destruction of Kama, the marriage of Siva and Parvati, the birth of the two sons, the killing of Taraka, the emanation of Bhadrakali and the cosmic dance of Siva (many verses for this enactment are adopted from Kalidasa's poem *Kumarasambhava*).

On the third day, the main character Satyasoma (the Kapalin) appears in a state of inebriation, drinking repeatedly from his cup and prattling incoherently on the virtues of intoxication. He sits on the stage and pays obeisance to Siva with elaborate rituals of propitiation. In between, he drinks from the cup of liquor meant as an offering to Siva. Though farcical at an obvious level, the performance is intended to make the spectator aware of the two levels of meaning in the play—the low comedy resulting from the drunken revelry of the main character and the deeper spiritual level, which equates his nonsensical extravagance with the cosmic dance of Lord Siva.

Mattavilasa is still performed as a votive offering in the temples of Kerala. Its performance is considered especially auspicious for the birth of a child. In the temple of Kottiyur, the play is traditionally staged as part of the festival and has special conventions that accompany its performance there.

Is Kutiyattam a 'ritualistic' theatre? The answer to this question lies in the nature of the ritual itself. Rituals are actions that are deeply ingrained into the culture of the people who observe them, conveying the meaning to the participants at a non-discursive and intuitive level. Through a series of signs, symbols, language and action, rituals transcend ordinary time and space through the power of imagination. It is an attempt by the human being to 'cosmocise himself'[43] in an attempt to get in touch with a deeper reality. Rituals, with an ensemble of meanings associated with them, are invested with the power to transform the physical space into the supernatural and ordinary time into the extraordinary.

In the Indian dramatic theory, the experience of a play is imbued with symbolic, larger-than-life meanings. The elaborate prayers and rituals that precede and accompany *natya* as prescribed in texts such as the *Natya Sastra* are aimed at representing something more than their physical formulations. In his *Concept of Ancient Indian Theatre* Christopher Byrski vividly brings out the association between *natya* and *yajna* or sacrificial ritual.[44] It argues for a mythological account of the origin of drama (*natyotpatti*), formulated in accordance with the idea of *yajna*. According to the description in the *Natya Sastra*, theatre emerged from festivities associated with the Indradhvaja festival and later got dissociated from it, forming a part of the preliminary conventions of a play at a later stage. While becoming an independent entity, it retained some of the elements of a sacred ceremony by adopting the conventions of *yajna*.

The consecration of the theatre, the actors, stage and even stage properties such as the *mizhavu*, through norms of purity and pollution and a strict code of rules and ritual observances, restricted other castes till recently from taking part or even observing the performance of Kutiyattam. The symbolic status given to *mizhavu* was equal to that of a great *brahmin* and this reverence for the drum sets it apart from other stage objects. The *mizhavu* is considered as a celibate *brahmin* (*brahmachari*) and accordingly it is consecrated with the traditional 'sixteen rites' (*shodasa samskaras*), including the *upanayanam*. In the same manner, a *koothambalam*, being part of the temple complex, comes under the same laws that govern the temple, with any incident of pollution requiring to be annulled through expiation rites for the whole temple. Chakyars, Nangiars and Nambiars have special rights to the performance of Kutiyattam, even exclusive rights for fixed temples and have their own initiation ceremonies. Apart from the traditional 'sixteen rites' that confirm a Chakyar's placement into and perpetration of the caste to which he belongs, he has to go through his debut performance (*arangettam*), which entitles him the status of a full-fledged actor. Usually the item selected for the debut performance is 'Purappadu' from Bhasa's *Balacharitam*. In the case of a Nangiar, the first performance is usually conducted before she reaches puberty. The initiation performance called 'Nangyar Koothu Purappadu' lasts for two days and is fixed on an auspicious day according to the girl's horoscope. A girl who has not had an *arangettam* is not entitled to use the name 'Nangiar', and is not allowed to take part in temple performances.[45]

The performance of Kutiyattam, because of its rootedness in a belief system and its emphasis on the sanctity of its ritual, is considered a

[43] Pillai, G. Sankara. 1991. 'Spatial Relationship in Ritual and Performance' in *Concepts of Space: Ancient and Modern*, pp. 437-439. New Delhi: Indira Gandhi National Centre for the Arts and Abihnav.

[44] Byrski, Christopher. 1974. *Concept of Ancient Indian Theatre*, p. 43. New Delhi: Munshiram Manoharlal.

[45] Daugherty, Diane. 'The Nangyar: Female Ritual Specialist of Kerala' in *Asian Theatre Journal* Vol. 13, No. 1, Spring 1996, pp. 54-67.

Mizhavu *players in action.*

'visual sacrifice' or *chakshushayajna*. Mani Madhava Chakyar in his *Introduction to Natya Kalpadrumam* strives to bring in similarities between a Kutiyattam performance and a *yajna*.[46] According to him, the theatre corresponds to a *yajnasala*, the sacrificial hall and the fire used in the form of three wicks, two directed at the actor and one at the audience, stands for the three sacrificial fires of a *yajna*. Instead of making it by the process of striking two pieces of *arani* wood against each other (as happens in a *yajna*), the flame in Kutiyattam is kindled from the sanctum sanctorum. Both the performances are presided over by two *brahmins*, one in the capacity of a priest and the other as a *sutradhara*, the director of the performance. Once the proceedings of a performance have been set in motion, the actor, like the priest, is above mundane considerations such as family or friends, and does not have purity bindings. At the close of the performance, like the ritualistic bath in a *yajna* (*abhavrthasnanam*), the actor sprinkles water on the stage as ritual purification. The *yajnasala* is burnt down at the end of a sacrifice but, in Kutiyattam, the actor symbolically takes two wicks from the stage, joins them together and puts out the fire in the concluding ritual called *mutiyakkitha*.

Before the starting of a performance in the temple, according to tradition, the Chakyar needs to take a purificatory bath in the pond attached to the temple. Then he goes to the greenroom and pays obeisance to the gods and preceptors. The main priest of the temple bestows his blessings on the actor and gives him a piece of consecrated cloth as well as a ring made of grass leaves (*kurayum*

[46] Mani Madhava Chakyar. 1996 (1973). *Introduction to Natya Kalpadrumam*, p. lxxiii. Cheruthuruthy: Kerala Kalamandalam.

pavithravum). The lamp on the stage and the lamp in the greenroom are lit with a wick brought from the sanctum sanctorum. The stage is decorated with fruit-bearing plantain trees (*kulavazha*), tender leaves of trees of coconut (*kuruthola)*, a vessel containing paddy (*nirapara*) and the traditional lamp. At the back of the stage stands the frame for the *mizhavu* (*mizhavana*), in which the *mizhavu* is placed.

The greenroom is decorated with the conventional 'eight auspicious items' (*ashtam-angalyam*). In the greenroom, the Chakyar changes into the cloth provided by a member of the washerman (*mannan*) caste, and ties an auspicious red cloth on his forehead. With this ritual, he has crossed the border from this life to a plane of meta-reality. The domain of this ordinary world does not pollute or affect him anymore, for he inhabits a privileged time and space till the end of the performance. He has (as a *vidushaka*) the freedom to ridicule or criticise anyone among the audience, including the king and this authority is accepted without question. As the preliminary step to make-up, he applies clarified butter on his face and then starts with the application of the colours.

The Nambiar takes his seat behind the *mizhavu*, sounds the drum (*mizhavu occhappeduthal*) and thus formally announces the play. The Nangiar, seated on the right side of the stage, recites the devotional *akkitha* songs praising Ganapati, Sarasvati and Siva to the drumming on the *mizhavu* and this duet is called *goshthi*. The Nambiar now comes forward, recites a benedictory verse and sprinkles the stage with holy water. With this, the small curtain is held for the preliminary dance. The *sutradhara* enters and with his back to the stage, performs dance steps behind the curtain, called *marayilkriya*. Now with the parting of the curtain, he turns around, faces the audience with a pleasant face, and dances 'chari' sequences, ending in the conventional 'five steps' (*panchapadavinyasa*). He opens his hands, which are laden with imaginary flowers and offers them to the gods and prostrates in obeisance. He goes on to symbolically enact a propitiatory ceremony on the stage, by offering flowers and water and invokes celestial Ganga water into the conch, sprinkling the place with the holy water. He worships Ganapati and Sarasvati. In a happy frame of mind, he proceeds to the stage and observes the presence of several well-bred, erudite spectators waiting for the show to begin. Paying respect to the learned audience, he recites the introductory verse (usually beginning with 'sankhaksheeravapuh...' from *Balacharita* and enacts its meaning in detail through gestures. But for other Sanskrit plays, the preliminary verse of each play is substituted with detailed enactment of the meaning.

Now comes a series of pure dance movements called by the general term 'daily rituals'. The dances are interspersed with songs of propitiation to different deities, sung by the Nangiar to rhythmical beats of her cymbals. The dances are different *charis*, including *dhruvam*, *cheriyakku* and *valiyakku*. The songs are respectively 'Ksheerasagara...,' 'Ambike Girije...,''Adrimavidruma...,' followed by a *kesadipadam* of Siva and Parvati. This is followed by songs beginning with 'Marasareeravinasakaram...,' with *bhramari* dance. There is a long propitiation to the *ashtadikpalas*. It finally ends in an all-embracing propitiation beginning with the lines 'Visvajanadhipa, vasava, jaya jaya...' ('Victory to you, Indra, the ruler of the world') with flowers and prayers to all the beings in the celestial, terrestrial and netherworlds, including *devas*, *rishis*, *siddhas*, *charanas*, *kinnaras* and *vidyadharas* of the heaven; *brahmins*, *kshatriyas*, *vaisyas*, *sudras*, birds and

Handing over the tradition: The master initiating the student.

animals of the earth; *asuras* and *nagas* of the underworld and ants, plants, grass, shoots and every other living being that inhabits the universe. This concludes the elaborate, tightly structured convention of *nityakriya*. The actor is by no means free to indulge in any improvisation or modification in its format. In fact, *nityakriya* is performed by the protagonist in the capacity of an actor—the shifting of his personality into the character/characters occurs only when the play commences.

At the outset of a play, the main character or the actor for the first day appears and narrates the story so far. This convention itself has four parts—*anvarambham*, *anukramam*, *samkshepam* and *nirvahanam*. *Anvarambham* is when a character, after the first day's commencement (*purappadu*) of a play, appears for the first time on the second day and starts with *anukramam*. *Anukramam* is the recapitulation of the previous story in the reverse order, starting from the last incident and going on backwards in time to the first, in the format of a volley of questions.

Samkshepam is a brief summary of the story in the normal order starting from the beginning and ending at the beginning of the day of the enactment of the play. The beginning of the actual play is usually through *nirvahanam*, a theatrical device crucial and unique to Kutiyattam, in which the main character or any other character narrates the past episodes in great detail.

There are several reasons for the prominent place given to *nirvahanam* as a dramatic technique in Kutiyattam. Stage conventions such as *nirvahanam* are aimed to project an 'imagined reality'.[47] In fact, this theatric convention

[47]Ayyappa Paniker, K. 1995. 'Introduction: The Aesthetics of Kutiyattam' in *Kutiyattam Special Issue*, pp. 7-11.

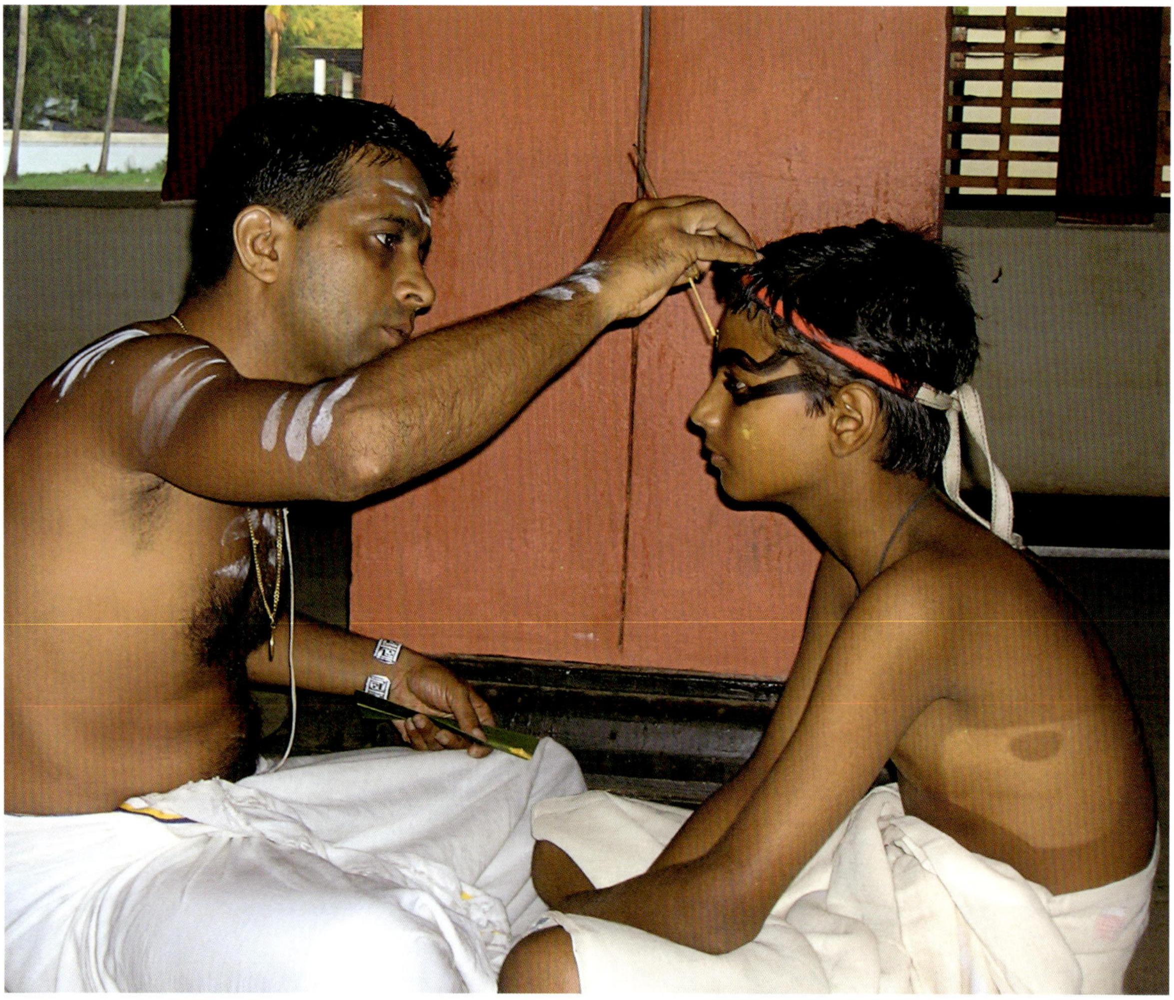

Passing on the mantle: The master applies make-up on the student.

contains the very essence of Kutiyattam. *Nirvahanam* is a detailed enactment, lasting for several days, of the story so far and the incidents leading up to the moment. While *anukramam* and *samkshepam* are rigidly codified and performed with the use of gestures alone, unlike *nirvahanam*, they are not elaborated. The *anukramam* of 'Balivadham', the first act of Bhasa's *Abhishekanataka* goes like this:

> Long ago, how did Sugriva, the son of the Sun-God, become a devotee of Rama, when he saw the feat of piercing the seven mighty trees? Before that, how did Sugriva, along with Rama, Lakshmana and Hanuman prepare for his fight with Bali?

The narrator now goes back to the origin of the demons, Dundubhi and Mayavi. While doing this, the actor-as-character ends his backward journey at one point and then takes forward the narration in the summarised form of *samkshepam*. In this instance, he narrates the origin of Bali and Sugriva. In *nirvahanam*, the narration is elaborate—it begins from the origin of Mayavi and Dundubhi and courses through several incidents and anecdotes with detailed enactment, till it reaches the incident of Rama destroying the seven *sal* trees, thus skilfully connecting it to the situation in the play. This is like an interpolated story—or stories—prefixed to the play by the

Gesture depicting 'you' by the male performer in an arrogant mood.

choreographers of Kutiyattam, with its own subtext. Usually, the actor recites the first lines of the text, arousing the interest of the spectator and then provides the background of the story through narration, histrionic or verbal. The play—the progression of the plot—is less important and there is no attempt at realism. Often *nirvahanam* goes on for several days together and the textual part where the actual play is enacted sometimes becomes meagre in comparison.

Perhaps initially introduced for establishing the background of a play, this 'flashback' technique evolved as the most important convention in Kutiyattam. There is a large corpus of *nirvahanam slokas* for each play—for example, Harsha's *Nagananda* has twenty-two, while for 'Anguliyankam', three hundred and thirty-one *slokas* are listed in K.P. Narayana Pisharoti's edition of *Ascharyachudamani*.[48] In 'Anguliyankam', Hanuman, in flashback mode, narrates the story of the previous five acts of the play *Ascharyachudamani* through *abhinaya* and integrates several other stories, anecdotes and descriptions. In plays such as *Nagananda*, Jimutavahana, the hero and Aterya, the *vidushaka*, both have their own *nirvahanam*. After the hero enacts his part through

[48] Narayana Pisharoti, K.P. 1988 (1967). *Ascharyachudamani*. Trissur: Kerala Sangeetha Nataka Akademi.

histrionic acting lasting for a few days with his assigned *slokas*, he withdraws, leaving the stage to the *vidushaka* who performs *nirvahanam* with oral action called Purusharthakkoothu. This appears in *Nagananda*, *Subhadradhananjaya* and *Tapatisamvarana* and is also a digression from the main play, which provides a comic counterpoint to the hero's high-flown action.

Purushartha in Kutiyattam is a comic imitation of the original idea of the 'four purposes' of life. For the enlightened *brahmin*, these, according to ancient texts, are the code of morality (*dharma*), wealth (*artha*), desire (*kama*) and salvation (*moksha*), but to the *vidushaka*, the *brahmin* impoverished in wealth and moral values, the *purusharthas* are entertainment (*vinoda*), deceit (*vanchana*), eating (*asana*) and service under a king (*rajaseva*). The context provided is the *vidushaka's* description of how he came to serve under the king. On the stage, the actor enacts the *stobham* of a *vidushaka* and recites a Sanskrit verse on destiny (*karma*). He explains the meaning of the verse in Malayalam, connecting the idea to his own impoverished state of affairs at home. This is followed by a detailed enumeration, lasting for four days, of the four purposes of life. The descriptions are long-drawn-out and wide-ranging. For example, the section called *asana* has an exhaustive account of culinary art, dwelling on the different vegetables and cereals, recipes, eating habits, feasts, manner of serving, qualities of good, bad and indifferent 'eaters', anecdotes on experiences relating to eating and so on. In 'Mantrankam', the *vidushaka* in the guise of a jesting beggar narrates his previous story through *nirvahanam* and reflects on the possibilities of saving his master from prison. Apart from rituals of propitiation of the deities, prayers directed towards the success of the play and preliminary sequences of theatric action, Kutiyattam has its own denotative codes and conventions, which are recognisable patterns of action for the initiated audience. A symbolic pattern of *abhinaya* is the convention of *varnana*, the description of various 'categories' of experience such as a tree, forest, mountain, garden or hermitage, with specified formal sequences of action. For example, the description of a mountain has details such as its girth, height, protrusions, rocks, streams, waterfalls, trees, caves, animals and so on. A garden is portrayed with images of plants and creepers with boughs wafting in the breeze; there are ponds where lotuses bloom, bees come to suck honey; there are creeper houses and simulated mountains, where peacocks dance and birds sing and creepers flutter in the breeze.

Another stock sequence is the description of love, which is shown in the conventional format of Kamadeva's relentless shooting of arrows (*kamasaram kollal*) at the lover to intensify the fire of erotic passion and the physical manifestations of extreme anguish. The cool rays of the moon and the wafting breeze serve to soothe the agony of desire, leading to a situation akin to swooning. These nuances of action belong to a conventional format, for they are not a 'natural' way of describing an event or situation and their meanings are determined by a repertoire of actions, embodying codes shared by the actor and the audience. In a completely different format is the description of the preparations for a battle (*patappurappadu*) in a vigorous mode, involving the gathering of weaponry, assembling of troops, repairing of chariots, getting ready with protective shields and weapons and commencing the journey, accompanied by the call of

Facing page: Gesture depicting the word 'name'.

Stage set with conventional decoration.

trumpets and bugles. In a *varnana*, within a given structure, the actor has the freedom to spread out, expand and indulge in details and move back and forth, for he has total control over the process of creation. These gestures and emotions, carefully presented, should not be performed mechanically, but presented in a spontaneous and graceful manner, with absolute control and mastery, to produce an aesthetic effect.

Almost all characters, including the hero, heroine, *vidushaka*, *brahmin*, demon and monkey, are role types with their own characteristic gestures, conventional signs of expression, gait, costume and oral delivery that they are easily recognisable on the stage by an initiated audience. The hero of a play, according to Sanskrit dramaturgy, needs to be suitable to the action that constitutes the play and can be of four basic types: *dheerodatta* (valiant and noble), *dheeroddhata* (valiant and arrogant), *dheeralalita* (valiant and gentle) and *dheerasanta* (valiant and serene). Kutiyattam has separate stylised enactment rules for each of them, as well as for heroines, demons, ogresses and monkeys. The conventional modes of interpretative action, known in Kutiyattam parlance as *attam*, are integral to the aesthetics of Kutiyattam. It has its own particular techniques such as moving forward and backward in time, in discontinuous, slow, fast, repetitious motion and offering different perspectives on the same theme.

Conventions such as *kettatal* (acting as though hearing another person's speech and responding to it) and *nishkramanam* (one actor temporarily leaves the stage while another indulges in elaborate action) break dramatic credibility and establish the illusory nature of this theatre. This is also the cause for the fact that the teachers insist on the actor not facing each other directly while engaging in dialogue. He is only supposed to look sideways towards the other actor. The most characteristic technique of the theatre language of Kutiyattam is the elaboration of action and multiple impersonation of the actor (*pakarnnattam*, literally, the *attam* of alternating roles), which have conventional meanings in Kutiyattam. Theatric action subsumes, dominates and transcends the text of the play. The extent of elaboration of action can be understood from the fact that though the lines are based on the text, the unravelling of the plot of the play is not as important in Kutiyattam, as the detailed exposition, histrionic or verbal, of specific situations and lines (or even words). The complex choreographic structure and acting strategies outlined in the performance manuals (*attaprakarams*) are communicated through the actor's capacity to express effectively and sustain interest through long stretches of time.

A World Outside the Temple

The decline of temple patronage and the loss of landed property as a result of reforms in Kerala and the depreciation of land value were factors that made a deep impact on the Chakyar community. In the post-land-reform context of Kerala, when art came out of the temple, the economic condition of the performers worsened and the grandeur of the form was at complete variance with the plight of its performers. The earnings of an actor who devoted his entire lifetime to the pursuit of the art became well below a minimal income needed for survival. This kind of uncertainty became a major constraint to the revitalisation of Kutiyattam. A new entrant, in spite of talent and creativity, was lured away to pursue other more lucrative professions.

Another factor was that Kutiyattam performances are time-consuming and elaborate and so it catered to only a limited section of people who had the time and energy to sit through the long hours of performance. This exclusivity itself became a constraint in terms of organising performances and devoting time to its pursuit and promotion. While considering financial support for the maintenance, promotion and revitalisation of this art, its special features had to be taken into account.

The attitude towards the arts such as Kutiyattam and Kathakali underwent a change approximately by the middle of the twentieth century. The shift in patronage from a feudal aristocracy to a more democratic order had a deep impact on these arts, which lost to a certain extent the moorings in a strictly sacred institution. It was the introduction of the school model for training in the classical arts such as Kutiyattam that revolutionised the traditional mode of *gurukula sampradaya*, which was the practice of the disciple learning the art by staying at his master's house and painstakingly imbibing the skills. In an effort to extend the viewership base of Kathakali, the plays were curtailed and edited from all-night performances to those lasting for about four or five hours. The shift of venue to large proscenium theatre halls minimised the reciprocity between the actor and the spectator.

Among the classical performing arts of Kerala, Kathakali was the first to register and receive attention from people outside the tradition. From the 1930s, there was a constant stream of visitors in Kerala, both non-Malayalis and international visitors who came to see performances and study the intricacies of the art. Kathakali troupes

Facing page: Gesture depicting 'Krishna'.

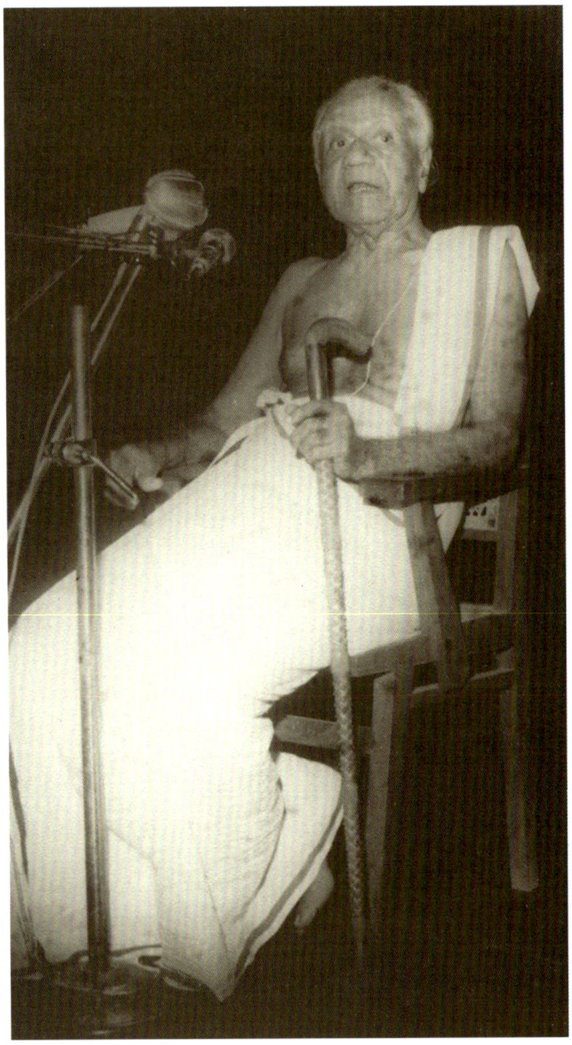

Mani Madhava Chakyar, one of the great maestros of Kutiyattam.

also started travelling to other places in India and abroad. The changes in format and content of the classical arts during this transitional time drew mixed reactions from the actor and sponsor groups across Kerala. Kalamandalam Ramankutty Nair, the Kathakali master, said that he felt gratified that the art has gained in status, which is directly reflected in the status in society and financial position of the artists. There is more appreciation for his art now than about fifty years ago, but paradoxically, the quality of appreciation has gone down.

The three established schools of Kutiyattam by the early eighties were the Kerala Kalamandalam in Cheruthuruthy, Margi in Thiruvananthapuram and Ammannur Chachu Chakyar Smaraka Gurukulam in Irinjalakkuda. These institutions, while incorporating changes in the pedagogy to suit the requirements of the modern age, have tried to keep the traditional content of Kutiyattam.

The starting of the Kutiyattam School in Kalamandalam in 1965, the admission of students from outside the Chakyar community and the introduction of the school system of learning with a fixed syllabus and specific duration of study, were some of the innovations brought about by Paimkulam Rama Chakyar. The transition of Kutiyattam from the *gurukula sampradaya* to the modern school system has resulted in changes in the system of admission. In the first place, the dwindling of the Chakyar families and their merging together has broken their privileged position as the sole custodians of the art. It has now by and large ceased to become the preserve of the Chakyar families, with more people from other castes joining the institutions to take up Kutiyattam as a profession. With the transformation of society on more democratic lines and the establishment of schools of acting, students from other castes have also enrolled themselves for Kutiyattam. Kutiyattam has now become open to all students irrespective of their birth status.

Kutiyattam in Kerala Kalamandalam incorporates a six-year diploma course and one-year post-diploma, while Mizhavu was structured as a four-year course and one-year post-diploma. The students are trained to learn all aspects of stage action and have a good grounding in Sanskrit. There is training in the Sanskrit and Malayalam languages and a well-designed course on Kutiyattam, which was originally planned by Paimkulam Rama Chakyar.[49] Great gurus such as Mani Madhava Chakyar and Ammannur Madhava Chakyar have served the institution as visiting faculty. Subsequently, the Kerala Government raised the Kerala Kalamandalam to the position of a 'deemed university' and this has resulted in the starting of a regular secondary school course in the institution. Apart from training in the art, the students also learn other subjects such as English, Hindi and Mathematics. Kalamandalam has a *koothambalam* designed by D. Appukkuttan Nair. Kalamandalam has published Mani Madhava Chakyar's book titled *Natyakalpadrumam*, which describes the theoretical as well as the practical aspects of Kutiyattam.

When an exclusive art such as Kutiyattam threw open its doors to large, heterogeneous audiences, total communication between the actor and the audience through a shared understanding of the codes and conventions of drama became a challenge. To aid cross-cultural communication and surmount problems of inscrutability of the intricate theatre grammar and narrative, lecture-demonstrations, where the dancer describes and demonstrates each dance movement, gesture and context, became common.

Kutiyattam troupes started travelling all over India and across the world, performing for new audiences. The first trip abroad for Kutiyattam was in 1980, headed by Paimkulam Rama Chakyar with a group of thirteen artists from Kalamandalam. Now there are frequent trips sponsored by institutions and universities in India and across the world.

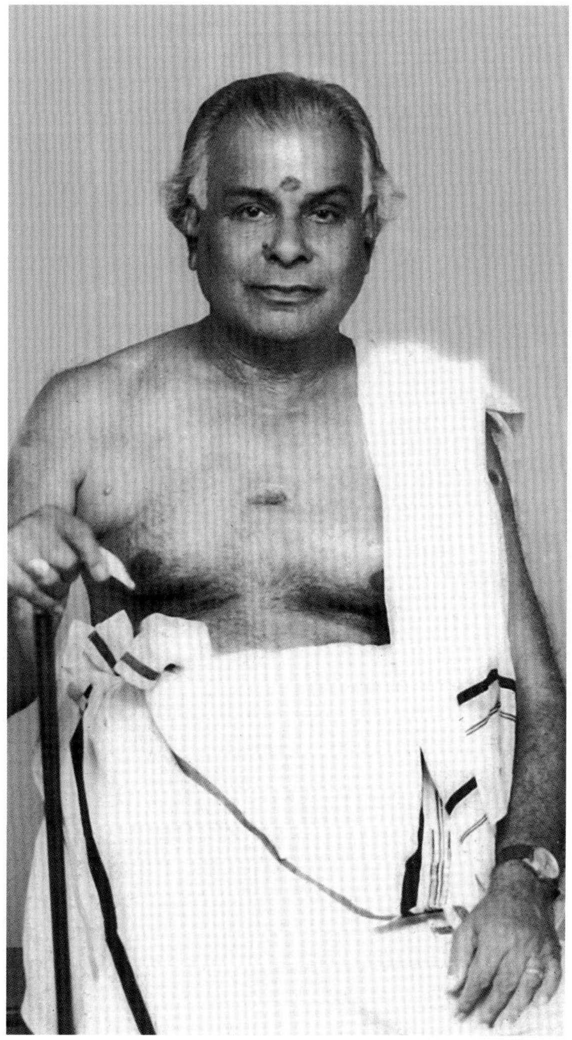

Paimkulam Rama Chakyar took the initiative to take Kutiyattam outside the temple.

Margi, based in Thiruvananthapuram, was started in 1970 as an institution devoted to the appreciation and preservation of Kerala's classical arts. Established by a few theatre enthusiasts with the pioneering efforts of D. Appukkuttan Nair as well as T.N.N. Bhattathiripad, Margi was initially focussed on the pursuit of Kathakali. However, by the late seventies, Margi took up a systematic campaign to revive Kutiyattam by organising a series of performances to expose the form to a larger audience. In 1981, Margi set up its own Kutiyattam school

[49] For a detailed information of the syllabus, see Sarma, V.S. 'Kutiyattam at Kerala Kalamandalam' in *Sangeet Natak Special Issue*, pp. 217-219.

Koothambalam *in Vadakkunnathan Temple in Trissur.*

to create a new generation of artists to carry on this performance tradition. The school evolved into a full-fledged repertory in the nineties.

Over the years, Margi has produced some excellent artists and pioneered the recovery and production of several plays, which had become extinct. At the outset, Margi had Ammannur Madhava Chakyar as the visiting teacher for eight years, with Ammannur Kochukuttan Chakyar as the resident teacher. Over the last fifteen years, the institution has trained twelve artists and runs a full-fledged repertory. It has given training to some outstanding performers and percussionists in Kutiyattam. Margi has performed all over India and abroad. One of the main efforts of Margi is to revitalise extinct plays such as *Mayasitankam*, *Agnipraveshankam* and *Parnasalankam*. Margi revived 'Mantrankam', which emphasises verbal action and *Sreekrishnacharitam Nangiarkoothu*. Margi Sathi is a talented actress who extended the repertoire of Nangiarkoothu by compiling *Sreeramacharitam*, a performance manual for the epic Ramayana. Margi exclusively devoted two issues of its journal to Kutiyattam and also published a monograph on the art form.

His descendants, Ammannur Madhava Chakyar and Parameswara Chakyar, started Ammannur Chachu Chakyar Smaraka Gurukulam in 1982, dedicated to the memory of the illustrious actor Ammannur Chachu Chakyar. The institution strives to preserve the Ammannur technique of Kutiyattam. The astuteness, passion and command shown by Ammannur Madhava Chakyar in giving training has paved the way for moulding a new generation of excellent young actors in the Gurukulam. Madhava Chakyar in his early years was unwilling to come out of a traditional mindset and resisted change in Kutiyattam. However, his years in Ammnuur Gurukulam gave him the opportunity to focus on a wider institutional context, train a group of promising young students, lead research through interpretation, re-create old *attaprakarams* and travel across the country and overseas disseminating his art. The artists have toured many parts of the world giving performances and lecture-demonstrations. The institution has revived the plays *Asokavanikankam*, *Jatayuvadhankam*, *Abhishekanataka*, *Kalyanasaugandhika* and *Sreekrishnacharitam Nangiarkoothu*. Every year, Ammannur Gurukulam organises a twelve-day Kutiyattam festival. The Gurukulam has published several books on Kutiyattam, including *The Production of a Play in Kutiyattam* by G. Venu and *Nangiarkoothu* by Nirmala Paniker.

These schools have come to be established as three *sampradayas* and are the springboard for opening new possibilities for Kutiyattam. With the shift of patronage in recent times from the feudal order to the Government and its agencies such as the Sangeet Natak Akademi and making the revival of the classical arts part of the avowed policy on culture and heritage, there have been some initiatives in recent years to encourage and support Kutiyattam. There are sponsors, though few, from the non-government sectors in Kerala, such as temple administrations and other private trusts. Over the years, the unique theatre language of classical theatre in Kerala has caught the attention of scholars and theatre people from all parts of the world. In recent times, cross-cultural studies have revitalised interest in classical theatres such as Kutiyattam and Kathakali. They also serve as routes to the discovery of tradition, leading sociologists and theatre scholars to search deep into roots of classicisation.

By the early nineties, the Sangeet Natak Akademi had come up with a restoration plan 'recognising that there exists a sense of high stake in the preservation of artistic traditions that appear to be threatened by the ever-changing socio-economic environment—and a fear of their loss to posterity'. The plan comprised strategies to ensure the transmission of Kutiyattam through revitalising the *guru-shishya parampara*, providing economic sustenance to the artists and performance opportunities. For achieving this, the Akademi made Margi and Ammannur Gurukulam its grant-in-aid institutions, the former primarily as a repertory providing ongoing performances of Kutiyattam and the latter as a training institution to create a new generation of actors. Financial assistance was also provided to P.K. Narayanan Nambiar, the *mizhavu* maestro, for training students in *mizhavu*. Another significant support was given to Ammannur Madhava Chakyar for transcribing and micro-filming the extensive manuscripts of Kutiyattam. At a time when the financial resources and internal capacities of these organisations were minimal, the Kutiyattam Scheme of the Sangeet Natak Akademi was a major boost to the revitalisation of the art form.

By the end of the nineties, apart from the three well-established institutions, new centres exclusively devoted to Kutiyattam mushroomed in Kerala. Among them, the Padmasri Mani Madhava Chakyar Smaraka Gurukulam started functioning in the memory of the late master-performer Mani Madhava Chakyar. Based in Lakkidi, the institution presently concentrates on giving intensive training in *mizhavu*. It has revived the play *Swapnavasavadatta*.

The International Centre for Kutiyattam, based in Thrippunithura, was established in 1995 with the purpose of promoting Kutiyattam, Prabandhakkoothu as well as Nangiarkoothu. It organises foundation courses and conducts classes with a detailed syllabus and evaluation at the end of the course. It has taken Kutiyattam to schools and colleges across Kerala and other places in the country for lecture-demonstrations and performances.

When cultural interaction took place in a colonial context of unequal powers, as it happened in India and the West, there was a tendency to assess its worth from the perspective of the dominant power. Initially, arts such as Kutiyattam and Kathakali appealed to the Western spectator for their fantastic, spectacular qualities. Seeing a performance of Uday Shankar in Paris in 1926, Alice Boner came looking for its roots in Kerala, went to Kalamandalam and described with wonder and passion the 'power of expression and melodious rhythm residing in the human body' in *Kathakali: The Religious Drama of Malabar.*[50] At first, Kathakali received far more attention from theatre people across the world, which resulted in the adaptation of several Indian stories and Western plays and narratives into the art form. Adaptations such as Shakespeare's *King Lear*, *Hamlet* and *The Tempest* and Goethe's *Faust* have evoked mixed reactions from the audience from being 'a tampering with tradition' to open admiration.

John Russell Brown, describing his first encounter with a Kutiyattam performance in his *New Sites for Shakespeare*, says: 'Unexpectedly I learnt about a part of the spectrum of theatre's possibilities that I had previously not known to exist and, increasingly, I began to understand that I had stumbled upon the key that would unlock some secret about Shakespeare's exceptional achievements.'[51] For him, the freedom of the actor to be what he chooses and the audience to imaginatively follow him through the fantasy of theatre began to 'challenge earlier ideas of Shakespeare's stagecraft and the almost unchanging background of Shakespearean theatre.'[52]

Peter Brook's experiment of extracting the essence of art through working with an international company for his celebrated *Mahabharata* finds a parallel in the cross-cultural experimental play *Desdemona*—Rio-Kishida's Japanese adaptation of Shakespeare's *Othello*, directed by Ong Keng Sen and produced by Singapore Theatreworks. An experimental production concerned with the issues of feminism and colonialism and involving artists from India, Korea, Indonesia and Singapore, the production emphasised the collaboration of the traditional artists with contemporary actors. The experiment, according to Margi Madhu, the Kutiyattam artist who played the role of Othello, resulted in the 're-invention of one's own theatre grammar for each actor and the emergence of a language, one through innovation and improvisation, to reach out to an international audience'. It was staged at the Adelaide Festival (March 2000), Munich Dance Festival (March 2000), Singapore Theatre Festival (June 2000) and Hamburg Theatre Festival (July 2000).

Another such venture was the cross-cultural mask dance *Dragon Bond Rite* staged by traditional artists from five Asian countries (India, Korea, Indonesia, Japan and Suva) based on a poem written by the famous American Buddhist poet Richard Armond and directed by Richard Emmert. The play depicts five scenes, which deal with the five stages of human development such as birth, suffering, lust, meditation, death and rebirth. This was staged in Washington, New York (1997) and at the 17th Asian Festival in Hong Kong (1998). Margi Madhu says that participating in such inter-cultural experiences has changed the perspective from which he looks at tradition: 'I feel

[50] Boner, G., L. Soni and J. Soni. 1996. 'First Encounter with Kathakali' in *Alice Boner on Kathakali*, p. 24. Alice Boner Foundation and Switzerland: Museum Rietberg.
[51] Brown, John Russell. 1997. *New Sites for Shakespeare: Theatre, the Audience and Asia*, p. 77. London: Routledge.
[52] *Ibid*, p. 84.

proud about my art and I have realised its potential for reaching across different audiences, but I also know that a blind adherence to tradition without being open to changes, wherever necessary, can lead to the decay of this age-old art form.' Most actors of Kutiyattam today share similar feelings and there are considerable innovative experiments taking place in the art, to cater to a wider viewership.

The awareness that the study of the classical arts such as Kathakali and Kutiyattam would lead to the discovery of lost links with traditional Indian theatre, has created renewed interest in the pursuit of these arts. With the recognition that tradition is not merely something venerable in itself, but is an ongoing process, contemporary playwrights such as Kavalam Narayana Panikkar have attempted to discover their 'roots' in the indigenous traditions of theatre. He has successfully integrated elements of Kutiyattam and experimented with creative interpretations of the Sanskrit plays of Bhasa and Kalidasa.

This going back to the roots[53] has, in fact, become a movement in post-colonial Indian theatre that manifested itself as a desire to reject an overarching Western theatric idiom and seeks to draw on the indigenous theatrical heritage. Apart from Kavalam, theatre people from Sankara Pillai to Arjun Raina and Maya Rao[54] in recent times creatively adapted the rich resources of the classical performances of Kerala in various ways.

[53] See Suresh Awasthi's paper 'Theatre of Roots' in *TDR: The Drama Review* 9 (34), pp. 48-69. 1989.

[54] Maya Rao's production *Khol Do*, performed first in 1993, dealing with a short story of Saadat Hasan Manto, draws inspiration from the acting technique of Kathakali.

An archival picture of the hero and the vidushaka.

The processes of change manifesting in classical theatres such as Kutiyattam in the present age have a counterpoint—a dialectic and reflexive tendency from 'within' the tradition that arrests the flow of rapid 'modernisation' and looks inwards for enrichment. While Kerala Kalamandalam under the leadership of Paimkulam Rama Chakyar, edited and choreographed plays such as *Jatayuvadham* and *Bhagavadajjukiyam* as shortened versions, fit for a single day's viewing, Margi retrieved performance manuals from masters such as Ammannur Madhava Chakyar and pioneered the revival of several plays that have long since become extinct. As a counter movement against the tendency of excessive reduction and editing of the plays for wider appeal, Margi resorts to go back to the original method of elaboration by extending the performance score as given in the old theatre manuals. It revived three extinct acts

Rama, Lakshmana and Surpanakha in Surpanakhankam.

from *Ascharyachudamani*—'Parnasalankam' (Act I), 'Mayasitankam' (Act II) and 'Agnipravesankam' (Act VII). Margi now boasts of being the only institution that performed the seven-act play *Ascharyachudamani* in its full form, stretching to a period of hundred and thirteen days of performance!

The first act of *Subhadradhnanjaya* was choreographed to extend to eleven days. Under the initiative of Diana Daugherty, the second act was also choreographed through a collaborative effort from Margi Sathi and Usha Nangiar. Margi also took the initiative to document, give training and perform 'Mantrankam', an elaborate verbal enactment stretching to forty days. Similarly, Ammannur Gurukulam revived *Kalyanasaugandhikam*, *Hanumaddutankam* and *Samudrataranankam*. All the schools now take up the revival of old plays on a big scale, with the result that the repertoire of Kutiyattam has become much richer than what it was fifty years ago.

Another manner of extension of the existing corpus of plays is to adapt new episodes in the Kutiyattam and Nangiarkoothu style of presentation. P.K. Narayanan Nambiar reconstructed *Sreekrishnacharitam Nangiar-koothu* for the Nangiar's presentation and Kalamandalam revived certain portions of the long-forgotten *Bhagavadajjukiyam*. Ammannur Gurukulam perfected Nilakantha's *Kalyanasaugandhikam* while Margi Sathi, through a Fellowship of the Department of Culture, Government of India, compiled the entire Ramayana story and codified its performance manual for Nangiarkoothu. This was soon followed by Margi Madhu's reconstruction of Bhasa's *Karnabharam*. Similar ventures have extended the performance score of Kutiyattam in recent years.

Kalamandalam introduced High School education for its students in 1990. The recent transition of Kerala Kalamandalam from a grant-in-aid institution under the Department of Culture, Government of Kerala, to a deemed university has made an impact in its structure and pedagogy. The institution now tries to harmonise the traditional training format with the requirements of a modern university system. It has introduced the AHSLC (Art High School Leaving Certificate course), Plus Two courses as well as a Bachelors course in the Performing Arts. Now the university also conducts a Masters course in Kathakali, Kutiyattam and Mohiniyattam, apart from MPhil and PhD programmes as well as integrated courses in Cultural Studies, Cultural Journalism, Multimedia, Mass Communication, Women's Studies and Documentation.

The impact of the electronic media on the classical arts such as Kutiyattam has perhaps not been analysed to a great extent yet. Preservation through audio and video documentation has made the classical arts accessible to a variety of people. Realising the potential of television to reach out to a wide viewership, channels from Kerala have started airing programmes on Kathakali and Kutiyattam. Presenting a Kutiyattam or Kathakali play on television calls for a combination of skills. Since the medium does not engage the attention of the viewer to the same extent as a live performance, there is a limitation in the presentation of such programmes that call for a focussed viewing. Only sections from plays can be presented at a time and even these episodes need to be selected carefully, to include self-contained, short pieces. Interviews with the masters of these art forms, as well as discussions, lecture-demonstrations and clips from the plays are often screened. These efforts have made the arts familiar to a large section of people. Directed at presenting a play in its entirety through a serialised format, showing only segments lasting for about one hour in one programme, a play takes a series of episodes to complete. As it is provided with a detailed commentary at the beginning and sub-titles in Malayalam, even the non-initiates can easily understand its complicated theatre language. This provides an opportunity for a wider dissemination of the art and is catering to the viewers who have lost touch with their own cultural heritage. Government agencies such as the Centre for Development of Imaging Technology (C.Dit), Thiruvananthapuram, educational institutions such as the Sree Sankara Sanskrit University, Kalady, along with international efforts such as the one made by Heidrun Bruckner, through a grant from the German Research Foundation and private initiatives from Invis Multimedia have already built up a good corpus of Kutiyattam plays. Like in other areas of knowledge, the classical arts have profited from the Internet as well. There are numerous websites with large volumes of data. The potential for the web as a medium to facilitate interest in the arts is obvious.

A linkage with tourism, especially mass tourism, whether domestic or international, can lead to both positive and negative outcomes. While it promotes exposure and ensures wider viewership for the art form, a casual tourist's motive in watching a play may be only as a spectacle-arousing curiosity or as leisure-time activity. Rather than providing standardised, homogenised 'packages' of experience to this market, a healthier, mutually beneficial option is to promote cultural festivals and periodically arrange performances to cater to a niche market. There is a need to create an appreciation base among the youth for the country's heritage, given the increasing trend of cultural homogenisation.

UNESCO Masterpiece

On 24 May 2000, I hired a taxi to go to watch a Kutiyattam performance, something I have been doing periodically. But today the taxi driver looked at me differently. 'Oh you are going to watch the Kutiyattam performance. You know it has won UNESCO recognition!' The taxi driver, who had apparently never seen a performance himself or heard about Kutiyattam before, was proudly informing me that Kutiyattam has won world recognition! Kerala, which prides itself on its hundred per cent literacy and has a population that reads newspapers and watches television, seems to have noticed its own art form after the UNESCO news...[55]

In 2000, a unique opportunity was created with UNESCO starting a new initiative called the Intangible Cultural Heritage and, within it, a programme for proclaiming outstanding forms of cultural expression as a collective heritage of the world. In view of the great awareness across the world of the urgent need to safeguard and preserve intangible cultural expressions, UNESCO created the Proclamation by UNESCO of Masterpieces of the Oral and Intangible Heritage of Humanity. The aim was to encourage governments, NGOs and local communities to identify, preserve and promote their intangible heritage. It was also intended to encourage individuals, groups, institutions and organisations to make outstanding contributions to managing, preserving, protecting and promoting the intangible heritage.

The information regarding this initiative reached the world of Kutiyattam by chance. In late 1999, a troupe from Margi travelled to Paris at the invitation of Mandapa, an organisation run by Milena Salvini. Having heard of the UNESCO programme, Margi took the initiative to request for a nomination. A meeting of the representatives of different schools, scholars and other practitioners was convened in Thiruvananthapuram to discuss the process and to invite suggestions for a ten-year action plan for the revitalisation of Kutiyattam. Adoor Gopalakrishnan made a video documentation of the art form. The production, lasting for more than ten hours, was done inside Kitangur Koothambalam, one of the oldest temple theatres in Kerala, with a performance history of about eight hundred years. I, as the Vice-President of Margi, put together the nomination dossier. The proposal, fielded by the Government of

Facing page: The vidushaka *in a characteristic pose.*

[55] Diana Daugherty, a scholar who worked on Kutiyattam for several years, in conversation with me.

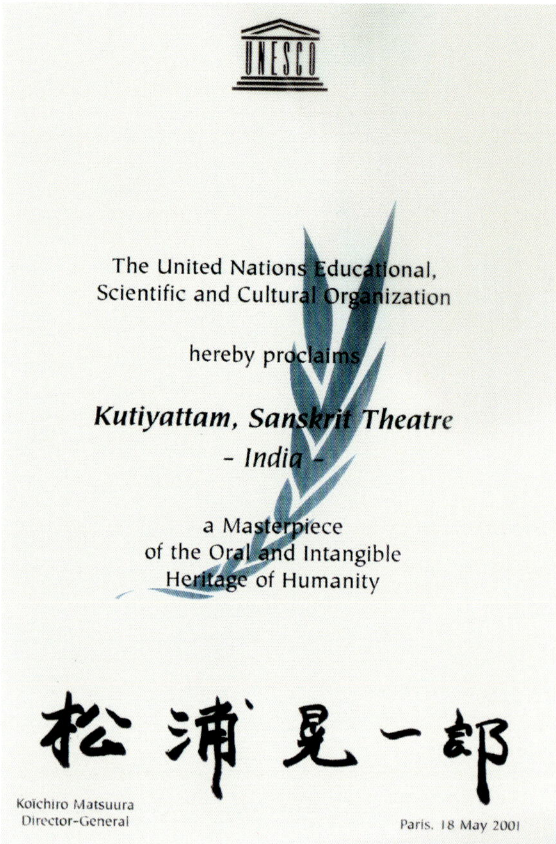

The United Nations Educational, Scientific and Cultural Organization

hereby proclaims

Kutiyattam, Sanskrit Theatre
- India -

a Masterpiece of the Oral and Intangible Heritage of Humanity

Koichiro Matsuura
Director-General

Paris, 18 May 2001

UNESCO Citation proclaiming Kutiyattam as 'Masterpiece of the Oral and Intangible Heritage of Humanity' in 2001.

India, was approved by an international jury in May 2000 when Kutiyattam, along with sixteen other expressions of heritage from across the world, was proclaimed as the world's heritage and accorded the status of the Oral and Intangible Heritage of Humanity.

The resurgence of Kutiyattam gained momentum with the UNESCO recognition. At the regional level, new initiatives were planned to safeguard the art form and reach it to a wider community of people. Performance opportunities increased, as did its cultural value.

After the announcement of the recognition, the Kutiyattam community came together for the first time to address the issue of its revitalisation. In spite of financial constraints, there is a renewed energy among artists in applying themselves to creative projects. The three major schools—Kalamandalam, Margi and Ammannur Gurukulam—have taken steps for the revitalisation of the art by creating new productions, reviving earlier plays and developing new choreographies. Margi revised the play *Subhadradhananjayam* (Act II), while Ammannur Gurukulam has already choreographed Kalidasa's famous play *Sakuntalam*.

With the extension of its base, in the present context there is a growing need to transmit the skills and knowledge to a wider community. One of the most important consequences of recognition is the establishment of more institutions dedicated to the pursuance and teaching of Kutiyattam in Kerala. Some of these worthwhile initiatives are the Paimkulam Ramachakyar Smaraka Gurukulam in Cheruthuruthy, the Krishnan Nambiar Smaraka Mizhavu Kalari by V.K.K. Hariharan and Usha Nangiar, Nepathya by Margi Madhu and Indu G. as well as Rangasree by Margi Sathi. Dedicated to training a new generation of students, reviving old choreographies, codifying new ones and transmitting the art through performances and lecture-demonstrations, these institutions play a big role in the consolidation and propagation of the tradition of Kutiyattam.

With the UNESCO recognition, the patrons and practitioners of Kutiyattam formed a network (perhaps for the first time in its history) under the celebrated Ammannur Madhava Chakyar and decided to come together for the common cause of rejuvenating the art. All the six centres made out their own action plans for the rejuvenation of their respective schools and chartered their individual needs. They also decided to have more interaction in the future and to support each other. Further, Kutiyattam caught the attention of people from a variety of fields in India including artists, media, theatre scholars and administrators and made big news across the country. This resulted in boosting its image to a national audience. In Kerala there is a feeling of pride that a sacred art belonging to the region has won international recognition. For the community of Chakyars and a small group of aficionados who strove to keep this art alive, it is a vindication of their commitment and efforts.

Efforts have also been made to link the performances with tourism activities, taking care not to dilute its content in the process. The Department of Tourism announced the recognition of Kutiyattam as a major landmark in Kerala and an international heritage. It has since started advertising performances through pamphlets and brochures. This has had the desired effect of attracting a segment of people, both domestic and international, to the art. The Department, while organising the annual tourism week, announced the heritage theatre of Kutiyattam as a prominent event. After the UNESCO proclamation, a comprehensive action plan was evolved at the national level, to revitalise Kutiyattam, to ensure its management and financial support. An Intangible Heritage Fund was created and, through this, funds were channelised. A budget line (head) was created in the Ministry of Culture as the Intangible Heritage Fund to give support to Indian art forms declared by UNESCO as Masterpieces of the Oral and Intangible Heritage of Humanity. Under this head, a series of activities that will lead to the promotion of Kutiyattam were budgeted. The Tenth Five Year Plan of India kept aside resources for the revitalisation of Kutiyattam. One of the most significant developments was that, in the National Budget for 2006, the Minister for Finance, Government of India, announced a special provision for the cultural expressions declared as Masterpieces by UNESCO. The announcement said, 'I am happy to inform the House that Kutiyattam, Vedic Chanting and Ramlila have been declared 'Oral and Intangible Heritage of Humanity' by UNESCO. These old art forms and oral traditions need to be safeguarded. Pending drawing up a detailed scheme, I propose to make an initial provision of Rs. 5 crore [Rs. 50 million] in 2006-07.'

Realising the importance of identifying activities for the safeguard and protection of Kutiyattam, the Department of Culture envisaged a detailed plan for its preservation. The proposal had the following components of assistance from the Department of Culture, Ministry of Culture, Government of India: The first was a Production Grant that sought to revive those plays that have gone out of active performance on the Kutiyattam stage, as well as choreograph new productions, keeping to the prescribed format of the art form and without tampering with its basic aesthetic and performative grammar. The second was a Grant for the Promotion of Performance Opportunities. This would bring artists from all the major schools of Kutiyattam on a common platform. It encourages practitioners to propagate and preserve their art and strengthen the common involvement and activities of safeguarding and disseminating Kutiyattam. Another component of the proposal included a Grant for Training and Promotion through Guru-Shisya Parampara. This was intended to conduct training of selected young people under eminent gurus and established teachers, for taking over and perpetuating Kutiyattam through generations. Under this programme, refresher courses, interactive workshops, lecture-demonstrations as well

Kalamandalam Sivan Namboothiri as Ravana in Kailasoddharanam.

as short performances would be part of the ongoing activity of each institution. Another activity would be the organisation of outreach workshops in educational institutions of Kerala and outside with the twin objectives of exposing young students to Kutiyattam and inducting talent to join the Kutiyattam schools. A Grant for Visual Documentation and Research was also proposed. This was directed towards the detailed documentation of Kutiyattam performances. It would include organising seminars, festivals, conducting research, translating theatre manuals and publishing books.

Through the Japan-Funds-in-Trust scheme, UNESCO made a comprehensive action plan for the revitalisation of Kutiyattam, which was part of the ten-year action plan projected in the nomination dossier. It sought to support and consolidate the network of Kutiyattam practitioners and to ensure its continued safeguarding. UNESCO identified the following objectives: assist intangible cultural heritage custodians and practitioners in their efforts to safeguard and transmit this heritage to future generations and to target young audiences and potential performers; assist and support the creation of a network of Kutiyattam institutions involved in the preservation of this art form; foster further academic research and produce publication of texts and audio-visual documentation; assist in establishing a centralised archive and library on Kutiyattam and raise awareness of young people in the local community of the important role they should play in ensuring the maintenance of their cultural heritage and also within Indian society at large.

The project sought to support local practitioners from the six Kutiyattam schools/institutions located in Kerala. This involved organising training courses, performances, lecture-demonstrations and workshops, Kutiyattam festivals and an international seminar. The promotion of performances was directed at bringing together artists from the major schools of Kutiyattam on a common platform. Other efforts included making traditional theatre houses available for public performances, conducting annual workshops with the participation of all the schools as well as providing refresher courses for all the artists and students from Kutiyattam institutions.

Further, the project emphasised the improvement of research facilities in the six institutions, with the creation of Academic Resource Centres in the schools. It envisaged the setting up of a centralised archive and library with cataloguing and electronic storing facilities to maintain the literature, documents, performance manuals and audio-video material on Kutiyattam. Other initiatives planned were the holding of seminars, bringing out publications including new research, translations of manuscripts and original writings on Kutiyattam. A programme of Documentation of Masters Series was directed towards the audio-visual documentation of distinctive artistic styles and techniques of the master-performers.

To put these comprehensive plans into practice, UNESCO identified two forms of assistance. The first was for supporting and facilitating the creation of the network (representatives of six institutions engaged in safeguarding of Kutiyattam) and for sustaining its activities for the preservation, conservation and dissemination of the Kutiyattam Sanskrit Theatre. It also recommended tapping private and public sources of funding at the local, regional and national level with a view to creating a Kutiyattam Fund. The other programme sought to sustain the specific needs, such as the ongoing activities of the six institutions of the network, to enable them to safeguard and transmit their art. Within the resources allocated from the Japan Funds-in-Trust scheme, financial assistance was given to individual institutions (Kalamandalam, Margi, Ammannoor Gurukulam, Mani Madhava Chakyar Gurukulam, International Centre for Kutiyattam and Sree Sankara University, Department of Ancient Theatre) for utilisation according to their own priority areas. These ranged from the upgrading of infrastructure facilities, production/choreography of new plays based on existing texts, organising training programmes/ lecture-demonstrations/performances to outreach activities and documentation.

With the tranferring of its earmarked funds from the Ministry of Culture, Government of India, towards the revitalisation of Kutiyattam and as a development of its earlier Kutiyattam project, in 2006 the Sangeet Natak Akademi, New Delhi, initiated Kutiyattam Kendram: National Centre for Kutiyattam in Thiruvananthapuram. It was intended as an institution with a wide-ranging agenda for Kutiyattam. Some of its objectives were the preservation and creative growth of Kutiyattam; the creation of an informed audience and *rasikas*; providing a platform for discussion and the exchange of concepts among gurus, artists and scholars; sponsoring training, as well as performance opportunities; encouraging research in affiliated theatric traditions; maintaining the genealogy of families of Chakyars and Nambiars; supporting traditional families and the conservation of traditional theatres. Under this programme, there are provisions for infrastructural support to all the existing institutions, annual grants, performance subsidies, monthly remuneration of each artist in all the institutions, scholarships to students, research and publication grants, as well as dissemination activities such as the organisation of Kutiyattam festivals. The National Centre for Kutiyattam now serves as a platform to address matters relating to Kutiyattam in a wide-ranging manner and to ensure its sustenance.

Revitalising a Tradition

How does a traditional art form create value in our age, in a new competitive context, when the dynamics between art traditions, processes of operation and patronage systems keep changing rapidly? In the present age, Kutiyattam confronts issues relating to adaptation to suit the demands of a new viewership. The last few years have necessitated the development of new insights and innovations in Kutiyattam to cope with a continuously evolving set of challenges and opportunities. The augmentation of resources through multiple funding agencies has to a certain extent lessened the vulnerability of the Kutiyattam artist. Exposure and interaction with larger art networks have broadened his understanding of what the world expects today from this age old traditional art form.

More than ever, rather than being a mere bearer and transmitter of a heavy load of tradition, the Kutiyattam artist is required to be an innovator and creator of new standards of acting and viewing. The gradual unfolding of the subtleties of *abhinaya,* which is crucial to the aesthetics of Kutiyattam, has now given way to two- or three-hour performances. The challenge before an actor today is to present the complexities of the art before a new viewer who does not have the patience or time for long hours of viewing.

There are two parallel trends working in this situation: on the one hand, long and time-consuming narrative portions with elaborate scope for acting get curtailed and edited, by making them more 'crisp' as well as 'dramatic'. On the other, apart from the existing plays and choreographic texts, there is the urge for the creation of new texts and choreographies. These include scenes with the potential for effective theatric communication and dramatic appeal, but which either avoid or reduce the scope of conventions such as *nirvahanamm* and *pakarnnattam*, and can be enacted within a couple of hours. While some of the new choreographies are re-inventions of extinct *attaprakarams*, many are creative interpretations of older plays, or totally new creations. This has resulted in the emergence of a significant body of 'new' texts in Kutiyattam.

Margi Madhu gives an exhaustive list of new choreographies (created between 1965 and now) in his article titled 'Ente Chittappeduthalukal'[56] (My Choreographies). These include the

Facing page: The innovative Kutiyattam artist is setting new standards for the discerning viewer.

[56] Margi Madhu, ed. K.G. Paulose. 2005. 'Ente Chittappe-duthalukal' in *Kutiyattathinte Puthiya Mukham*, pp. 67-90. Trippunithura: International Centre for Kutiyattam.

experiments by repertories in Kerala Kalamandalam ('Kalyanasaugandhikam,' the second act of *Nagananda*, 'Bhagavadajjukam', the fourth act of *Swapnavasavadattam*), Margi ('Agnipravesankam', 'Parnasalankam Mayasitankam' and 'Agnipravesankam' of *Ascharyachudamani*) and Ammnuur Gurukulam (*Jatayuvadhankam, Hanumaddutankam, Samudrataranankam, Mayasirassankam*, apart from new productions such as *Saundaryalahari, Vikramorvasiyam, Sakuntalam*) as well as by Mani Madhava Chakyar Smaraka Gurukulam (*Kaliyankam*) and Paimkulam Rama Chakyar Smaraka Gurukulam (Bhasa's *Pancharatram*).

There are also experiments by individual artists such as Kalamandalam Rama Chakyar, Margi Madhu, Margi Sathi and Usha Nangiar. Rama Chakyar's revitalisation of the *attaprakarams* of Bhasa's *Dutavakyam* and the individual productions of Margi Madhu (*Karnabharam* with support from the Sree Sankara Sanskrit University and *Kanchukiyam*, supported by the International Centre for Kutiyattam) are significant.

Margi Sathi produced an acting manual for the Ramayana story in the Nangiarkoothu format, called 'Sreeramacharitam,' through a fellowship of the Ministry of Culture, Government of India. 'Sreeramacharitam' is Sathi's attempt at a broad-span narrative in which she encapsulates the story of Ramayana through obtaining two hundred and twenty verses from different literary sources. Later, she choreographed 'Kannakicharitam' and the recent 'Sitayanam' in Nangiarkoothu mode.

Margi Madhu's experiment with *Macbeth* is an innovative attempt to introduce the celebrated Shakespearean play into the context of Kutiyattam. He took up the challenge by first translating the play into Sanskrit and, through the theatric device of *nirvahanam*, recapitulated the story in solo-acting mode.

On the other hand, the choreography of *Abhijnanasakuntalam*, a four-day format by Ammannur Gurukulam, under the direction of G. Venu, was done in a manner of co-creation with the active collaboration of the performers of the *gurukulam*, the *Sakuntalam* scholars as well as the Kutiyattam experts.

Usha Nangiar developed choreographies based on women in Indian mythology who feature as important characters in Kutiyattam. In collaboration with Margi Sathi, she also re-invented the *nirvahanam* of Subhadra in the fifth act of *Subhadradhanjayam*.[57]

Usha Nangiar's consistent efforts paved the way for the reconstruction of several episodes that focus on the female performer. Some of these remarkable reinventions include those of Lalita in *Surpanakhankam*, Mandodari in 'Asokavanikankam' and Subhadra in the fifth act of *Subhadradhananjaya*. She has also revived the text and performance of Karttyayani whose character shows unique traits, which pose a challenge to the performer.

All these experiments have undoubtedly added richness and depth to the Kutiyattam corpus; new experiments, however, need to be based on stringent principles of the pursuit of excellence. They should also be open to a rigorous process of the critical evaluation of the performance. The

[57] For this exhaustive information on new choreographies, I am indebted to Margi Madhu's article cited above.

Percussion instruments: mizhavu *and* edakka.

test of a good production is its robustness and time is, no doubt, the best judge of sustainability. For, it is only when the old blends harmoniously with the new can we safely conclude that this heritage theatre of India will be assured its rightful place in the hearts of those who love the classical arts.

existing manuals. In August 2008, at a time when the performance of an entire act from a play as a continuous sequence had become rare, if not extinct, elsewhere, Nepathya, the Centre for Kutiyattam run by Margi Madhu and Indu G., volunteered to do a complete performance of the single act over fifteen days. The event was made possible by financial assistance from the Indology Department of Hebrew University, Jerusalem, through the involvement of Professor David Schulman.

Ascharyachudamani depicts episodes from the Ramayana. It details Surpanakha's disfigurement at Lakshmana's hands, Ravana's abduction of Sita, the killing of Jatayu, the love-struck Ravana's total surrender to Sita and Sita's rejection of his passion. The minimal text of the play gains unparalleled dramatic grandeur at the hands of the Kutiyattam artist. A single actor in the costume of Ravana holds the the stories as well as a powerful depiction of the intensity and the progression of Ravana's love for Sita. It is a challenge for the actor to retain the basic character of Ravana and 'get into' the roles of other characters deftly and in quick succession without losing the dramatic inspiration and focus. Only an actor with a full command of imaginative, histrionic and intellectual resources can pull off these sequences.

Margi Madhu, the actor who played Ravana for the sequence, shares his experiences of intensely engaging with the epic character: 'In the first few days, I was enacting the role as it was taught to me by my teachers. However, as the days advanced, I felt a change in my own attitude towards Ravana. Gradually, the feeling towards Sita as an object of romantic obsession was transforming in my mind to a deeper feeling of admiration mixed with reverential love. This, perhaps, may have been the real reason why Ravana could not bring himself to 'touch' her. My problem here was to conform and match these thoughts to the verses in the Sanskrit text.'

Facing page: Ravana's grand entry.

DAY ONE

When the curtain is removed, Ravana appears in a reflective mood, with his arms resting on the head of Varshavara, the pageboy. At the end of the ritual drumming, the woman chanter (Nangiar) recites a verse, which signifies the mental disposition of the character. Simultaneously, Ravana enacts the different moods as depicted in the verse.

When Varshavara retires, Ravana meditates on Sita. He describes her physical form from head to feet, as an imaginative recapitulation. He is lovesick, struck by the arrows of Kamadeva. The pangs of his love intensify by the cool rays of the moon and the gentle breeze. In agony, he looks up towards the moon and thinks, 'It is not the moon. Then who could it be? It is the sun.' In anger, he hits his own thighs and performs a dance movement depicting anger (Pravesikam).

He tells his pageboy, 'O Varshavara, there is no chance that the sun can enter Lanka. Why? The trees in my garden cannot tolerate the rays of the sun and as a result I have banished him. How did that happen? I was living in a state of happiness and one day, I went to my court after my daily chores such as bath, prayer and food. I sat on my throne adorned in all the regalia, under the royal umbrella and other regal services, surrounded by my chieftains and other royalty. Later, to spend some time in leisure, I reached the royal garden. Noticing that the trees were not looking fresh, I questioned the gardener, 'Why aren't you looking after the trees carefully?' The gardener replied, 'O lord, we tend the plants carefully. We never leave the roots of the plants without water.' After a careful examination, Ravana concurs with him and looking up, notices the sun shining brightly in the sky. He realises that the heat from the sun makes the trees dry. In anger, suddenly, Ravana draws his sword and lunges towards the sun to kill him. The sun bows at his feet and begs pardon. Ravana says, 'O sun, promise me that you will never come to Lanka again'. The sun obeys him and Ravana throws him out with his legs and banishes him from Lanka.

Then Ravana continues, 'So, this can't be the sun. I will kill him.' On second thoughts, he decides that it is better to kill him after consulting with Chitrayodhi, his minister. Ravana now orders Varshavara to summon Chitrayodhi. While waiting for Chitrayodhi, Ravana realises that it is the moon and he is embarrassed at his mistake.

In conclusion, as this is the first day, the actor performs a series of dance rituals, called purappadu.

DAY TWO

The second day starts with Ravana entering the scene after performing his rituals. He is facing the drum (mizhavu). *Now he proceeds with the* anukramam, *the narration of the story, from the present to the past. The format in the* anukramam *describes the incidents in reverse chronological order in the form of questions, as follows:* 'How did Ravana, born in the Pulastya race behold the moon and mistake him as the sun? Prior to that, how did he abduct Sita and take her to Asokavanika and place her beneath the *simsipa* tree? Before that, how did he reach Lanka with Sita and cut off the wings of Jatayu who blocked his way by stopping his chariot? Prior to that, how did he disguise himself as the illusory [*maya*] Rama, force Sita into the chariot and

Facing page: Ravana in a reflective mood, meditating on Sita.

proceed towards Lanka? Before that, how did Ravana start from Lanka with his charioteers and Surpanakha?'

With this the anukramam *is completed and now the* samkshepam *(abridged narration) follows:*

Once upon a time, Ravana, born in the Pulastya race, was residing peacefully in Lanka. At that time, accompanied by the army of titanic demons (*rakshasas*), he prepared for a battle with the serpents, in the netherworld. In the battle, Vidyutjihva, the husband of Surpanakha, was killed by mistake.

Upon hearing the mourning of Surpanakha, Ravana assures her, 'O Surpanakha, you shall marry any man you wish in the three worlds, whoever he may be.' With these words he entrusts the *rakshasas*, Khara and Dushana, and an army of fourteen thousand demons for her assistance. However, Surpanakha, after a few days, comes to Ravana with a bruised nose and ears, wailing loudly. From the afflicted Surpanakha, Ravana understands that Lakshmana attacked her, cut off her nose and ears and also killed Khara and Dushana. He also comes to know about the extraordinary beauty of Sita. With great desire and longing, he reaches the abode of Maricha, gives him the task of disguising as a golden deer and returns to Lanka. *Thus ends the* samkshepam. *Now the actor places the vest cloth on his arms and enacts the convention of* panchangam, *the five-point description (hair, eyes, face, breast and feet) of the heroine, Sita, and is afflicted by the arrows of Kamadeva.*

Overpowered by desire, Ravana decides to leave for Sita's place and starts the preparation. He takes his bath, wears fresh garments, adorns himself with royal insignia, such as his crown and bangles, chews betel leaves with areca (*paan*), inspects himself in the mirror and again thinks of Sita. Deciding to go to her immediately, he stands on the stool (*pitha*) and ties the waistcloth, tightens his armour, takes his sword, called Chandrahasa, and commands Surpanakha to accompany him in the chariot. He turns right, gestures as though seeing Surpanakha seated in the chariot and gets into the chariot himself.

Now he depicts the conventional stage behaviour, corresponding to the journey on a chariot, and standing before the lamp describes the *panchangam* of Sita. Though he is struck by Kama's arrow, on seeing Surpanakha seated near him, he is embarrassed at his own open demonstration of his desire for Sita. He also looks around to see whether anyone else has seen his frailty. He happens to see the *devas* mocking him and he threatens them with dire consequences. He gives instructions to the charioteer to go faster and again describes Sita's *panchangam*. He urges the charioteer to go faster and tells the mocking *devas* that he would soon have Sita with him in Lanka and then he would avenge them. Turning to the charioteer, he says, 'Hey charioteer, lead the horses fast. Why so? My sister is in agony, as her nose and ears have been cut off. Why did I say 'my sister'? Because, nobody addresses her as Kumbhakarna's sister or Vibhishana's sister. She is known as *my* sister. Even with me in this world, she had to suffer at the hands of a mere mortal. What a pity! If it was done by Indra, the king of *devas*, or by any one of the *devas*, or by a mighty king on earth, I may have tolerated it. But it was done by none of them, but by a mere human being with long matted hair, who is living in the woods, eating just fruits and roots and spending his days suffering the wind, the sun, the rain and the snow. What a pity! It would have been better had she died at his hands, at least I would not have had to see her always like this. He has done this deliberately, so that I see her in this state constantly.

'Look at what will happen now. I will kill that Rama right now and drag Sita away with me. How? With my armour and sword fastened tightly around me, I will approach Rama and call him for a duel. He will then confront me, fully armed with bow and arrows. I will then realise that to kill him, I don't need any weapons and will keep the sword aside. I will then kill Rama by just squeezing his neck. I will then approach Sita who might appear to be sad and will tell her, 'O lovely Sita, please don't be sad thinking of that silly Rama; come with me to Lanka and live happily. You have been struggling here in these forests with that Rama for a long time. Now that I have killed Rama, you don't have to be sad thinking of him. You can live happily with me. I will make all your wishes come true.' Seeing no change on Sita's face, I will then drag her away by her hair. At that time, the sorrow in Surpanakha's mind will vanish. So charioteer, please steer the horses faster. Don't be slow; please go faster! Why? The world should say that Ravana dragged away Sita. For what reason? As Surpanakha's ears and nose were cut off, Ravana dragged away Sita. Everybody should say first that Ravana dragged away Sita and it was because Surpanakha's ears and nose were cut off. So you steer the horses fast.'

Gesture to stop the drums and render the verse.

What did Surpanakha say? *The actor transforms himself to Surpanakha and continues as the demoness.* 'O lord, please don't get angry. Rama won't be subjected to your anger. You are not a weak person; after all, you are greater and more powerful than Indra. Therefore, you should not take Rama's life; rather you could steal his wife Sita, dearer to him than his own life, away from him.'

Back to his own self as Ravana. He thinks, 'What she said is true. Why is it so? When I call Rama for a duel, he will come with the armour tightened around him and ready with all his weapons. While fighting, I will keep aside my sword and will kill that puny Rama by squeezing his neck. Then I will drag Sita away. But then Sita will kill herself due to her dear husband's death. How?' *The actor enacts the role of Sita.* Sita lives in the forest happily with Rama. She sees Ravana calling her husband for battle and their furious fight with each other. She prays to God, 'O God, please let my husband be safe. Destroy that wicked Ravana.' However, seeing Ravana kill her husband, she closes her eyes in agony. When Ravana comes near and blabbers something, she shuts her ears also. The enraged Ravana pulls her by her hair and drags her away.

Here the detailed enactment of Sita being dragged away is shown. The actor alternates himself as Sita and Ravana and finally as Sita. Sita thinks, 'Why should I live any more? My husband has been killed. I am in the hands of the wicked Ravana. I cannot live anymore, even for a second'. And then she will commit suicide.

Back as Ravana. 'Sita will surely kill herself. She does not even know me. What Surpanakha said is true. To kill that weakling and human Rama, why should my hands touch a weapon? No, never! How are my hands? With my vanquishing the *devas*, everyone is praising me that there is none as powerful as Ravana. How?'

The actor elaborately depicts the description of the battle between Ravana and Rama. Ravana decides that his hands will not touch a weapon to kill a human being. Why? He gestures to stop the drums and recites the verse.

DAY THREE

Ravana listens to what his charioteer has to say. He takes the role of the charioteer who says, 'My lord, there are many bad omens. Your horses are shivering, and tears are rolling down from their eyes. Their minds are wavering and, while galloping through the sky, their legs are stumbling. There is no reason, for your horses are not of poor quality at all. They are much more adept than the horses of Aditya [the Sun God]. Yet these bad omens appear again and again.' *Ravana says to the charioteer,* 'Hey charioteer, we are only going to the hermitage of Rama. If these omens were seen while we were going to the Kailasa Mountain, the abode of Lord Siva, we definitely need to be worried. But of what consequence is it now, since we are merely going to Rama's place? You steer the chariot faster.'

The charioteer replies, 'My lord, what did you say? I just informed you about those bad omens. I am not at all worried. Let me steer the horses.'

With this, the actor depicts the stage conventions for the journey and renders the verse. At the end of the verse, the actor as Ravana stands on the *pitha* and listens to Surpanakha. Then, as Surpanakha, he enacts Surpanakha's words, 'O lord, what the charioteer said is true. We have reached Rama's hermitage.' *Back as Ravana,* 'O Surpanakha, where is Sita, the life support of that Rama who bruised your ears and nose?' He listens to Surpanakha. 'Did she say, 'Here is Sita'? Then let me see Sita'. With these words, he surveys himself in the mirror and then searches for Sita, and finds her. In a reflective mood, he enacts the *panchangam* description, but at the description of the breast he stops, unable to go further. Finally pulling himself together, he resumes, struck with wonder and awe. 'Here she is, famed in all the three worlds as the most beautiful woman! It is marvellous! If she were from the celestial world, then definitely all the thousand eyes of Indra, the King of *devas*, would have become fruitful. If she were from the netherworld, from the serpent clan, then that place would not be without the moon. Why so? Her face is comparable to the moon itself. If she were born as one among us, then we would have definitely astonished all the other races. If she were born in the Sidha race, then that race would have become famous in all the three worlds.'

Recites the verse again.

Ravana continues, 'I have never seen any other lady with such beauty and desirable qualities as complete as Sita. I have seen several ladies. After defeating Indra, I have dragged all the celestial damsels and even Sachidevi, Indra's wife, to prison and at that time, seen them all clearly.

'Once, after completing my routine chores, I was seated on the throne with the royal umbrella and the fans, when I asked my ministers, 'O ministers, what sort of fun shall we have?' They replied, 'O lord, let us go to the prison today. You haven't seen the prison after the celestial damsels were brought in. So let us go there.' Hearing their words, I decided to go and reached the prison and gave orders to open the gates of the prison. I went inside and saw that all the women were tired and worried. I told them, 'Hey, don't be afraid. I won't harm you. I just came here to see you and divert myself.' All of a sudden, seeing one of them, Ravana asked the minister, 'Hey, who is she?' The minister replied, 'My lord, she is Urvasi, the renowned celestial damsel.' Ravana appraises her carefully and also shows his appreciation. Then he sees the celestial damsels Menaka, Rambha and Tilottama and finally seeing Sachidevi amid them, asks the minister, 'Who is she?' The minister replies, 'O my lord, don't you know her? She is Sachidevi, the wife of Indra.' Ravana acknowledges her and moves on.

'In this manner, I have seen all those ladies and also when I returned after conquering the ten worlds in my chariot, I abducted several women and observed all of them very well. Among them, one had beautiful hair, another had an excellent face, yet another had an astonishing breast and so on. Moreover, when I lifted the Kailasa Mountain, I have seen Parvati, the daughter of Himavan, in a vexed mood. How was it? Once, when I was residing in Lanka, I killed the messenger of Vaishravana and with all the *rakshasa* forces set out for a battle with Vaishravana. Reaching Alaka [the abode of Vaishravana] I defeated him in a battle and plundered his flying chariot from him. While I was returning to Lanka, the chariot was blocked by the peak of the Kailasa Mountain. I gave orders to the charioteer to tell the mountain to move away from my path.'

He replied, 'O lord, it is Lord Siva who resides there!'

As Ravana, 'Is that a reason for it to block my way? Tell it to move out of my way.' *As the charioteer,* 'My lord, it is not moving.' 'Hearing this, I descended from the chariot and surveyed the mountain in detail. This mountain is not a trifling matter at all.' *The actor as Ravana elaborately depicts the girth, breadth and height of the mountain and summons the energy and strength to lift the mountain. Slowly, with great effort, he displaces the mountain a bit, and ultimately lifts it off the ground and heaves it up the air several times. The actor continues his mono acting with role transformations into the characters of Siva, Parvati, Ravana and others.*

Meanwhile at the top of the mountain, Siva is shown to be sitting with Parvati on his lap. Parvati happens to see Ganga inside the matted hair of Siva and thinks, 'Let me ask my husband about her.' She then asks Siva, 'O my lord, what is there in your hair?' *As Siva,* 'It seems that she has seen Ganga. What should I do to hide this?' On reflection, he decides to say, 'O lovely one, don't you know that there is water locked up on my head?'

As Parvati, 'What did he say? Water?' She looks at Ganga closely and again asks Siva, 'O husband, I can see a face there. Does water have a face?' Siva replies, 'My dear, it is not a face, it is a lotus.'

As Parvati, 'He said it is a lotus?' Again looks at Ganga and asks, 'O husband, I can see curled hair there; how can a lotus have got curls?'

To this, Siva replies, 'Those aren't curls, but bees, that suck honey from the lotus. They look like curls, but are not actually.'

Parvati says, 'I can see two eyebrows there; what are they?'

Siva says, 'They are not brows, they are just ripples in the water.'

Parvati in growing consternation, 'O husband, there are also two eyes!'

Siva pacifies her by saying, 'They are not eyes, but two fish.'

Parvati is angry now. 'I can see two breasts there, what do you have to say now about them?'

Siva, 'My dear, they are not breasts, but a couple of *chakravaka* birds.'

Now, an irate Parvati thinks, 'Did he say that those are birds? Alas! He is deceiving me. He has no love left for me anymore. So I have had enough, I should leave this place.'

She looks at Siva with anger, sadness and frustration and glances at Ganga with jealousy and finally decides to leave the place. She tells her maids, 'Dear friends, let us go to see my father. I have not seen my father for a long time.'

The actor depicting the mood of Parvati stands on the pitha *and enacts different emotional states—with frustration and jealousy towards Ganga, anger towards Siva and grief at her own plight. Finally, she begins her journey (here, the particular dance movements for the journey of a woman is depicted). At this point, the mountain shakes violently because of Ravana's actions. Though she tries hard, she cannot control herself anymore and she runs back to Siva to hug him tightly in an embrace.*

Then again back into the original role as Ravana.

'In this manner, I've seen Parvati in a state of agitation. Thus I have seen many other women, but none as beautiful as Sita. As a result of this vision, my eyes have become blessed. Indeed, it took a long time for this.'

'What a wonder!'

Recites the verse.

Ravana completes the head-to-foot description (*padadikesavarnana*) of Sita continuing from the breasts. Struck by Kamadeva's arrows, he swoons. Later, reviving himself, he describes the *panchangam* of Sita and concludes the day's act.

DAY FOUR

After the preliminary rituals, Ravana is seen sitting on the *pitha* in an introspective mood. He reflects on the beauty of Sita and performs her head-to-foot description. Ravana then looks to his right and left, surveys his own ten faces and feels gloomy at their plight. 'On seeing Sita, all my ten faces have now adopted ten different expressions and moods. One sighs long and deep, while the next is despondent. The other head is bowing shamefacedly and another is oscillating. Yet another face has expanded with joy and the next one is in a complaining mood. One is at a loss for words and another is in a meditative mood. While a head out there is in ecstasy, another is in tears. In this way all the ten faces are in ten different moods.' Looking at them mockingly, he recites the verse.

Again in a reflective mood, Ravana happens to see his faces having a fight. One face says to the other, 'You move out of the way, now let me see Sita.' Another says, 'Now it's my turn to see her.' Ravana now tells his faces, 'Hey faces, you don't have to fight. I will divide her body parts for you to see properly. How is it? One will be given her hair.' *Here the actor enacts Ravana giving the hair to one face.* The face denies it. Then Ravana says, 'This is the hair that has defeated the feathers of a peacock.' It seems that it had defeated the peacock's feathers in beauty and was honoured by Brahma. How is it?'

The peacock's feather looks with jealousy at Sita's hair and says, 'Don't to be too proud. I am more beautiful than you.'

Sita's hair, 'You go away.'

Feather, 'Let us go to Brahma and ask him.'

Reaches Brahma's abode, Satyaloka.

Feather, 'O, Brahma, am I not beautiful?'

Brahma, 'You are beautiful.'

The feather becomes swollen with pride. Brahma, seeing the hair approaching him, receives it with love. He puts it on his lap and starts caressing it.

Feather, 'Brahma, you should not do this.' Brahma gets irritated and says, 'Didn't I tell you that you are beautiful?'

Feather, 'O! You are making us compete with each other!' At this point, Brahma gets angry and drives the feather away by pushing its neck. He then adorns the hair with flowers and sends it away in a kindly manner. After hearing this, the face receives the hair happily. Now, another face takes a look at Sita's long eyes, another at her eyebrows, yet another enjoys gazing at her ears while another looks at her red lips. One of the faces opts to gaze at her neck. Now Ravana happens to see one of the faces begging, 'O let me see her breasts.'

Thinking for a while, Ravana agrees, and decides to have the loins for him to enjoy. This way each one of the faces enjoys gazing at different parts of Sita.

Recites the verse.

Ravana is seen literally devouring the beauty of Sita. Here he shows ten faces drinking her beauty in ten ways through the eyes. 'In this way, enjoying her beauty, my mind has become much happier. Is it that I enjoyed it just once? No, I enjoyed gazing at her many times! As a result, my mind has again become happier. My weary eyes have now become fruitful.' Thinking for a while, 'When will I be able to hug her beautiful body with my hands? How are my hands? They have great scars on them.'

The recitation of the verse. The actor once again performs Sita's panchangam *and ends the act for the day.*

DAY FIVE

After the *kesadipada* description of Sita, Ravana gets struck by Kamadeva's arrows. Then he gazes at Sita longingly and notices Lakshmana standing near her. Ravana asks Surpanakha, 'O Surpanakha, who is that fellow? He looks a dumb fellow, standing there as though he is going to fight with Sita. He has tightened the armour and has taken the bow in the left hand and the arrow is also ready. Who is he? Idiot!'

Recites the verse.

After hearing Surpanakha's words, Ravana remarks, 'What did Surpanakha say? Did she say, 'He is the man who bruised my ears and nose?' Ravana is amazed. 'These humans are audacious enough! How? Rama, after bowing at the feet of his father, reached the forest of Tataka with Viswamitra and on seeing Tataka, fearfully hid himself behind a tree and sent the arrow and killed her.'

Recites the verse.

Again Ravana asks Surpanakha, 'Whose is the noise that we hear?'

Listening to Surpanakha's words, 'O brother, he is that Rama.'

Ravana on seeing Rama, 'O! This is that Rama! He is not insignificant.' He faints.

After reviving, he notices that the charioteer has seen this and feels shy. Thinks, 'O, the charioteer has noticed my worry. What can I do now?' In arrogance, he looks at the charioteer and says, 'Your body looks as if you are frightened.' He listens to the charioteer and says, 'What did he say? O lord, her body even without any ornaments looks wonderful. Then how much more captivating will she be all decked up in finery?' Looking at Sita, Ravana replies, 'O Surpanakha, she doesn't need any ornaments. A thing that has real charm need not be purified. Thinking that the scar on the moon reduces its charm, we need not wipe the scar off. Do we need to polish the *kausthubha* diamond thinking that it is dull? Is there any reduction in the charm of the lotus perched in the middle of the moss? No! The scar does nothing to the charm of the moon. Like that even if she wears the bark of a tree it doubles her charm.'

Recites the verse.

He listens to the charioteer, 'What did the charioteer say? 'O lord, no there is none with such a steadfast sense of virtue as her', I believe.'

Ravana, 'O charioteer, how do you know it?'

Recites the verse.

Ravana listens to the charioteer and says, 'Are you saying that, 'As she had left all her relatives and came to the forest with Rama and lives happily.' O stupid one, you don't know how fickle a woman can be. When they possess rare and exceptional things, they are happy. How?'

Ravana transforms into the role of a woman. He depicts how a woman who is living contentedly with her husband gets attracted to a stranger, leaves her husband and follows the latter. The same woman then gets attracted to a prince and absconds with him. In this manner, women are enamoured by worldly things. 'Sita, too, will certainly leave Rama and live with me happily. How? I will approach her and say pleasantly, 'O lovely one, living in the forest with Rama, you are miserable. You need not suffer anymore from the sun, snow and wind, living here in this hermitage. Come with me to Lanka and live happily.' On hearing this, Sita will agree with me. I will take Sita with me and will reach Lanka. One day after finishing my bath and other chores, I will put Sita on my lap. Then Sita will tell me, 'O, I wish to see the heaven. I have only heard about it. I wish to go and live happily there.'

'Then I will take her and after reaching heaven, we will sit on the banks of the River Mandakini enjoying the wind, which comes with the fragrance of the golden lotus in the river. Then I will see Indra bowing at me. I will say, 'O, Indra, go and fetch the things for our bath.' Then to Sita, 'O lovely one, you take a bath.'

After oiling herself, Sita takes the things brought by Indra and has her bath in the river. The *kalpaka* tree brings ornaments and garments in front of Ravana.

On seeing them, he says, 'O beauty, take these things and adorn yourself.' 'After that, I will place Sita again on my lap. At that time, Sachi, Indra's wife, will stand in terror in front of us and Sita will allay her fears saying, 'Don't worry. I will look after you.' Like this, Sita will leave Rama and live happily with me.'

After the panchangam *the actor ends the performance of that day.*

DAY SIX

Ravana sits on the *pitha* and performs the *kesadipada* of Sita; gets struck by Kamadeva's arrows and is in a meditative mood. He listens to what Sita says and thinks, 'What did Sita say?' *Enacting as Sita*, 'O Lakshmana, my right eyes are now fluttering. This indicates some danger.' Did she say so? *Happens to hear what Lakshmana says and recites the verse.*

'What did Lakshmana say?' *Then as Lakshmana*, 'O dear sister, don't be afraid of any bad omens. We have left our country and our relatives, and come here in this forest as hermits and hence no harm can come to us. Did you mean that whenever there is prosperity, there is the presence of an enemy?' *As Ravana enacts Sita's role.* 'Dear Lakshmana, while I was sitting in the hermitage, I had heard about a brother of Khara and Dushana from the wives of hermits. He seems to be a dreadful demon with twenty arms.'

Hearing this, Ravana becomes happy that by God's grace Sita has heard about him. *Now hears what Lakshmana says*, 'Dear sister, you don't have to be worried. Don't be scared that Ravana will come and harm us.' *Then back as Ravana*, 'What is he about to say' *and recites the verse.*

Again as Lakshmana, 'Dear sister, even if he has many arms, there is no use. Why so? Karttaviryarjuna defeated Ravana in a war. He has one thousand arms. However, Sage Parasurama cut off all those thousand arms with his axe, just like cutting down trees. Brother Rama has defeated that Parasurama. So, there is no use of those arms.'

Then as Ravana, 'You mortal! You will regret these words of yours.' *Listens to backstage voice*, 'O Lakshmana...' Is it heard so? *Then as Sita*, 'O, it sounds like my husband.' *Ravana enacts Lakshmana's role*, 'What did Lakshmana say?' 'Dear sister, will my brother ever cry like this?

'Never, for sure.' Did he say so? *As Sita*, what did Sita say, 'Lakshmana, what are you thinking about?' As Lakshmana, 'I believe this as something fake.' As Ravana thinks, 'What a wonder, he is smart. He has a strong mind.' *Again hears the sound from the back (as Sita).* 'Why are you hesitating to go? O Lakshmana, even after hearing your brother's cries, you are still standing here. How is this earth tolerating you?'

As Lakshmana, 'O sister, is this what you think?' *Sita*: 'Is your brother not worth being saved by you?' *Ravana hears what Lakshmana says*, 'How am I to protect the one who has the ability to save and protect all people?' *As Ravana hears Rama's sound and again as Sita says*, 'O Lakshmana, I know the reason for you still standing here. Is it because of your desire for the country and also for me? I won't live with anyone other than my husband, you please understand that.' *As Ravana, recites the verse.*

After the verse, Ravana goes on to enact the role of Lakshmana. Hearing Sita's harsh words, Lakshmana closes both his ears with his hands and says, 'O sister, please don't say such vulgar words. You are not an ordinary woman. You are well-bred and chaste. How can you say these offensive words without thinking at all? As a result of this, a danger is sure to befall on us. Imminent hazard undoubtedly diminishes our wisdom.'

As Ravana, 'Idiot, no harm is going to happen to her, suffering in this forest. She is going to prosper. You don't know it.' Sita and Lakshmana leave in search of Rama. Now in a reflective mood Ravana hears the words of Surpanakha, 'What did Surpanakha say? O lords, see this, a jewel is coming out herself! Where is she?' Sees Sita coming out from the hermitage. 'Let me not waste this time. I will approach her as Rama and block her way.' What did Surphanakha say? Did she say, 'I am also going to take Sita's role and keep Rama in my thoughts.' Let it be so.

'What did the charioteer say, 'O lord what should I do?' Then Ravana whispers into the ears of the charioteer, 'You take on the role of Lakshmana's and bring the chariot.' *Then stands on the* pitha *and assumes Rama's guise, looks at himself, sees the long matted hair and gets angry with himself. Then descends from the* pitha *and as Rama takes the bows and arrows and hears Sita's words,* 'Long live my lord'. Then asks Sita, 'O lovely one, why are you alone here in this forest? Your feet are so soft and what is the reason for walking around with those? Did Lakshmana leave you? You are the subject discussed by those demons. How could Lakshmana leave you like that?'

Renders the verse.

Looking at the charioteer, 'I saw Lakshmana coming with the chariot. What is he saying?' 'O my lord, the great sages have come to know through their meditation that the enemy kings had a war with Bharata and took over Ayodhya. So they made this chariot and sent it with me to go to Ayodhya. So you please enter the chariot with your wife.' On hearing this, Rama (*Ravana as Rama*) decides to enter the chariot and tells Lakshmana to seat Sita in front of him. Then he enters the chariot (performing the conventional dance movements of a chariot journey) armed with bow and arrow (stands in front of the lamp) and decides to touch Sita. When he is about to touch her, he sees that he is unable to do so and feels sorry for himself. 'Even if she believes that I am Rama, I am not powerful enough to touch her. It is a wonder why it is not possible, because it is unlike the ladies whom we have seen earlier. Let me see what I can do.'

Recites the verse.

Ravana, thinking, 'What should I do to please her?' Thinks harder and finally strikes on an idea. He tells Lakshmana, 'O Lakshmana, you steer the horses faster. Why so? Let Bharata be relieved. Now he might be worried and confined to the palace, after the enemy kings have beaten him in war and captured Ayodhya.' How? *Now enacts as the various enemy kings, sits on the* pitha, 'Hey didn't you hear? Rama's coronation has been cancelled! What is the reason for that? Kaikeyi wanted the coronation of Bharata and as a result Rama's coronation was cancelled. Didn't you hear? Rama has left Ayodhya with Sita and Lakshmana for the forest. Didn't you hear? King Dasaradha died because of the grief.' 'Are you sure?' 'Sure,' 'Then let us go and loot the country.' 'Hey, but Bharata is there.' 'What if Bharata is there? He is nobody.' 'Hey, let the army get ready for the war.' (Stands on the *pitha* and acts as though they reach Ayodhya. Calls Bharata for war.)

As Bharata, sits on the *pitha*, worried and grief-struck due to his father's death as well as his brother's absence. He hears the call of the enemy kings for the war. Stands on the *pitha* and prepares for the war and with his army, reaches the battlefield and fights with them. After being defeated by them, he returns to the palace. Then Rama enters the field and fights with the kings. Seeing Bharata returning to the palace in defeat, the kings scoff at him, but suddenly seeing

Facing page: Ravana's presence dominates the scene.

Rama coming and, getting frightened, they run away.

When Bharata hears that Rama has come and the enemies have fled, he rushes to Rama, falls on his feet and urges him to take over Ayodhya.

Rama (*Ravana in Rama's guise*) wants Bharata to divest himself of his burden of power. That burden is not small. To protect the world surrounded by the four oceans is a burden, which he should get rid of. Seeing us let our mothers be happy. How? *In the guise of royal mother,* 'What a pity! Our husband is dead. Our children have gone to the forest. When will we be able to see them again?' *Then as Rama,* goes near them and bows at their feet. *The mothers see Rama, Lakshmana and Sita, bowing at their feet, become so happy that milk starts oozing from their breasts.*

As Rama, 'Let the mothers be happy. And Sita also would be happy to leave the forest. She has suffered a lot in the forest, with proximity to wild animals such as lions and tigers, from the rocks, thorns, huge demons, from the sun, wind, snow and rain. On many occasions, she also had to go without food. So let her now live in Ayodhya and enjoy herself.'

Renders the verse and ends the act for the day.

DAY SEVEN

The actor, as Ravana, enters the stage armed with bows and arrows and stands in front of the lamp and enacts the meaning of the verse, which starts with 'Lakshmana thoornam'. Now listens to what Sita says, 'What did Sita say? Does she say, 'O lord, I don't want to go to Ayodhya. I prefer to sit here in this hermitage itself.'

Ravana depicts the *panchangam* of Sita and is afflicted by Kamadeva's arrows. He wonders how it is possible for him to overcome the sufferings caused by the desire for a mortal lady. But then he decides to delight himself by touching her. He attempts to touch her, but comes back, unable to do so. He thinks, 'Her power is enormous. Why so? My hands are unable to touch the wife of a mere mendicant mortal. When I went to the heavens to fight with Indra and the other celestials, all of them ran away in terror. While I was looking to see whether anybody else remained to confront me, I happened to see Airavata [the celestial white elephant]. Deciding to fight him single-handedly, I called him for a duel.' *Then as Airavata,* sees Ravana and in fury, runs towards him for the fight. Then shows the fight between Airavata and Ravana. At the end of the fight, Airavata runs away from the battlefield.

'In this manner, I am capable of striking even at the head of the powerful Airavata. How is the head of Airavata? It has long ears like fans, with traces of the fluid of rutting. My hands have no hesitation to torture such a head, but they are really inept to touch the wife of a mortal. What a pity!'

Recites the verse.

Now depicts the movement of a chariot journey. At that time sees Sita's hair getting untied and exclaims, 'O lovely one, your hair is undone from its knot due to the speed of this chariot. How is your hair? It is matted due to the *trishnavasnana* [a specific type of bath]? It is also decorated with flowers and creepers of the forest. Now your hair is untied. Shall I do it up for you?'

Recites the verse.

Then again tries to touch Sita. Listens to what Sita says, 'O dear, Lakshmana is standing near us.' Saying this she prevents him from tying her hair and just touches him. *Now as Ravana*, 'What does Sita say? 'Is he not my husband?' Now Sita starts crying. Seeing her crying, Ravana comforts her, 'Dear Sita, please do not worry. Am I not your husband Rama?' Then again listens to what Sita says, 'Let your mighty power be destroyed!' Then he says, 'O Lakshmana, what is this?'

Recites the verse.

Ravana listens to what Lakshmana says and enacts, 'Is he saying like this, O lord, there is no use of you saying that I am Rama, for you have gone back to your real self of Ravana. How is your body? It is with ten furious faces, with long protruding canine teeth, enormously large like the moon and black as a cloud, which can belittle the moon.' Ravana, 'Did he say, 'You have gone to your real self!'

Ravana surveys himself and feels embarrassed that his real features have revealed themselves. Reflecting, he decides to remain in his real self. He is at ease now since he has rid himself of the guise of that stupid Rama.

Ravana, seeing Sita in tears, thinks to himself, 'How sad! This lady is crying her heart out! Let me try to comfort her.' Ravana asks Sita, 'Lovely one, what is this? Do not feel sad. It is not that nobody needs to be scared of me. Hearing the name of Ravana people in all the three worlds should shiver. But you don't have to get worried. Why, you may ask.' He continues with the rest of the portion in a reflective mood. 'There is none as beautiful and prized as you are. So you need not be frightened about me. Instead, please be cheerful.' Then looks carefully at Sita and thinks to himself, 'What is this? Even after this, there is no response at all. She is crying disconsolately.' To Sita, 'There is no use for you to cry like this. There is nobody to save you. When I am here, not even a single person, whether it be a *deva* or *asura* from all the three worlds, can save you.

'Leave the matter of saving you. They can't even think of saving you. Why so? It is because I am not a paltry being. My chest is so strong as if it is marked with the ends of the furious tusks of the eight elephants that guard the eight worlds. How is that? When the guardian elephants stray here and there, I call them for a fight. When they rush towards me angrily, I hold their tusks with my hands and wield my sword, scratch them on my chest and throw them away. In this manner, my chest has the marks of tusks. When I am here with you, there is none to save you. So all your cries are in vain.'

Recites the verse.

Ravana now listens to what the charioteer says, 'O lord, please look! A mighty bird is coming towards us. How is this bird? It has a furious demeanour. It has a long beak, bent like a hook and a neck like a beautiful pillar of gold. Its eyes are shining like the *vidruma* diamond. The lapping of its wings causes trees and leaves to fall and scatter away. Look at the bird coming towards us.'

Recites the verse.

Ravana, 'What is the bird saying?' *As Jatayu*, 'O dear Sita, I am there for you. Please don't distress yourself. I am Jatayu, the friend of Dasaratha, the scion of the race of the Sun. I have come here to save you.' To Ravana, 'Hey Ravana, please do leave her. I pardon the mistakes of those who are ignorant. So if you want to be alive, please do leave her.' As *Ravana*, 'This bird says that he is going to pardon my mistake! O charioteer, kill him with your whip and throw his wings out of the chariot. He doesn't know my strength.'

Recites the verse.

As Jatayu, 'O evil one, I know very well all about your strength. While you were juggling with the Kailasa Mountain, it fell on your chest. I know that. I also know that Karttaviryarjuna had once caught you and put you in prison. Also how Bali had tied all your hands with his tail. I know about your prowess. You are an evil meteor for all the three worlds.'

As Ravana, 'O charioteer, don't drive the chariot anymore, and let it be stationary. Why so? Let Sita see my real strength. With my sword, I am going to cut off the wings of this bird and let them fall from the sky to earth. Just as Indra chopped off the wings of mountains, I am going to hack the wings of this bird down. Let Sita watch this.'

Recites the verse.

Ravana listens to Jatayu, 'What is Jatayu saying?' *As Jatayu,* 'Then just you wait. Ravana, I am going to tear off all your ten faces with my beak in front of Sita and I will then throw them away in ten different directions. How do you look now? Your body is as black as the clouds of the flood season. I am going to cut off your ten faces. How are your faces? They are bristling with brown hair just like the peaks of Anjana Mountain burning in the forest fire during the night.

'When in rage I cut off your neck, veins will break out and the outpouring of blood shall make your faces red. Then I am going to cut off your faces. I won't delay, but will do the act presently. Just see.'

Ravana, 'Did he say like this?'

As Ravana, exhorts Jatayu for a fight. The demonstration of the fight follows. As Ravana, to himself, 'It is not normally possible to defeat him in the war. It is feasible to kill him only by resorting to treachery. What shall I do?' Thinks and finally strikes at an idea. Then he asks Jatayu, 'O Jatayu, which is your most sensitive point?' Jatayu replies, 'Which is yours?' Ravana replies, 'It is on my right leg's toe.'

As Jatayu, 'It is on my right wing.' Now they continue fighting and as Jatayu flies down he hits Ravana on his right toe. In the process, Ravana catches hold of his left wing and chops it off. As Ravana to charioteer, 'O charioteer, you drive the chariot faster.' Shows the movement for the chariot journey and reaches Lanka.

He takes Sita to *Asokavanika* (Ravana's royal garden), places her under the *simsapa* tree and engages demonesses as guards to take care of her. *Recites the verse and ends the act.*

DAY EIGHT

This day is known as 'The Brief Garden Entry' (cheriya udyana pravesam). *Ravana enters and does the usual stage conventions and starts 'Samkshepam'.*

'Long ago I, Ravana, born in the Pulastya race, lived in Lanka in great comfort. At that time a messenger came from Vaisravana. I killed him and went with my army to Alakapuri, the abode of Vaisravana and defeated him in battle. I plundered Vaisravana's flying chariot and on the way dislocated and played with the Kailasa Mountain. Siva was pleased and gave me Chandrahasa, the great sword. I defeated King Marut and the God of Death, reached the netherworld and defeated the Serpents. Vidyujjihva, the husband of Surpanakha, was killed during the encounter. Seeing her state of grief, I said, 'O Surpanakha, do not worry. You can marry whoever you like in the three worlds.' I sent Khara and Dushana along with fourteen thousand demons to accompany her.'

Later, when Ravana was sitting peacefully Surpanakha came to him crying, with her nose and ears chopped off. From her words, Ravana came to know about the death of Khara and Dushana and the unrivalled charm of Sita. With mounting desire towards Sita, Ravana approached Maricha in his hermitage and sent him to Sita in the guise of a golden deer. Through deception, Maricha sent Rama and Lakhmana away, and Ravana disguised as fake (*maya*) Rama took Sita in the chariot. On the way to Lanka, Ravana cut off the wings of Jatayu. He came to Lanka and placed Sita in the Asoka garden beneath the *simsapa* tree. Here ends 'Samkshepam'.

In a reflective mood Ravana decides to go to see Sita. Ravana shows the stage movements, which denote the journey, placing his hands on the head of Varshavara. After reaching the garden, he enacts the foot-to-head description of Sita.

Afflicted by Kamadeva's arrows, fainting and reviving himself, Ravana tells Sita: 'O, lovely one, why are you in a despondent mood? Do not be so. I came here out of my love towards you. Your beauty is exquisite. Your eyes shine like the long petals of a lotus and resemble the eyes of a frightened fawn. Don't be afraid, I am your saviour. Your face is as bright as the full moon. My mind is full of joy on seeing you. Your thighs are like the stalks of a banana tree, smooth and cool. You are unparalleled in beauty and the *rakshasa* clan is famous for plundering and forceful acquisition. But I will not touch you, since you have no love towards me. Discard your grief and fear and live with me happily.'

Recites the verse.

'Seeing your beautiful face with long eyes and eyebrows, Kamadeva tortures me (*verse*). Seeing your forehead decorated with curls, Kama tortures me (*verse*). O daughter of Janaka, there is no use, sitting here bereft of bath, food and adornments. See, I have wealth, power and fame. Rama has no wealth, no appeal and no fame. He is merely a mortal who wears matted hair and lives in the forest to do penance. So leave him and accept me, the most handsome person in the world.'

Recites the verse.

'People who have become frail by the arrows of Kamadeva cannot recognise the moon from the sun. Both give grief to them. Then, to know the moon, the only way is the scar.' Then shows *panchangam* of Sita and thinks, 'I created this grief myself.'

Recites verse.

'Without my command, the moon is not brave enough to wither the lotus. Does this mean that he does not wither the flowers near to me? No. Even the flowers that exist far from me, he will not shrivel.' *As the moon,* requests Ravana to wilt the lotus. *Then as Ravana,* gives permission to wilt only five or six flowers. *Then the moon bows to Ravana and starts wilting the flowers. When he was about to wither the seventh flower, he thinks,* 'No! Ravana has given permission only for a maximum of six flowers.'

As Ravana, 'The moon who is terrified of me, is now torturing me so. Is he doing this, hiding himself? No. He is here in front of me and torturing me. Even if he is weak, he gets power at this particular state. He gets the power due to Sita.'

Here he performs the panchangam *of Sita and concludes that day's performance.*

DAY NINE

This day starts with the 'Entry' (purappadu) *of Chitrayodhi, Ravana's minister. Before removing the curtain Chitrayodhi does some conventional movements on the stage, signifying the entry of the character. After the removal of the curtain he starts the performance:* Chitrayodhi sees Varshavara, the pageboy, approaching. 'What did he say?' 'O, the Lord has ordered to bring you with me. So please start soon.' 'Is that so?' *Then, as Chitrayodhi* starts showing the dance movement of *kalappurathunadakkal,* which denotes the journey. He sees the full moon shining above. He looks around amazed. 'O the *rakshasa* has enjoyed the smooth feel of the rays of the moon after a long time. What a surprise! Why? The moon does not dare enter these premises in fear of Lord Ravana. Now, because of the order of the Lord itself the moon has appeared and the people, sighting the moon, exclaim to each other, 'O friend, what a sight in the sky? It's very nice to see. I have never seen this kind of a substance. Did you know what it is?' *As another person,* 'O dear, no. I haven't even heard about it.' *The former,* 'So, what shall we do? Let us ask our elders.' Then they reach the place of an old *rakshasa* who says, 'O, there are two things, known as the sun and the moon. The moon usually does not come to Lanka in fear of our Lord. Now, as the Lord has ordered, he has come.' Hearing this, the *rakshasas* become very happy and reaching their own homes, spend the time in merriment, drinking liquor and playing chess. In this manner, the *rakshasas* are enjoying the appeal of the moon after a long period.

Here ends the day's sequence and after some ritualistic dance steps the 'Entry' is completed.

DAY TEN

The act starts with the actor sitting on the pitha *and starting the playback mode of narration* (anukramam).

How did Chitrayodhi, seeing the moon, become surprised? Before that, how did the full moon rise as ordered by Ravana? Before that, how did the moon come out when the *devas* and *asuras* were churning the Sea of Milk? Before that, how were the damsels of heaven created? How did the wish-fulfilling *kalpaka* tree come into being? Before that, how did Varuni *devi* emerge? Before that, how did Surabhi originate? Before that, how did the *devas* and *asuras* churn the Sea of Milk? Thus finishes the *anukramam* and now starts the 'Encapsulation' (*samkshepam*).

Even after defeating the demon, Pura, the wrath of Lord Siva did not subside. Out of that rage, he created Durvasavu, the sage. *As Durvasavu, to Siva,* 'O lord, what is my duty?' Siva replies, 'Hey, you travel around the world, giving curses and boons to all.' Accordingly, Durvasavu started travelling, giving curses and boons to people. At that time, a celestial damsel was making a flower garland of the *kalpaka* tree and the sage asked her, 'O lovely one, who is this garland for?' She replied, 'It was for you yourself' and gave it to the sage.

He received the garland, blessed her and tied it around his hair. Wafting bees surrounded the garland to suck honey and the sage became irritated by the murmur of the bees. Wishing to give it away to someone, he saw Indra mounted on Airavata, his white elephant. Seeing the sage, Indra descended from the elephant and bowed to him. Durvasavu gave the garland to Indra, who placed it on Airavata's head. Unable to suffer the bees, Airavata caught hold of the garland on his head and threw it away. Indra, who was about to adorn this garland on his hair, saw Airavata throwing it down. In anger, he hit Airavata, who started wailing loudly. The sage, hearing the sound of Airavata, looked back and happened to see the garland thrown on the ground and became furious. He cursed Indra, 'Hey Indra, you will be devoid of your heavenly glory from now onwards. May you become old, with grey hair and wrinkles.'

Indra approached the sage, narrated the story of what had happened and pleaded for mercy. The sage then told him to have *amrita* (celestial potion, which grants eternal youth and emancipation from death) to restore his former self. Indra, along with the gods, reached Satyaloka, the abode of Brahma, and pleaded with him to create *amrita* and give it to him.

Brahma replied, 'O Indra, I am helpless; I can't make *amrita*. Please go to the Sea of Milk and tell Srinarayana [Vishnu] to create and give *amrita*.'

Indra, along with the *devas*, approached the Sea of Milk and requested Srinarayana to make *amrita* and give him. To this Srinarayana replied, 'O *devas*, alone I won't be able to create *amrita*. Please go to Kailasa and bring Sriparameshwara [Siva] also. The *devas* then went to Kailasa and urged, 'O lord, please create *amrita* for us.' Siva replied, 'O *devas*, I can't make *amrita* alone. Didn't you tell Vishnu?' Then the *devas* told him that they had informed Srinarayana and it was he who instructed them to bring Lord Siva with them to the Sea of Milk. Siva replied 'Let it be so' and went with the *devas* to the Sea of Milk. Vishnu received Siva graciously.

With this, the samkshepam comes to a close. Siva told Srinarayana, 'O Vishnu, the *devas* want to have *amrita*. What can be done?' Srinarayana replied, 'O lord, please invite the *asuras* also.' Siva then said, 'O Bhringeeradi, you go to the abyss and bring the *asuras*.' *As Bhringeeradi*, bows to the lord, listens to his words, sets out and reaches the netherworld, and tells the *asuras*, 'O *asuras*, please come fast, Siva has ordered thus.' *As asuras*, shows the special conventional manners of *asuras*, such as drinking liquor and playing chess. They hear what Bhringeeradi says and deciding to start immediately, throw away the chessboard and follow Bhringeeradi to the Sea of Milk. As Bhringeeradi sees the *asuras* going to Mount Kailasa, he tells them, 'O *asuras*, our Lord Siva is not in Kailasa, but is presently at the Sea of Milk.' *As the asuras* tell each other, 'All right, then let us go the Sea of Milk and when we reach there, we will bow at the feet of our Lord Siva, but we should definitely dishonour Vishnu.' Deciding this, they reached the Sea of Milk and bowed to Lord Siva in great respect. Siva then beckons the *asuras* to bow to Vishnu also. *As asuras* initially hesitate to do so, but at the instance of Lord Siva, they also bow to Vishnu. *As Vishnu*, 'O *devas* and *asuras*, you should not have rivalry between you until we create and possess *amrita*.' Siva then tells the *asuras*, 'O *asuras*, obey whatever Vishnu says.' *As Vishnu*, 'O *asuras*, you should not have rivalry with the *devas* until we have created and had *amrita*' and makes them promise. Then Vishnu tells the *asuras*, 'O *asuras*, go and bring the Mandara Mountain'.

As the *asuras* start from there, they reach the premises of the Mandara Mountain and with all their strength try to lift it, but in vain. Now they tell each other, 'It is not moving at all. We are not able to lift it, so let's go back.' They go to Vishnu and say, 'We tried hard, but couldn't move the mountain'. *As Vishnu,* on hearing these words, tells the great Serpent Ananta to go and bring the mountain. *As Ananta*, listens to what Vishnu says and sets out to bring the mountain. He lifts the mountain with just one of his ten hoods, places it in the middle of the Sea of Milk and tells Vishnu, 'O lord, I've brought the mountain.'

Vishnu then sees the great falcon Garuda standing in an arrogant manner and thinks to himself, 'This Garuda is too arrogant; what could be done to destroy his pride?' He tells Garuda, 'O Garuda, please bring Vasuki, the great Serpent.' *Then as Garuda*, stands on the *pitha*, and flies to the netherworld and starts searching for Vasuki. Finding him, Garuda flies towards him and picks him up, but finding that he is too long, winds him around the beak and the body. However, finding that the length of the serpent is still more, he flies out of the netherworld. So he flies high up in the sky (stands on the *pitha*), only to discover that he cannot still be in full control of the length. Discarding Vasuki, he goes back to Vishnu and tells him. 'O Lord, I am incapable of bringing Vasuki.' Vishnu tells Siva, 'O Lord, please bring Vasuki.' Siva listens to the words of Vishnu and then taps his fingers twice and at once Vasuki, who happens to be Siva's insignia bangle, comes down to them.

Vishnu instructs Garuda to coil him around the Mandara Mountain. But Garuda expresses his inability to do so and Vishnu urges him again, comforting him and telling him not to be afraid. *As Garuda*, stands on the *pitha*, bows in front of Vishnu, catches hold of Vasuki and coils him around the mountain. He reports back to Vishnu who now gives the order to the *devas* and *asuras* to start churning the Sea of Milk. *As the devas and asuras*, descend from the *pitha*, listens to the words of Vishnu and start churning the mountain. Thus, by keeping the Mandara Mountain as the churning stick and Vasuki as the rope, the *devas* and *asuras* started churning the Sea of Milk.

Recites the verse.

Now the description of the churning of the Sea of Milk by the *devas* and *asuras*. The *asuras*, seeing that the *devas* are stationed at the head of Vasuki and they at the tail, are incensed and release the tail. Vishnu sees the *asuras* releasing the tail of Vasuki and says, 'O *devas*, go and hold the tail of Vasuki, and you, *asuras*, hold the head.' Saying so, he placed the *devas* at the tail side and the *asuras* at the head side of Vasuki.

Recites the verse.

As the *asuras* and *devas* churn the Sea of Milk, Vishnu sees the mountain slide down: 'Why has the mountain slipped? What can be done now?' An idea strikes him. Enacts as though he has disappeared from the scene, he takes on the guise of a tortoise (descends from the *pitha*) and lifts up the mountain. *Shows the stylised movement of aerial flight* (ambarayana) *and recites the verse. After the verse, as Vishnu,* 'Hey, both of you [parties] continue the churning.' *Then as devas and asuras* they continue with the churning. *As asuras*, 'Hey, let us play a trick on the *devas*.' Telling this to each other all of them drag Vasuki away from the mountain. *Then as devas* go to Vishnu and tell him, 'O lord, Vasuki slipped away from our hands.' *Then as Vishnu* disappears, then takes the form of one of the *devas*, and descends from the *pitha* and looks carefully.

While churning, the *devas* pulled out Vasuki and defeated the *asuras*. Vishnu now takes the form of one of the *asuras* and saves the situation and starts churning again.

Recites the verse.

The churning process continues. Suddenly a big sound is heard. How is the sound? It is similar to the sound of the great clouds.

Recites the verse.

Again shows the churning and meanwhile Vasuki vomits the terrible poison (*kalakuda*). All *asuras* begin to burn from the hot rays of the poison. Vishnu, at that time takes a vessel made of skulls (*kapala*) and collects the poison. He then goes to Siva and asks, 'O lord, where shall I keep this poison?' *Then as Siva* sits on the *pitha*, listens to Vishnu and says, 'O Vishnu, let it be kept on earth.' *As Vishnu*, 'O lord, if it is kept there, the human race will be finished. Therefore, it is not possible to keep it there!' *As Siva*, sits on the *pitha* and says, 'Then you keep it in heaven.' Vishnu replies, 'No, it is not possible. This will cause the destruction of the *devas*.' *As Siva*, 'Then keep it in the netherworld.' *As Vishnu*, 'It is not possible as it will destroy the *asuras*. So it can't be kept there or in the three worlds. Where else shall we keep this? Please do tell us.' *As Siva* sits on the *pitha* and replies, 'I don't know.' Vishnu then pours the poison into the mouth of Siva, who tries to swallow it. But Parvati, Siva's wife, holds firmly on his neck. Siva tries to spit it off. Vishnu promptly shuts his mouth. The poison gets stuck in Siva's neck and forms three lines on his neck. In this manner, he comes to be known as the One with a Blue Neck (*neelakantha*).

To protect the three worlds, Siva consumed the poison, causing him to have three dark lines on the neck.

Recites the verse.

The churning continues. After some time, Surabhi, the divine cow, emerges from the sea. The *devas* received Surabhi with great respect.

Recites the verse.

Then emerges Varuni Devi. How is she? Her eyes are red with pride. The grant-giving *kalpaka* tree emerges, followed by the *apsaras*.

Recites the verse.

The moon appears. Siva on the *pitha* sees, 'While churning for *amrita*, emerged Surabhi, who was well received by the *devas*. Then emerged the *kalpaka* tree, then *apsaras*.' He sees each of these things surfacing one by one, and finally the moon with all its glory. *Then as Siva* descends from the *pitha*, and takes the moon and comes back to the *pitha*.

Recites the verse.

Siva watches the moon carefully and wonders. And shows the meaning of the verse starting with '*Aho chandrapada...*'

Recites the verse.

'Here appears the moon, the abode of pleasantly cool rays. The cool touch of the rays of the moon makes everyone happy. How is this moon?' The actor recites '*anangajanmasenapati*' and enacts its meaning. He is the head of Kamadeva's army. How else is he? He is the vessel suitable to hold *amrita*. When the moon rises, its rays spread all over the world, giving the feeling that everyone submerges into the Sea of Milk.

Again recites the second part of the verse. And ends the act for the day.

DAY ELEVEN

Ravana enters, seats himself and meditates on Sita from hair to feet. He is excited with passion for Sita. The moonlight falls on him and the slight breeze make him think, 'Alas! This moonlight falling on my forehead is indeed saddening me. What shall I do? I had better say so!' He gestures to the right uttering '*Himakara*' in a low voice. He looks at the moon and thinks. 'There is no response. Has he not heard me? I will call once again.' He calls again, '*Himakara*', in a slightly raised voice. 'Have you not heard me?

Have you become deaf?' Then for the third time, he calls out loudly, '*Himakara*!' He looks pointedly at the moon who defiantly looks back at him. Ravana decides to tell him anyway, and renders the verse while depicting it through hand gestures.

'Your rays are like fire on my body. My body is burning under your light. It is as though embers of fire are being thrown at me. Your cool rays suppress heat. All people shiver with cold when your rays fall on them. However, it is not so for me. Your rays that fall on me are not cool, but I feel scorching heat. How is it so?'

Recites the verse.

'I am a slave of Kamadeva. He has conquered me with his love arrows. In such a situation, your rays exhaust me.' (*Recites the verse.*) 'It is not your power. What is it? You are insignificant. You are the discharge from the eye of the saint Atri. It is not your power.'

Recites the verse.

'It is not your power. Nor is it Kamadeva's. Then whose power is it? It is the power of Janaka's daughter. How is she? She is the seat of sorrow. He repeats 'sorrow'. 'Sita came to the jungle with Rama and had to survive on the fruits of the jungle. I abducted her and brought her here, and therefore she is definitely sad and downcast. This power could only belong to the sorrow of Sita. You are aware of that.'

Recites the verse.

'You are the husband of the night. You are familiar with the sorrow of separation.' *Ravana exits.*

Chitrayodhi, the minister, enters and recites the verse.

'Shall I leave Ravana and meet my death at the hands of Rama? How? I will go to my lord and tell him, 'You have confined Sita, the wife of Rama, to wreak vengeance for the act of maiming Surpanakha, your sister,' and my lord will be highly pleased. At that time Rama will come with Sugriva and his army of monkeys, and will destroy Ravana along with his army of *rakshasas*. Then I need only to reject Ravana and die. What kind of a being is Ravana? He has surpassed the limits of decent conduct.'

Recites the dialogue.

'So saying I will earn the displeasure of my Lord Ravana. Yes, I will go to my Lord and ask him to return Sita to Rama. If not, Rama will come here accompanied by Sugriva and his army of monkeys, and destroy all that is ours. On hearing this, my lord will get angry and behead me. What kind of being is Ravana?'

Recites.

'One who indulges in cruel acts.' *Recites*. 'He is crueler than the Rudra the Destroyer. Causing destruction, or earning the displeasure of Ravana.' *Recites.* 'Both options are not good for me. Of these, destruction in the hands of Ravana is more glorious for me. Why?' (*Recites.*) 'I am not the one who pretends not to see danger when it comes. (*Recites.*) Alas, my lord's condition is so distressful. What is his condition? (*Recites.*) My lord is tied with a mere thread of hair and is going to be killed with a pestle made of iron. Sita is the hair, which is used to tie, and Rama is the pestle.'

Now he goes to Ravana and sees him bright and shining. Watches carefully and enacts.

'He [Ravana] after his bath, prayer and food is meditating on Lord Siva. The time at which I came to see the Lord is wonderful.' *Again watches carefully and exclaims.* 'O! He is not meditating on Siva.' (*Recites.*) 'He is always meditating on Sita. How is it certain? '(*Recites.*) 'He is pumping himself up; because of deep sighs, his lips are seen lean; his body which was shining like a blue lotus is pale, resembling the last cloud of the rain. What is the reason for all these? Kamadeva, hiding himself, is burning Ravana's body, like the great raging underwater fire [*badavagni*], unrevealed to strangers.'

Ravana enters the stage, sits on the *pitha* and enacts Sita's *panchangam* and is afflicted by Kamadeva's arrows. He feels as if Sita has come near to him. (*Enacts as though embracing Sita.*) At the same moment Chitrayodhi enters and bows, 'O lord, long live Your Highness!' Ravana, without hearing this, continues the act of embracing Sita. Suddenly, he feels like he heard a sound. He thinks, 'What is that sound? Yes, this is the lament of cuckoos separated from their lovers.' Again Ravana continues, as though embracing Sita. Chitrayodhi again announces, 'O lord, long live Your Highness!' Now Ravana realises, 'O! I am indeed hearing a sound. It is not that of a cuckoo. It resembles the voice of my minister. I had ordered Chitrayodhi to come. Has he come?' On seeing Chitrayodhi, Ravana is embarrassed, and thinks to himself, 'He has disturbed my happiness. Let me send him away soon.' He looks at Chitrayodhi in a supercilious manner. Ravana and Chitrayodhi engage in the following dialogue:

Ravana: 'O Chitrayodhi, is there any news which is unusual?' Chitrayodhi: 'Yes.'

Ravana: 'Yes, there are many unusual things. I have lifted and played with the Kailasa Mountain; I have defeated the Lord of Death [Antaka]. I haven't asked you about all that [dialogue]. After I have dragged Sita and placed here, has something unusual happened?'

Chitrayodhi: 'Yes.'

Ravana mocks him, saying, 'Yes, Yes, Yes' and angrily asks 'What yes?' [What has happened?]

Chitrayodhi: 'People are talking about...'

Ravana: 'O, Rama has killed Bali. Is that so? How is that? Did he kill Bali by fighting him face to face? No. While Bali and Sugriva were engaged in fight, Rama hid himself behind a tree, sent an arrow surreptitiously and killed Bali. After that, he took refuge with Sugriva. How was it? Rama reached Sugriva and begged 'O, please save me.' At that time, Sugriva jumped to the branch of another tree. Rama standing beneath the tree again begged, 'Please save me, please save me....' (*When Ravana renders 'Rama' he mockingly shows the gesture of a worm and for 'Sugriva', the gesture 'monkey'.*) This is what I heard.' Then Chitrayodhi tells Ravana that he has extraordinary news.

Ravana commands, 'Then tell me that!'

Chitrayodhi: 'To all places....'

Ravana: 'What, to all places? Why don't they come here?'

Chitrayodhi: 'Will come here also.' Ravana: 'What is the reason for coming here?'

Chitrayodhi: 'Searching for Sita.'

Ravana: (*repeats*) 'Searching for Sita' *and enacts* 'I have dragged her and placed here. Then why search?'

Chitrayodhi: (*repeats*) 'Searching for Sita' and shows the meaning as 'You have stolen her' and with that renders 'as per his order...'

Ravana is furious. Chitrayodhi continues: 'The army of monkeys is moving....'

Ravana: (*angrily*) 'What? The army of monkeys is moving! Is that so? Then you see.'

He recites the verse and enacts.

'O Chitrayodhi, your reference to a group of monkeys as an army is not fair. In front of a mighty army of *rakshasas* who get ready for war and deal with enemies in the battlefield, how can a mere herd of monkeys withstand it? How is the *rakshsa* army? (*Recites.*) Their weapons are the mountains that are used to close up the netherworlds. They are not an inadequate lot. (*Recites.*) They have conquered Indra and all the *devas*.

While they pluck out the huge mountains and use them as weapons, the monkeys cannot withstand such prowess in the battlefield. How are the monkeys? They crush buds in their hands and on seeing the red colour, get frightened and run away, mistaking it as blood. Therefore, mentioning monkeys as an 'army' is not reasonable. O Chitrayodhi, now change your reference as 'army of *rakshasas*, herd of monkeys'.'

Chitrayodhi : 'Let the monkeys be numerous, but...'

Ravana: 'Then say that' *and retires to the greenroom.*

Chitrayodhi: 'Among the great warriors proficient in archery, Rama is invincible.'

DAY TWELVE

Ravana enters and is seated, in the same mood as the previous day. (*Recites.*) 'What did Chitrayodhi say? 'Among the great warriors who are experts in archery, Rama is the mightiest. Is that so?' 'O Chitrayodhi, consider my valour.' (*Recites.*) 'You referred to Rama, my enemy. But how am I? There is none in the three worlds to stand in front of me. Even Indra, the King of *devas*, is not capable to do that (*Recites.*). Does it mean that he cannot stand in front of me at all? No. (*Recites.*) When I am angry, he cannot. Does it mean when I am angry only towards Indra? No. Even if the anger is directed towards anyone else, Indra cannot stand. How is that? I, after my bath, prayer and food, adorned myself with royal insignia and was seated on the throne. When I spat into the spitting vessel, I saw that in my *paan*, the lime was less than what I had wanted. I got angry. Indra, bowing at that time by my side, ran away frightened. How am I? (*Recites.*) My hands are not trivial. I am the one who lifted the Kailasa Mountain. How was that? Once when I was living in Lanka, I killed the messenger of Vaisravana and when the *rakshasa* army reached Alaka, the abode of Vaisravana, waged war against him and defeated him. I plundered his flying chariot from him. While I was returning to Lanka, mounted on the chariot, it was blocked by the peak of the Kailasa Mountain. I told the charioteer to tell the mountain to move out from my path. But then the charioteer replied, 'O Lord, it is Lord Siva who lives on the peak of the mountain.' *As Ravana*, 'So what? Can it block my way? Tell it to move out.' *As the charioteer*, 'It is not moving.' Hearing this, I descended from the chariot surveyed the mountain carefully. 'This mountain is not trivial at all.' [Shows the greatness of the mountain and then gets ready to lift the mountain and having done so, playfully throws it up in the air and catches several times.] Thus I have played with the Kailasa Mountain. (*Recites.*) Also, I have thrown out the nine planets from their spaces because they tried to humiliate me. So your words are extremely entertaining to me.'

Chitrayodhi: 'What! Are you are still thinking that Rama is a human being? Do not think so. (*Recites.*) Rama is Narayana himself, the lord of all the three worlds. How is Narayana? (*Recites.*) Now he is born in the Race of the Sun as the son of the King Dasaratha. Before that, he has taken many births. (*Recites.*) *Here enacts the ten incarnations of Vishnu elaborately.* When Hayagriva, the demon, stole the four Vedas and hid at the bottom of the sea Vishnu took the birth of a fish, killed Hayagriva and retrieved the Veda from him. After that, when the *devas* and *asuras* together churned the Sea of Milk to lift the Mandara Mountain from the sea, he took the birth of a tortoise to lift it up. After that, when Hiranyaksha the demon rolled up the earth like a leaf and wore it in his ear, Vishnu took the birth of a pig, killed Hiranyaksha and saved the earth.'

The story of Hiranyakasipu is enacted in detail. One day, Hiranyakasipu after his bath, prayer and meal went to the court wearing a crown and other ornaments and was seated on his throne, surrounded by his obedient vassals. At that time a messenger came there. The king listened to him, 'What? My son Prahlada is singing the praises of Srinarayana?' He gets angry and orders that Prahlada be brought to him. At that time, Prahlada approaches and bows to Hiranyakasipu: 'O tell me, who is that you praise?'

Prahlada: 'Vishnu, who is the lord of all. He is my lord.'

Hiranyakasipu: 'Where is your Vishnu?'

Prahlada: 'He is everywhere.'

Hiryanakasipu: 'Is he present in this pillar?'

Prahlada: 'Yes, he is.'

In anger, Hiranyakasipu strikes at the pillar. At that time, Vishnu appears as Narasimha, a man-lion incarnation, breaking out of the pillar. He engages in a combat with Hiranyakasipu at the end of which Hiranyakasipu is killed. Narasimha in rage plucks out his vital organs and drinks his blood.

Again, Vishnu took the birth of Vamana during the Treta age. Here also the scene is elaborated in detail. Vishnu, in the guise of Vamana, reaches the sacrificial chamber of Mahabali, the great *asura* king. At that time, as Mahabali bows to Vamana and asks, 'What can I do for you?' Vamana replies, 'I need three feet of land to offer the oblations in the holy fire.' Mahabali laughs at him and says, 'Only three feet of land? Ask for a whole country!' Then Vamana says, 'No. I need only three feet of land.' Mahabali in an attempt to give it, takes a pot of water. Sukra, the preceptor of the *asuras* in an attempt to prevent the act, comes as a bee and sits at the mouth of the pot so that the water could not be poured. Mahabali takes a sharp grass and with its tip makes the hole for the water to flow freely, and thus gives the land to Vamana. All of a sudden, Vamana starts to grow to such a scale that he touches the sky.

With gigantic feet he measures the heavens, earth and netherworlds with the measure of his two feet. Then he demands, 'Where shall I place my third foot?' A humbled Mahabali shows his head and with the third step, Vishnu banishes him to the netherworld.

Chitrayodhi says, 'Now he has taken birth as the son of Dasaratha. How did he come to the forest? He came here to obey the orders of his father. So do not consider him as a mere mortal. People will speak ill of you. This undue passion for Sita will cause you disgrace only. So please leave her.'

Ravana gets angry and says, 'What did you say? That he is 'Vishnu'? That is a wonder! As though I need to be frightened of him! There is no one who is afraid of me as him. Why? (*Recites.*) Along with the *rakshasas*, I reached heaven and defeated Indra. I have stolen his precious elephant, horse and women. I have made the *rakshasas* permeate heaven. At that time Sachi, the wife of Indra, accompanied by all the other celestial damsels, stood frightened. If Vishnu, the brother of Indra, were capable, he would have come and defeated me. Where did his valour go hiding then?'

Chitrayodhi: 'O lord, who has defeated the *devas*?'

Ravana: 'What? Don't you know who defeated the *devas*?'

Chitrayodhi: 'No.'

Ravana: 'I myself.'

Chitrayodhi: 'It is not true. It is a lie. Why? O lord, you have defeated the Lord of Death, the Lord of Sea, the Lord of Monkey, Indra and others without any difficulty. Even then, you are not capable of enduring the arrows of flowers sent by Kamadeva. So it is a lie.'

Ravana: 'What did you say, 'Kamadeva is beating me'? Is that so?'

Chitrayodhi: 'It is evident.'

Ravana tells Chitrayodhi, 'What you said is true' and continues, 'Please think' and then retires to the greenroom.

Here ends the day's performance.

DAY THIRTEEN

When the enactment starts, the actor sits on the pitha *and as Ravana says*, 'What did you say? It is obvious that Kamadeva is worrying me and that all the people see that. 'Is that so? Hey, what you said is true.'

Recites the verse.

'How is Kamadeva torturing me? He has nothing to beat me with, not even a body. Why so? The fire emitted from the eyes of Siva killed Kamadeva. How was it? One day, Kamadeva, on Indra's words, went to the Himavan, the great mountain, to halt the penance of Siva. He reached near the hermitage of Siva and aimed his arrow [*sammoanastra*] at Siva. At that time Siva woke up from the meditation and was disturbed to see that somebody had weakened his penance. Then he saw Kamadeva with his arrows aimed at him. He became furious and opened his third eye, and the fire that emitted from that eye turned Kama into ashes. Thus how can Kamadeva beat me? And if this is so, what else is the reason for my distress? I will tell you now. You just listen. (*Recites the second part of the verse.*) It is not these paltry things that disturb me. It is nothing but Sita's face that is disarming me. How is Sita's face? Awesome. It kills the hearts of all. How? It is as beautiful as the moon of the autumn season. In autumn, the moon spreads his beautiful rays all over. Seeing that moon, make us happier.' Again thinks of Sita's face. 'It is beautiful, with those eyebrows bent like bows. Her eyes are like arrows. Seeing this splendid face, my longing increases.'

Chitrayodhi: 'What a pity! His mind does not digress from Sita. What is the way out this?' (*Recites the verse.*) 'O lord, aren't you the grandchild of Lord Brahma and have learnt all the Vedas and Sastras [sciences] and have known the truth of all things. It is not worthy of you to be besotted with the wife of another person. Everyone will speak ill of you. Your obsession with Sita can bring nothing else but harm to you. Please understand this.'

Ravana thinks, 'Even this precious thing can cause disgrace?'

Recites the verse.

Chitrayodhi: 'There is no disgrace greater than this.'

Ravana: 'If it is so, Indra would have been disgraced due to Ahalya, the wife of Gautama. When the people do sacrifices [*yajna*], they address Indra as the paramour of Ahalya. Indra with pleasure appears in front of them hearing this and after receiving the offerings, gives them his blessings. If the desire towards the wife of another person is a sin, the sages would not have addressed Indra like this and he would not have been happy enough to go there and accept the offerings. How is Indra? He has done hundred *yajnas* as prescribed. You have said, 'Lord, you have studied all the Vedas and *sastras*. So it is not fair for you.'

Just think about Indra. Indra is the one who knows all the Vedas and their inner meanings. He has done hundred *yajnas*. I have studied the Vedas and Sastras. But I haven't done many *yajnas*. So Indra has more greatness than me. The greatness of Indra is said clearly in the Vedas. He is the sovereign ruler of the *devas*. You have also said, 'Lord you are the grandchild of the Lord Brahma. So this disgrace is not fair for you.' You think about Indra. He is the elder brother of Vishnu. This Indra receives the offerings when he is called upon as the paramour of Ahalya. How is it? The sages did all the preparations and started *yajna*. When they addressed Indra as 'Hari', Indra didn't come. Then they addressed him as king of the *devas* and after that the elder brother of Vishnu. He didn't come. At last they called upon 'Ahalya's Hari'. At that time Indra was sitting on his throne in heaven. He heard 'Hari'. But he was enjoying the dance of a heavenly woman. He thought, 'If I go now the joyful moment will break. I can't go now.' Again after some time he heard, 'Come Indra, who had done many *yajnas*'. He sat enjoying the music of *veena* [a musical instrument] played by a beautiful lady. When he heard, 'The Lord of the Devas, please come' he was enjoying the sweetness of the *amrita* served by a heavenly beauty. He didn't go. Now he heard, 'Come Indra, the brother of Vishnu.' Indra thought, 'What shall I do?' Then he heard, 'Indra, the paramour of Ahalya, please come.' Indra becomes extremely happy. He went there, received the offerings and blessed them. If attaining another's wife is a sin, it is not fair for Indra. So this is not a sin.'

Chitrayodhi: 'Do not concern yourself about disgrace. You gave up the right path [*dharma*], which is the basis of your prosperity, only because of Sita. Is it fair?'

Ravana: 'All people receive one thing to attain another goal. Please think about this [*recites verse*]. If there is a desire to get the leadership of the *devas*, the sword the Chandrahasa is the friend. How is Chandrahasa? Even if it has touched the Vajra, the weapon of Indra, its sharpness is not diminished. Let righteous action [*dharma*], the weapon of the powerless, be discarded. Powerful men like me have the right to do anything.'

Chitrayodhi: 'O lord, you are powerful. Is it fair for someone as powerful as you to give up *dharma*? Rama who has abdicated his power and doing penance in the forest is not to be harassed.'

Recites verse.

Ravana: 'What? Did you say that Rama is right? Just think. Long ago, Rama, according to the words of Dasaratha, went to the forest with sage Visvamitra and reached the forest of Tataka. On seeing her terrified, he sent arrows and killed her. Is that fair for a warrior? After that, while Bali and Sugriva were engaged in fight, Rama hid behind a tree and sent arrows to kill Bali while his own brother Lakshmana was observing this. Also, he wears matted hair like hermits and holds a bow and arrows like a warrior. Is it fair? How can Rama, a man of such character, be called noble? It is a pity that you speak like this.'

Chitrayodhi: 'O lord, this is my duty.'

Ravana: 'What is your duty?'

Chitrayodhi: 'To help you to attain the three type of wealth [*trivargaprapanam*].'

Ravana: 'Which are they?'

Chitrayodhi: 'They are duty, wealth and desire.'

Ravana: 'Tell me about each one of them.'

Chitrayodhi: 'Duty...'

Ravana: 'I am punishing the God of Death who punishes all. The prosperity of the heaven is my own. Then why shall I do duty?'

'What is the next?'

Chitrayodhi: 'Wealth.'

Ravana: 'Wealth is for what purpose?'

Chitrayodhi: 'It is to expand the army and the treasury.'

Ravana: 'My soldiers are those who travel in the air. My treasury is my custody of the Lord of Money [*Kubera*]. All the three worlds belong to me. Then what do I need money for? Which is the next?'

Chitrayodhi: 'Desire [*kama*].'

Ravana: 'Yes. That is what I search. Fulfill my ambition.'

Chitrayodhi: 'The workings of the mind are remarkable.'

Ravana: 'Yes, it is true.'

Chitrayodhi: 'Even then she does not belong to you. She is the one who came out from soil. She has no passion towards you. You have access to women more desirable than the wife of Indra. Then why do you need to have her?'

Ravana: 'A matter like this is not to be decided by others. Do we leave money thinking that others have also used it? And do we give up jewels only because they are produced from the earth? Do we give up the use of language even if it is difficult to master?'

Chitrayodhi: 'Now the only way is the use of weapon. My master has no sense of discrimination anymore.'

Ravana: 'Go and arrange a spy to gather news about Rama.'

Chitrayodhi: 'As you wish, my lord. I have spoken these words that go against your wishes, neither because I was afraid of the battle nor because of partiality towards the enemy. The persons who are real well-wishers say things that are in the interest of their master, even if there is a sword above their neck.'

Chitrayodhi retires to the greenroom after bowing to Ravana. After that, Ravana also retires and ends the day's performance.

DAY FOURTEEN

This day is known as Udyanapravesam *(Entry into the Garden). The royal and spectacular procession of Ravana going to Sita is the main attraction of this day. The procession starts from the left side of the stage. Ravana appears, placing his head on the hand of Varshavara, the pageboy. The acting starts with Ravana describing a* padadikesa *of Sita. He is afflicted with Kamadeva's arrows. By the end of this description, he has come to the front of the stage, near the lamp. Now he gives orders to Varshavara to make the way to Asokavanika, the garden where Sita is seated.*

Accompanied by Varshavara, Ravana retires to the greenroom. Again comes back asking, 'Where is the Asoka garden?' Looks around and sees the garden. Walks around and looks closely. 'Marvellous! I haven't seen a garden like this. How is that?' He describes the beauty of Asoka garden elaborately. He marvels at the beautiful trees, describes their width, height, branches, flowers, leaves, buds, fruits, creepers and so on. Then he sees a peacock dancing. He elaborates on the dance. Ravana thinks, 'This state of mind is wonderful! Even familiar things look good. Even if Sita sits here, she thinks about Rama. That is fair. She has spent a lot of time in the hermitage of Rama. Is she thinking about this place? No. She thinks about the hermitage of Rama only. The hermitage of Rama is pervaded by wild animals such as lions and tigers. How is this place? These trees are brought here and planted by me. How are the trees? They were the ornaments in heaven. Without these trees, heaven has no charm. Heaven is attractive only when these trees adorn the place. From where did I bring these trees? From the bank of the heavenly River Mandakini. There are many *kalpaka* trees spread in the bank of Mandakini. Did I go there only to pluck these trees? No. Did I steal these trees? Not at all. Indra was watching when the trees were uprooted. Was he alone watching? No. He was sitting in his throne surrounded by all the *devas* bowing at him. Did Indra resist me? No. While I was plucking them he remained there, bearing it. Did he close his eyes? No. He can't bat his eyes. So he sat without blinking his eye. Did he turn back? No. He has eyes at the back. What was the cause of bringing the trees? There are no such trees in the earth. So I plucked them to have such trees on the earth also. How was that? Once I was living happily in Lanka. One day I went to heaven along with the *rakshasa* army to conquer the *devas*. In the war, I defeated the *devas*, who fled from heaven. Then I looked around, and saw *kalpaka* trees on the banks of the Mandakini. I ordered the *rakshasas* to go and uproot them. On seeing their unsuccessful attempt, I descended from the chariot and drew them out without losing their roots. After that I brought them here. I tended to them properly.'

Ravana surveys the garden closely. He sees a couple of swans drinking honey, and cuckoos nibbling at the sprouts of flowers. He enacts the scene, first through the movement of eyes alone and then through gestures and reciting the verses. After that Ravana retires to the greenroom. Here ends the first half of Udyanapravesam.

DAY FIFTEEN

This is the continuation of Udyanapravesam. *The day starts with Ravana describing the* panchangam *of Sita. He is afflicted with Kamadeva's arrows.*

Recites verses.

'Kamadeva has won over the universe with the five flowers. What will be his power if he got the flower of *kalpaka*?'

Ravana (to Varshavara): 'Is Sita still sitting beneath the *simsapa* tree?'

Ravana listens to Varshavara saying, 'Yes, she is.' Ravana thinks, 'Alas! [*recites verse*] When I gaze at Sita with my twenty eyes, she looks at me with disgust. When I try to woo her with sweet words, she closes her eyes with her hands as if she can't bear me. When I request her, 'O Sita, please be kind to me', she meditates and chants the name of Rama. I am not experiencing her kindness. Where is Sita?'

Looks around and sees Sita and enacts her *padadikesa* description. By the time the description reaches Sita's breast, Ravana has moved near the lamp. Now he moves towards Sita with rhythmic steps. Sita is not physically present on the stage. There is a lamp lit on the right side of the stage that symbolises Sita. Ravana tries to win her over with presents such as garments and ornaments, betel leaf, etc. He completes the *padadikesa* description, is struck by Kamadeva's arrows and swoons. After waking up, again he offers *paan* and ornaments and pleads, 'O Sita, if you adorn yourself with the ornaments given by *kalpaka* trees and come with me, you can enjoy the Kailasa Mountain or the garden of heaven. Your sense of chastity has become a hurdle on the path of our heavenly pleasure.

(Here onwards, Sita's verses are rendered by the Nangiar)

Sita: 'O Ravana, your path to heaven is spread with sin. I wish to go to hell with my husband.'

Ravana: 'O Sita, only because of you, I am giving up my wives.'

Sita: 'Not only the wives, but you will also give up your life.'

Ravana: 'Yes, Kamadeva is taking away my life from me.'

Sita: 'Not Kamadeva. Rama who is more handsome than Kamadeva will take your life from you.'

Recites the verse.

Ravana: 'My chest is so strong that the Vajra of Indra has only left a speck there. So how can the weapon of a mere mortal living like a hunter face up to me?' Ravana bows to Sita who is sitting on the floor. Sita takes her feet back. Ravana then prostrates before her, saying, 'O Sita, your feet are my only shelter.'

Ravana in a happy mood as he ruminates on Sita's beauty.

Sita: 'Go and seek shelter at the feet of my husband.'

Now Ravana gets angry [*recites the verse*]. 'O Sita, your mother is the wife of all the kings in the world. You are the daughter of the earth; why do you then think about your chastity?'

He draws out the Chandrahasa sword and attempts to kill Sita. Suddenly, he notices the presence of his wife Mandodari there and feels embarrassed. He listens to the announcement from his aides that the night is over.

Finally, Ravana says, 'Let it be, for now. I will show you in the morning.'

Here ends the performance.

Glossary

aharya — one of the four-fold divisions of acting (*abhinaya*), it signifies the physical elements of acting, such as costume, make-up and stage properties

akasa — literally meaning 'space', it is one of the five elements (*mahabhutas*), which in Indian tradition is considered as the origin of all things

akasa charis — dance step in Kutiyattam, with thrusting movements into the air, integrating leaps and jumps

akkitha — invocatory songs in praise of different deities, sung by the Nangiar at the opening of a play

ambalavasi — communities who are attached to the temple in Kerala, assigned with different duties related to the temple

ambarayanam — dance steps, which indicate travelling in the sky, such as flying

angikabhinaya — one of the four-fold divisions of *abhinaya* or acting, it involves the communication of ideas through body movements such as dance, gestures and facial expression

arangettam — the first performance of an actor, indicating the commencement of his career as a full-fledged actor

arangu perumattam — dance step in Kutiyattam, with a intricate pattern of movements

arangutali — literally, 'sprinkling of water on the stage', it is one of the invocatory rituals in Kutiyattam

artha — means both, 'meaning' and 'wealth' in Sanskrit

ashtamangalyam — eight auspicious objects associated with Hindu religion in Kerala. These are gold, rice, sandalwood, small casket containing vermillion, *vaal kannadi* (a special kind of handled mirror), small lamp, *kindi* (metal water pot with a spout) and *kasavu mundu* (dhoti with a gold brocade border)

asramavarnana — literally, 'description of a spiritual abode'. In Kutiyattam, description of an *asrama* has a fixed convention of stock characteristics such as its tranquil atmosphere, spirituality, peaceful co-existence of different animals with contradictory traits, among others

atiyantharakkoothu — performances of Kutiyattam fixed as a matter of routine according to the annual calendar in specific temples of Kerala

attam — literally 'movement'. A general term in Malayalam signifying 'performance'

avabhrtasnanam — ritual bath taken at the end of a sacrifice

bhaumika chari — dance step in Kutiyattam, with movements of the feet close to the ground

chakshushayajna — literally, 'visual sacrifice'. A term adapted from Kalidasa's *Malavikagnimitra*. Drama is said to correspond to a sacrifice and, therefore, each and every component has sacred associations with it

chakyar — community of actors in Kerala who traditionally perform Kutiyattam

chari — refers to the movements from the feet to the torso, and are in fact dance steps described in the *Natya Sastra*. However, the terms *chari* and *gati* (gait) of Kutiyattam do not correspond to those mentioned in the *Natya Sastra*. In Kutiyattam, there are two varieties of *chari*, *akasa* and *bhaumika*, depending on whether the feet touch the ground or are kept above; there are many movement patterns for each of these

chayilyam — red colour from vermillion, used for make-up in Kutiyattam

chunda — herb placed on the lower eyelid of the actor as part of make-up, to give a red colour to the eyes

dharma — moral and ethical code of conduct, according to Hindu tradition

dheeralalita; dheerasanta; dheerodatta and *dheeroddhata*	different 'types' of characters of a heroic nature, representing mild, tranquil, sublime and valorous traits, respectively
dhvani	literally meaning 'resonance' in Sanskrit, it refers to the element of suggestion in poetry. Anandavardhana, in *Dhvanyaloka*, considers *dhvani* as the soul of poetry
edakka (idakka)	cylindrical small drum used as accompaniment in Kutiyattam
gati	refer to *chari*
goshthi kottal	part of the preliminaries of Kutiyattam, when the Nambiar performs a conventional drumming on the *mizhavu*, to the accompaniment of the devotional *akkitha* songs by the Nangiar praising deities such as Ganapati, Sarasvati and Siva
gurukula sampradaya; guru-shishya parampara	practice widely prevalent throughout India when knowledge in particular disciplines was transmitted through the disciple learning the art by staying at his master's house and painstakingly imbibing the skills through learning and assisting him
hamsapaksha;	varieties of hand poses (*hastas*) used in Kutiyattam, based on the text *Hastalakshanadeepika*
hastamudras	complex code of hand gestures through which the actor communicates the meaning of the verses in Kutiyattam
hastas	refer to *hamsapaksha*
kailasoddharanam and *parvativiraham*	literally, 'the lifting of Kailasa'. An interpretative acting sequence from Bhasa's *Abhishekanataka* in which the actor in the guise of Ravana elaborately depicts the lifting of the Kailasa Mountain and the subsequent turbulence and reconciliation in the marital life of Siva and Parvati
kalakalavadyam	part of *bhaumika chari*, with steps in which the legs are in a position close to each other
Kama, kamasaram kollal	Kama is the presiding deity of love in Indian mythology. *Kamasaram kollal* is a conventional acting sequence in which the hero expresses his love for the heroine (or vice versa). He describes the beauty of the heroine, acts as though he suffers the shafts of love. The fire of love intensifies his passion, leading to swooning and the cool breeze revives him a little
kazhchakkoothu	performances of Kutiyattam conducted in earlier times purely for the purposes of aesthetic enjoyment and not as a votive ritual
kesadipadam	literally, 'from head to foot'. A convention in Kutiyattam when the actor as hero describes the beauty of the heroine with a detailed description of each part of her body
kettatal	convention in Kutiyattam when the actor performs as though hearing another person's speech and responding to it
koothu	literally means 'acting' in Malayalam. In the context of Kutiyattam, there are three varieties of *koothu—Prabandha koothu*, the verbal narration, *Nangiar koothu*, the performance of the female performers called the Nangiars and Kutiyattam in which the male and the female performers act together
koppaniyikkal	theatric convention in Kutiyattam, when the actor elaborately represents the action of maids adorning the heroine with make-up and attire. In this context, the same actor usually acts as the heroine as well as the maids who adorn her
kramadeepikas	theatre manuals handed down through generations, in which physical details such as stage properties used in Kutiyattam and remuneration to actors were discussed in detail. These texts still remain as source for eliciting information on how Kutiyattam performances were held in earlier times
kriyas	acting sequences in Kutiyattam
kurumkuzhal; kuzhal, kuzhitalam	different musical instruments in Kutiyattam
marayilkriya	preliminary dance done by the actor behind the curtain
mayilattam	conventional dance representing the characteristics and gait of a peacock

meysadhakam	physical exercises and patterns of body movement through flexing, leaping and stretching in the air, hand stretching and rotation, which give strength and fitness to the body during training
mizhavocch appetuthal	first drum beats signifying the commencement of a play
mizhavu	main percussion instrument used in Kutiyattam, played by Nambiars, a community specialised in drumming. *Mizhavu* is a huge pot made of copper, with its mouth covered by leather
mutiyakkitha	concluding action at the end of every act, when the main character comes forward, takes off his crown, wears the red band of cloth on his forehead and after customary salutations, removes the wicks of the lamp to signify the conclusion of the performance
nataka	one of the ten forms of drama, according to the Sanskrit text *Dasarupaka*. According to definition, *nataka* is a play consisting of a well-known plot and a noble hero. It has a well-constructed body consisting of five or more acts, consisting of five stages in the development of the plot
natya	in Sanskrit corresponds to 'dramatic art'; the *Natya Sastra* has given an elaborate treatment of the different components of *natya*
natyotpatti	literally, the 'origin of dramatic art'. In the *Natya Sastra*, the origin of *natya* is discussed in detail, in which Bharata has established that it has a divine origin
navarasas	in Indian aesthetics, the word *rasa* suggests 'delight' and in the context of drama, it is the experience of joy derived from a performance. According to Bharata, *rasas* are nine in number
nepathya	backstage of a theatre hall, where the actors don make-up
netrabhinaya	theatric communication through the eyes, which the Kutiyattam actor has taken to great heights, to display subtle nuances of expressions
ninam	literally, 'blood'. In Kutiyattam, *ninam* refers to a scene in which specific characters such as Surpanakha in *Surpanakhankam* appear with maimed bodies and blood-spattered clothes, evoking terror and revulsion in the spectator. The 'blood' in this case is made with a mixture of lime and rice paste
nrittam	pure dance movements, without the aid of facial expressions and gestures
pakarnnattam	fundamental theatric device in Kutiyattam in which a character singlehandedly takes on the roles of other different characters to represent a situation, without changing costumes
panchangam	characteristic description of five organs such as head, eyes, chest, hands and feet of the hero/heroine as a mode of passionate remembrance in a romantic situation
panchapadavinyasa	conventional dance of 'five steps' in the opening of a play
parikrama	types of gaits associated with the entry of different characters in Kutiyattam
patappurappadu	literally, 'preparation for battle'. In Kutiyattam, the preparation of a hero for battle follows a conventional mode of performance, with specific dance movements and the description, repairing and wielding of each weapon
pathakakkayyukal	hand manipulations of a Nambiar, the *mizhavu*-drummer, during his training. The preparation to become a good drummer starts each morning when he practises the rhythm vocalisations (*vayttari*) in different tempos, starting with the slow, gradually reaching the fastest and coming back to the slow
prahasana	one of the ten forms of drama, according to the Sanskrit text *Dasarupaka*. It is characterised by the predominance of *hasya rasa*, the comic sentiment. Unlike the other varieties of dramas, it is of popular origin and vogue, and the subject matter is the dramatist's invention
prakarana	one of the ten forms of drama, according to the Sanskrit text *Dasarupaka*. It has an imaginary plot, and the predominant theme is love

purvaranga — preliminaries of a play, according to the *Natya Sastra*, which elaborately discusses the subject. In Kutiyattam, the *purvaranga* component is ritualistic and very elaborate

rajadhanivarnana — one of the set conventions in Kutiyattam where the details of a palace, such as the towers, halls, inner quarters and military arrangements, are elaborated in detail as 'descriptions' (*varnana*)

rajaseva — counter-interpretation to the original *purusharthas* (aims of life) in Indian classical tradition, the *vidushaka* in Kutiyattam has adopted his subversive aims, which include entertainment (*vinodam*), deceit (*vanchanam*), excellent food (*asanam*) and service under a king (*rajaseva*). *Rajaseva* also refers to acting as the king's friend and minister-of-sport (*narmasachiva*)

rasabhinaya — communicating the *rasas*, the appropriate emotions on the stage

rasika — an involved spectator who understands and appreciates the nuances of the play

sadhakam — practice by constant repetition, as part of training in Kutiyattam

sakhachankramanam — literally, 'branching out and spreading'. The cyclical narration in Indian tradition, where events are narrated not in a linear manner, but through a process of branching and sub-branching out into other different stories and events, without affecting the core of the narrative or registering any change in the axis of time. Kutiyattam has effectively used this non-linearity as a theatrical device

samapada — basic body posture of balance, closer to a sitting mode

sampradaya — manner, a tradition handed down through generations, which becomes the fixed characteristic of that school

samudravarnana — one of the set conventions in Kutiyattam where the details of an ocean, such as the great waves, ships, fish and whales, are elaborated in detail as 'descriptions' (*varnana*)

shodasha kriya — sixteen rites of passage enumerated in the classical tradition of Kerala, which include formal procedures to be conducted for a *brahmin* from birth to death

stobham — characteristic expressions adopted for different classes of characters in Kutiyattam, for example, for a bird (*pakshistobham*), monkey (*vanarastobham*), ogress (*rakshasistobham*)

sutradhara — literally, 'holder of a thread'. Applied to drama, the manager of a play who controls and directs the action on the stage

svarga; svargavarnana — heavens; one of the set conventions in Kutiyattam where the details of heaven, such as the palace of Indra, the great wish-granting tree (*kalpavriksha*), the divine elephant (*Airavata*), the gardens, the enjoyment of the celestial damsels, are elaborated in detail as 'descriptions' (*varnana*)

tala — literally, a 'clap'. In Indian classical arts, *tala* signifies the rhythmic pattern of a composition or movement

tayambaka — percussion performance prevalent in Kerala, using the instrument called *chenda*. In *tayambaka*, the main player at the centre starts in a slow tempo, improvises the rhythm and assisted by about half-a-dozen or more assistants, takes the percussion to a crescendo. Popularly performed during the temple festivals in Kerala

timila — drum shaped like an hourglass, which is used as a percussion accompaniment in Kutiyattam

tirassila — handheld curtain used in Kutiyattam

udyanavarnana — literally, 'description of a garden'. One of the set conventions in Kutiyattam where the details of a garden, such as the lovely trees, creepers and flowers, cuckoos and peacocks, ponds with full-blown lotuses swarming with bees, are elaborated in detail as 'descriptions' (*varnana*)

upanayanam — one of the *samskaras* (rituals) in the life of a *brahmin*, where he is initiated into the life of an ascetic student, by the tying of a sacred thread called *yajnopavita*

uzhichil	rigorous body massage done while training a student, to make his body supple and flexible
vachikabhinaya	one of the four-fold methods of acting (*abhinaya*), in which communication takes place through speech or the verbal medium
vanavarnana	literally, 'description of a forest'. One of the set conventions in Kutiyattam where the details of a forest, such as the huge trees, creepers, animals (lions and elephants), are elaborated in detail as 'descriptions' (*varnana*)
vasukeeyam	headgear with a slanted top, used for characters such as Bhima and Rama
vattattil chadi	gait with a circular movement, indicative of travelling some distance, which comes under the category of *akasa chari natakkal*
vayttari	vocalisation of rhythms in different tempos, memorised by a student for easy access and recall
vayu kodukkal	mode of infusing breath manipulation in acting, practised in Kutiyattam. Makes the actor achieve unbelievable elasticity in performance. Adapted from the psycho-physical gymnastic tradition of Kalarippayattu from Kerala, this relates to the channelling of vital energy into different organs of the body, thereby enlivening the performance. In specific terms, applying the breath to the eyes creates different *rasas* (*rasavayu*), to the voice (*svaravayu*) and to the other parts of the body, such as the torso or the fingers, also enhances their vigour
vazhipadukoothu	Kutiyattam plays performed in the olden days, strictly as votive offerings
vidushaka	comic character in a Sanskrit play who displays multi-faceted humour by subjecting himself and the world to ridicule. Plays a vital role in Kutiyattam, and is both inside and outside the situation in a play. He ridicules the king and the audience alike, interprets the Sanskrit verses into Malayalam, and acts as both a wit and a butt
vyayoga	one of the ten forms of drama, according to the Sanskrit text *Dasarupaka*. It has a well-known plot and usually consists of vigorous action
yajna; yajnasala	signifies a Vedic sacrifice. *Yajnasala* is a temporary structure erected for conducting the performance of the ritual

Acknowledgements

For the writing of this book, I am grateful to Margi, the institution I grew up with, especially Rama Iyer, my supporter who keeps Margi going; D. Appukkuttan Nair, my mentor; Ayyappa Paniker, my teacher and guide; the Kutiyattam community and the great gurus Paimkulam Rama Chakyar and Ammannur Madhava Chakyar for their vital insights and inspiration; P.K. Narayanan Nambiar for concrete ideas on training and the use of the *mizhavu*; Moozhikkulam Kochukuttan Chakyar for helping with the complexities of Kutiyattam's theatre grammar; Margi Madhu especially, for giving photographs, as well as valuable suggestions and comments on vital aspects in this book, and for the *attaprakaram* (choreographic text) of 'Asokavanikankam' for inclusion in this book; Margi Sathi for her unstinting support, as ever; all the performers and practitioners who participated in performances for the UNESCO nomination dossier; Adoor Gopalakrishnan, for taking up the visual documentation of Kutiyattam for the UNESCO Proclamation as a labour of love; K.K. Gopalakrishnan, for generously offering photographs from his private photo collection on Kutiyattam; Leah Lowthorp for freely sharing those amazing pictures for use in the book; Killimangalam Kunchu Namboothiripad, for accessing archival pictures and the Sangeet Natak Akademi, for allowing me to use select photographs.

I am also grateful to the Niyogis, Bikash and Tultul, who are not just publishers but art lovers; Ritu Khanna and Navkala Roy of Write Media, my parents, who helped deepen my interest in classical arts; my daughters, Amulya who diligently went through the final draft and Aditi, with the optimism that she will not let her work come in the way of her love for Kutiyattam; and finally Gopal, my husband, to whom I dedicate this book.

Bibliography

I. Primary Sources

A. Sanskrit

(1) Books

Bhasa. *The Thirteen Trivandrum Plays Attributed to Bhasa.* A.C. Woolner and Lakshman Sarup, trans. 1930. London: Oxford University Press.

Plays ascribed to Bhasa. C.R. Devadhar. 1937. Pune: Oriental Book Agency.

Bharatamuni. *Natyasastra with Abhinavabharati.* 1975. Varanasi: Banaras Hindu University.

Bodhayana. P. Anujan Achan, ed. 1924. *Bhagavadajjukam.* Trichur.

Ganapati Sastri, T. *Nagananda, Tapatisamvarana, Subhadradhananjaya.* Reprints with introduction by Unni N.P. 1987. Delhi: Nag Publishers.

Harsha. *Sri Harsha's Plays.* Bak Kunbae, trans. 1964. Delhi: Asia Publishing House.

Kulasekharavarman. *Subhadradhananjayam.* T. Ganapati Sastri, ed. 1912. Trivandrum Sanskrit Series XIII. Trivandrum.

—. *Tapatisamvaranam.* T. Ganapati Sastri, ed. 1911. Trivandrum Sanskrit Series XI. Trivandrum.

Mahendravikramavarman. *Mattavilasa Prahasana.* T. Ganapati Sastri, ed. 1917. Trivandrum Sanskrit Series LV. Trivandrum.

Nandikeswara. *Abhinayadarpanam.* Manmohan Ghosh, trans. 1975. Calcutta: Manisha Granthalaya.

—. *Natankusa.* ed. 1993. Tripunithura: Govt. Sanskrit College.

—. *Kutiyattm Theatre: The Earliest Living Tradition.* 2006. Tripunithura: International Centre for Kutiyattam and D.C. Books.

Ramachandra and Gunachandra. 1959. *Natyadarpanam.* Baroda Oriental Institute.

Raghavan Pillai, K. ed. 1961. *Abhijnanasakuntalacarcca.* Trivandrum Sanskrit Series.

Sagaranandin. 1972. *Natakalaksanaratnakosa.* Varanasi Chaukhamba Vidyabhavan.

Saktibhadra. *Ascharyachudamani.* K.P.A. Menon, ed. 1968. Delhi: Nag Publishers.

Saktibhadra. *Ascharyachudamani.* M.P. Narayana Pisharoti, ed. 1967. Trichur: Kerala Sangeeta Nataka Akademi.

Saradatanaya. *Bhavaprakasana.* Vadodara: Gaekwad Oriental Series, 45.

Sarngadeva. *Sangitaratnakaram.* Subrahmanya Sastri, ed. Madras: Adayar Library.

(2) Attaprakarams and Kramadeepikas

(i) Malayalam

Krishnachandran, V.R., ed. 1978. *Purusharathakoothu.* Trichur: Kerala Sahitya Akademi.

Kunjan Pillai, Suranat., ed. 1968. *Asokavanikankam Attaprakaram.* Bhashagranthavali 95. Trivandrum: Kerala University.

Narayana Pisharoti, K.P. ed. 1967. *Ascharyachudamani.* Trissur: Sangita Nataka Akademi.

—. *Subhadradhananjayam Onnamankam.* 1954. Geeta Press.

Narayanan Nambiar, P. K. *Sreekrishnacharitam Nangyarammakkoothu.* 1984. Trichur: National Book Stall.

Narayanan Nambiar, P.K., ed. 1980. *Mantrankam.* Trichur: Kerala Sahitya Akademi.

Narayana Pisharoti, K. P. 1965. *Toranayuddham Kutiyattam.* Trichur.

Narayana Pisharoti, K.P., ed. 1967. *Ascharyachudamani: Attaprakara and Kramadipika.* Trichur: Kerala Sangeetha Nataka Akademi.

—. *Subhadradhananjayam -Onnamankam.* 1954. Trichur: Geeta Press.

—. Abhishekanatakattinte Kramadipika, *Keli.* Trichur: Sangeetha Nataka Akademi (being serialised).

Satyavratan, Aranmula, ed. 1967. *Asokavanikankam Attaprakaram.* Kottayam: National Book Stall.

(ii) English

Jones, Clifford Reis and Namboothiripad, Leela, eds. 1984. *Ascharyachudamani: The Wondrous Crest Jewel in Performance.* New Delhi: Oxford University Press.

Paulose, K.G. 2000. *Bhagavatajjuka in Kutiyattam.* Text with com. New Delhi: Bharatiya Book Corporation.

–. 2000. *Bhima in Search of Celestial Flowers–Kalyana Saugandhika in Performance*. New Delhi: Bharatiya Book Corporation.

–. 2006. *Kutiyattam Theatre: The Earliest Living Tradition*. Thripunithura: International Centre for Kutiyattam and D.C. Books.

Venu, G., ed. 1989. *Production of a Play in Kutiyattam*. Documentation of Kutiyattam Series 1. Irinjalakkuda: Natanakairali.

II. Secondary Sources

A. Malayalam

(1) Books

Ammaman Tampuran. *Koothum Kutiyattavum*. Trichur: Vellakkal Narayana Menon, 1110 (M.E.).

Appukkuttan Nair, D., ed. 1976. *Margi Souvenir*.

Das, Bhargavinilayam. 2000. *Manimadhaviyam* (Biography of Mani Madhava Chakyar). Thiruvananthapuram: Cultural Publications, Govt. of Kerala, Thycaud.

Kalyanikutty Amma. 1978. *Mohiniyattam*. N.B.S. Kottayam.

Kerala Kalamandalam. 1968. *Kutiyattam Souvenir Abstracts*.

Krishnankutty Poduval. *Melappadam*. N.B.S. Kottayam.

Krishna Warrier, P.V. 1952. *Tolamahakavi*. Calicut: P.K. Bros.

Krishna Warrier, N.V. 1980. *Paripreksyam*. N.B.S. Kottayam.

Kumar, Ajit, N. 2004. *Kerala Samskaram*. Thiruvavanthapuram: Cultural Publications Department.

Kuttikrishna Menon, V.M. 1957. *Keralattile Natanakala*. Trissur: Mangalodayam.

–. 1997. *Kalayum vidyayum kazchappatukaliloote*. Trissur: Kerala Sahitya Akademi.

Madhava Chakyar, Mani. 1975. *Natyakalpadrumam*. Kottayam: National Book Stall.

Madhu, Margi. 2002. *Aattathinte Vazhiyatayalangal*. Trichur: Current Books.

Menon, Sreedhara, A. 1982. Rpt. 1992. *Kerala Samskaram*. Kottayam: National Book Stall.

Narayanan Nambiar, P.K. 1984. *Nangiarammakuttu*. Kerala Kalamandalam.

Narayanan Nambissan. 1958. *Hastalaksanadeepika*. Kozhikodu: K.P. Bros.

Narayana Pisharoti, K.P. *Koothambalangalil*. 1981. Trichur: Kairali Press.

–. 1960. *Kalalokam*. Trissur: Mangalodayam.

–. 1984. *Bharatamuniyuta Natyasastram*. Tr. 3 Vol. Trissur: Kerala Sahitya Akademi.

–. Ed. K.G. *Kutiyattattinte Puthiya Mukham*. 2005. Thripunithura: International Centre for Kutiyattam.

Payyanad, Raghavan, ed. 1997. *Kerala Folklore*. Payyannur: Folklore Fellows of Malabar.

Pisharoti, K.R. 1958. *Nammute Drsyakala*. N.B.S. Kottayam.
Prabhakara Warrier, K.M. 1985. *Kalakeli*. Kottayam: D.C. Books.

Ramavarma, K.T. 1981. *Ammannur Chachu Chakya*. Sukapuram: Vallathol Vidyapitham.

Sankunni Nair. M.P. 1987. *Natyamandapam*. Calicut: Matrubhumi.

Usha Nangiar. 2003. *Abhinetri*. Mumbai: Keli.

Varier, Raghava and Rajan Gurukkal, *Kerala Charitram*. 1991. Sukapuram: Vallathol Vidyapeetham.

Viswanathan, Nair, tr. *Chilapatikaram*. Trissur: Kerala Sahitya Akademi.

(2) Articles

Appukkuttan Nair, D. 1971. 'Kutiyattam', *Margi Souvenir*, pp. 21-41.

–. 1976. 'Kutiyattattile Abhinayam', *Margi Souvenir*, pp. xv-xvi.

–. 1976. 'Koothambalangal', *Margi Souvenir*, pp. xi-xiv.

–. 1976. 'Likhitangalilum Pracheenasahityattilum Koothineyum Kutiyattatteyum Pattiyulla Paramarsangal', *Margi Souvenir*.

–. 1976. 'Kutiyattattinupayogikkunna Adharagranthangal', *Margi Souvenir*, pp. vii-ix.

–. 1976. 'Prabandhakkoothu', *Margi Souvenir*, pp. xvii-xix.

–. 1976 'Nambiar, Nangiar Ennivarute Pankalittam', *Margi Souvenir*, pp. xx-xxii.

–. 1976. 'Natankusam Enna Kulsitakriti', *Margi Souvenir*. p. xxiii.

Ayyappa Paniker, K. 1985. 'Keraltile Vachikhyanaparamprяam', *Kalakeli Dr. S.K. Nair Samaranika*. Kottayam: D.C. Books, pp. 22-41.

Bhattathiripad, Ammini. 1976. 'Kutiyattam', *Margi Souvenir*, pp. 1-6.

Ezhuttachan, K.N. 1950. 'Koothum Kutiyattavum', *Matrubhumu Weekly*.

Kunjunni Raja, K. 'Natankusam', *Kalakeli. Dr. S.K. Nair Smaranika*.

Gopalakrishnan, Sudha. 1998. 'Kutiyattathile Aharyabhinayam'. Paper presented at Seminar on Kutiyattam Cheruthuruthy.

Madhava Chakyar, Irinjalakkuda. 1976. 'Kutiyattam Kshetrangalil', *Margi Souvenir*, pp. 7-10.

Madhava Chakyar, Ammannoor. 1976. 'Kutiyattam Kshetrangalil', *Margi Souvenir*.

Madhava Chakyar, Mani. 1967. 'Kuttum Kutiyattam', Tali Temple Kalasam Souvenir.

Madhu, Margi. 1999. 'Atiyantarakkothu' in *Kutiyattam*. Trivandrum, pp. 58-62.

Menon, K.P.S. 1976. 'Pramukha chakyar kudumbangalum chakyanmarum', *Margi Souvenir*.

Narayanan Nambiar, P.K. 1976. 'Kutiyattathile thalamelangal', *Margi*.

Narayana Paniker, Kavalam. 1980. 'Natakathile pazhamayute putuma', *Malayalamanorama, Annual*.

Narayana Pisharoti, K.P. 1976. 'Kutiyattathile Vidooshakan', *Margi*.

Menon, K.P.S. 1976. 'Pramukha Chakyar Kutumbangalum Chakyanmarum', *Margi Souvenir*, pp. 11-22.

Narayanan Nambiar, P.K. 1976. 'Kutiyattattile Talamelangal', *Margi Souvenir*, pp. 55-57.

Narayana Pisharoti, K.P. 1976. 'Kutiyattattile Vidushakan', *Margi Souvenir*, pp. 33-36.

Paulose K.G. 1992. 'Kutiyattavum anubandha kalakalum', *Bhashasahiti*. Journal of the University of Kerala, Trivandrum, Vol. 16.

–. 1993. 'Kulasekharanum kutiyattavum', *Sahityalokam*, Journal of Sahitya Akademi. Trichur.

–. 1995. 'Pakarnattam,' *Kaladarpanam*, Aluva.

–. 1995. 'Malayalathile adyathe Nirupanagrandham', *Bhashaposhini*. Kottayam: Malayala Manorama.

–. 1995. 'Kutiyattathile Vidushakan', *Kaladarpanam*.

–. 1997. 'Kutiyattathinte Caritram', *Keli*. Trichur: Kerala Sangita Nataka Akademi.

–. 1997. 'Kutiyattathile Parusha Saundaryam', *Desabhimani*. Kochi.

–. 1998. 'Kutiattathinte Adhunika Mukham', *Desabhimani Keraliyam Special*.

–. 2000. 'Kutiyattachintakal', *Desabhimani Keraliyam Special*.
Pisharoti, K.H. 1967. 'Ksetrakalakal', *Tali Temple Kalasam Souvenir*.

Rajagopalan, L.S. 1974. 'Samavedavum Sangitavum', *Guruvayoor Temple Renovation Souvenir*.

Rama Chakyar, Paimkulam. 1976. 'Kutiyattattile Ragangal (Svarangal)', *Margi Souvenir*, pp. 23-32.

Ramnarayan, Gowri, 'Rukmini Devi: Dancer, Reformer, A Profile', Part 2 in *Sruti 9*, pp. 17-29.

Sankunni Nair, M.P. 1977. 'Kallum Poovum', *Matrubhumi Weekly*. Calicut.

–. 1977. '*Tozhano Tolan?*' *Matrubhumi Weekly*, Calicut.

Sarma, V.S. 1980. 'Talavum Melavum Kutiyattattil', *Sangeetika*, pp. 75-99.

B. English

(1) Books

Rangacharya, Adya. 1971. *The Indian Theatre*. Delhi: National Book Trust.

–. 1966. *Introduction to Bharata's Natya Sastra*. Bombay: Popular Prakasan.

Mitra Sastri, Ajay. 1975. *India as Seen in the Kuttaneemata of Damodaragupta*. Delhi: Motilal Banarasidass.

Coomaraswamy, Ananda and Gopalakrishnayya Duggirala. 1997. *The Mirror of Gesture: Abhinaya Darpana of Nadikeswara*. Third edition. New Delhi: Munshiram Manoharlal Publishers.

Ratnam Rangary, Anila. 1979. *Natyabrahman–The Theatre Universe* (A Concept of Ancient Indian Theatre). Madras: Society for Archeological Historical and Epigraphical Research.

Bhat, G.K. 1959. *The Vidushaka*. Ahmedabad: The New Order Book Company.

–. 1975. *Sanskrit Drama–A Perspective on Theory and Practice*. Dharwar: Karnataka University.

Bhat, S.C. 1961. *Drama in Ancient India*, New Delhi: Amrit Book Co.

Byrsky, M. Christopher. 1974. *Concept of Ancient Indian Theatre*. Delhi: Munshiram Manoharlal Publishers.

–. 1997. *Natya and Yajna*. Tripunithura: Govt. Sanskrit College.

Chaitanya, Krishna. 1972. *Kerala*. New Delhi: National Book Trust.

Dange, Sadashiv A. 1963. *Critiques on Sanskrit Drama*, Moradabad: Darsana Printers.

Eswaran Namputiri E. 1983. *Balaramabharatam–A Critique on Dance and Drama*. Trivandrum: Kerala Samskrtam Publications.

Byrski, M. Christopher. 1974. *Concept of Ancient Indian Theatre*. Delhi: Munshiram Manoharlal Publishers.

Guha-Thakurta, Tapati. 1992. *The Making of 'New' Indian Art: Artists, Aesthetics and Nationalism in Bengal, c. 1850–1920*. Cambridge: Cambridge University Press. p. 147.

Gupta, C.B. 1954. *Indian Theatre*. Delhi: Motilal Banarasidass.

Haas, George C.O. trans. 1962. *The Dasarupaka of Dhananjaya*. Delhi: Motilal Banarasidass.

Keith, A.B. 1924. *Sanskrit Drama*. Oxford: Clarendon Press.

Kunjunni Raja, K. 1964. *Kutiyattam: An Introduction*. Delhi: Sangeet Natak Akademi.

Kuiper, F.B.J. 1979. *Varuna and Vidushaka*. New York: North Hill and Publishing Co.

Kulkarni, K.P. 1927. *Sanskrit Drama and Dramatists*.

Kunjunni Raja, 1964. *Kutiyattam: An Introduction*. Delhi: Sangeet Natak Akademi.

Mankad, D.R. 1960. *Ancient Indian Theatre*. Charotar Book Stall.

Michael Lockwood et al. 1991. *King Mahendravarman's Plays*. Madras: Chidambaram Research Associates.

Mehta, Tarla. 1995. *Sanskrit Play Production in Ancient India*. Delhi: Motilal Banarsidass.

Paniker, Nirmala. 1992. *Nangiar Koothu*. Documentation of Kutiyattum Series 2. Irinjalakkuda: Natanakairali.

Panchal, Govardhan. 1996. *The Theatre of Bharata and Some Aspects of Sanskrit Play Production*. New Delhi: Munshiram Manoharlal Publishers.

. 1984. *Kuttampalam and Kutiyattam*. Delhi: Sangeet Natak Akademi.

Paulose K.G. 1998. *Kutiyattam–A Historical Study*. Govt. Sanskrit College.

–. 2000. *An Introduction to Kutiyattam*. Tripunithura: International Centre for Kutiyattam.

Raghavan, V. 1993. *Sanskrit Drama; its Aesthetics and Production*. Madras.

Rajagopalan, L.S. 1997. *Women's Role in Kudiyattam*. Chennai: K.S.R. Institute.

–. 2000. *Kudiyattam: Preliminaries and Performance*. Chennai: K.S.R. Institute.

Rajendran, C. 1989. *The Traditional Sanskrit Theatre of Kerala*. Calicut: University of Calicut.

Richmond, Farley, ed. 1990. *Indian Theatre: Traditions of Performance*. Honolulu: Univ. of Hawaii.

Sekhar, Indu. 1960. *Sanskrit Drama: Its Origin and Decline*. Leiden: E. Brill.

Subrahmania Iyer. 1984. S. *Sanskrit Dramas*, New Delhi: Sundeep Prakasan.

Shulman, David Dean. 1985. *The King and the Clown in South Indian Myth and Poetry*. Princeton: Princeton University Press.

Tarlekar, G.H. 1991. *Studies in the Natya Shastra, with Special Reference to the Sanskrit Drama in Performance*. Second ed. Delhi: Motilal Banarsidass.

Unni, N.P. 1977. *Sanskrit Dramas of Kulasekhara*: A Study. Trivandrum: Kerala Historical Society.

Unni, N.P. and Bruce M. Sullivan. 1995. *The Sun God's Daughter and King Samvarana: Tapati-Samvaranam and the Kutiyattam Drama Tradition*. Delhi: Nag.

Varad Pande M.L. 1981. *Traditions of Indian Theatre*. New Delhi: Abhinav Publications.

Varma K.M. 1957. *Natya Nrtta and Nrtya–Their Meaning and Relation*. Bombay: Oriental Organisation.

Vatsyayan, Kapila. 1977. *Classical Indian Dance in Literature and the Arts*. Second ed. New Delhi: Sangeet Natak Akademi.

–. 1980. *Traditional Indian Theatre–Multiple Streams*. New Delhi: National Book Trust.

–. 1983. *The Square and Circle of Indian Arts*. New Delhi: Roli Books International.

Wilson, H.H. 1935. *The Theatre of the Hindus*. Calcutta: Susil Gupta.

Yajnik, R.K. 1933. *The Indian Theatre*, London: George Allen and Unwin.

Yarrow, Ralf, 2001. *Indian Theatre: Theatre of Origin, Theatre of Freedom*. London: Cusron Press.

(2) Articles

Appukkuttan Nair. 1977. 'Abhinaya in Kutiyattam'. *Theatre India*. Trichur: Kerala Sangeetha Nataka Akademi.

–. 'Bhasa's Plays in Kutiyattam.' Unpublished Paper.

Bhat, G.K. 1954. 'The Mahabharata Plays of Bhasa'. *Annals of the Bhandarkar Oriental Research Institute (35)*.

–. 'Bhasa's Stage', *Journal of Oriental Institute*, Vol. 2, Parts 1- 4.

Byrski, Christopher M. 'Is Kutiyattam a Museum Piece?' *Sangeet Natak* (5).

Chandrahasan, K.A. 'Kutiyattam: The Traditional Sanskrit Theatre of Kerala'. *Purnatrayi*. Vol. XVII, No. 1.

Chari, V.K. 'Lokadharmi and Natyadharmi.' *The Adayar Library Bulletin*. Vol. 49.

Daugherty, Diane. 1996. 'The Nangyar: Female Ritual Specialist of Kerala.' *Asian Theatre Journal* 13:1, pp. 54-67.

–. 2000. 'Fifty Years On: Arts Funding in Kerala Today.' *Asian Theatre Journal* 17:2, pp. 237-252.

De, S. K. 'The Curtain in Ancient Indian Theatre', *Bharatiya Vidya*. Vol. 9.

Enros, Pragna Thakar. 1981. 'Producing Plays in the Tradition of Kutiyattam.' *Sanskrit Drama in Performance*, ed. Rachel Van M. Baumer and James R. Brandon. Honolulu: University of Hawaii Press.

Ezhuttassan, K.N. 1966. 'Inscriptional and Literary References to Kuttu'. *Kutiyattam Seminar Abstracts*, Kerala Kalamandalam.

Feistel, Hartmut-Ortwin. 'The Purvaranga and the Chronology of Pre-classical Sanskrit Theatre', *Samskrita Ranga Annual* (6), pp.1- 26.

Gopalakrishnan, Sudha. 1988. 'Kutiyattam and its Correspondence to the *Natya Sastra'. Sangeet Natak 88*, pp. 32-38.

–. 1991. 'Kutiyattam and Noh: Commonalities and Divergences'. *Sangeet Natak 99*, pp. 35-43.

–. 1997. 'Rasa in Kutiyattam and Kathakali'. Paper presented at 'Seminar on Rasa' in Performance. Varanasi.

–. 2006. 'Expression and Impersonation in Kutiyattam, Krishnattam and Noh', *Masked Ritual and Performance in South India*. ed. David Shulman. Centres for South and South Asian Studies, Michigan University.

Gonda, Jan. 1967. 'The Indra Festival according to the Atharvavedins', *Journal of American Oriental Society (87).*

Jefferds Keith N. 1981. 'Vidushka versus Fool: A Functional Analysis', *Journal of South Asian Literature (16)*, p 61-73.

Jones, Clifford R. 1966. 'The Kuttampalam or Temple Theatre in Kerala'. *Kutiyattam Seminar Abstracts.* Kerala Kalamandalam.

–. 1972. 'Temple Theatre and the Sanskrit Tradition in Kerala.' *Sanskrit Ranga Annual.*

–. 1975. 'Notes on the Restoration of a Temple Theatre for Sanskrit Drama.' *Journal of the National Centre for Performing Arts. Vol. II, No. 2.*

–. 1983. 'Notes on Comparison of Vedic Mudras used in Kutiyattam and Kathakali' in *AGNI: The Vedic Ritual of the Fire Altar 2 Vols.*, ed. Frits Staal. Berkeley: Asian Humanities Press, pp. 380-381.

–. 'A Pattern for Survival: Literary and Epigraphical References to the Chakyars, Custodians of Sanskrit Drama in the Temple of Kerala.' Univ. of Pennsylvania.

–. 1973. 'Source Material for the Construction of the Natyamandapa in the Silparatna and tantrasamucchaya, Silpabhagam.' Journal of the American Oriental Society. Vol. 43, No. 3, pp. 286-296.

Krishnan Namboothiripad, P.C. 1966. 'The Ritual and Religious Aspects of Kutiyattam', *Kutiyattam Seminar Abstracts.* Kerala Kalamandalam.

Kuiper, F.B.J. 1975. 'Worship of the Jarjara on the Stage', *Indo-Iranian Journal* (16), pp. 241-268.

Kunjunni Raja K. 1964. 'Kutiyattam–Its Form and Significance as Sanskrit Drama', *Samskrita Ranga Annual 5*, pp. 77-87.

–. 'Natankusa–A Goad On Actors', *Samskrita Ranga Annual 8*, pp. 118-123.

–. 1959-60. 'The Staging of Sanskrit Plays in the Traditional Sanskrit Theatre', *Samskrita Ranga Annual* 2.

Madhava Chakyar, Mani. 1966. 'Means of Editing or Condensing Kutiyattam Plays within the Traditional Structure'. *Kutiyattam Seminar Abstracts.* Kerala Kalamandalam.

Madhava Chakyar, Irinjalakkuda. 'Lineages of Chakyar Families'. *Kutiyattam Seminar Abstracts.*

Mathur, J.C. 1973. 'Inside a Temple Theatre.' *Sangeet Natak*, No. 26.

Menon, K.P.S. 'Aspects of the Development of Kathakali in Relation to its Protoform in Kutiyattam'. *Kutiyattam Seminar Abstracts.*

Narayanan Nambiar. 'Thalam and Vadyam in Kutiyattam.' *Kutiyattam Seminar Abstracts.*

Narayana Menon, V.K. 1977. 'The Place of Music in Indian Dance Drama', *Theatre India*, Trichur Sangeeta Nataka Akademy.

Narayana Panikkar, Kavalam. 1977. 'Thouryathrikam on the Traditional Stage of Kerala.' *Souvenir of the All India Theatre Festival.*

Narayana Pisharoti, K.P. 'Attaprakarams and Kramadipikas: Their Dates and Contents'. *Kutiyattam Seminar Abstracts.*

Oleksiw, Susan. 1977. 'Mantrankam at Peruvanam'. *Sangeet Natak 45*, pp. 43-46.

Panchal, Govardhan. 'Kuthambalam–Sanskrit Stage of Kerala'. *Sangeet Natak 8*, pp. 17-30.

–. 'Many Splendered Theatres of India'. *Purnatrayi.*

–. 1977. 'Kutiyattam and its Links with the Classical Sanskrit Drama.' *Journal of the Oriental Institute*, Baroda, Vol. 26, No. 2.

–. 1977. 'Kuttampalam and its Links with Bharata's Stage'. *Journal of the National Centre for Performing Arts*, Vol. VI, No. 1.

—. 1984. 'Kutiyattam: The Sanskrit Dramatic Tradition of Kerala. *The India Magazine*.

—. 'Kutiyattam: A Historical Study' *Purjatrayi*. Vol. XVII, No.2.

—. 1992. 'Vyangyavyakhya.' *Sri Ravi Varma Samskrta Granthavali Journal* 19:2, pp. 1-12.

Paulose, K.G. 'Vyangyavyakhya'—with notes and English Translation. *Purnatrayi, Journal of Ravivarma Samskrta Grandhavali*, Vol. 19 (1992) and Vol. 20 (1993).

—. 1993. 'Presentation of Inner Meaning—A Tradition Peculiar to Kerala Sanskrit Theatre'. All India Oriental Conference, XXVI, Pune.

—. 1997. 'Buddhism and Sankrit Theatre'. *Journal, South Indian History Congress*, Kalady, Kerala.

—. 1998. 'Natya and Attam—A study on the origin of Kudiyattam based on Vyangyavyakhya'. *Purnatrayi, Journal of Ravivarma Samskrta Grandhavali*, Vol. XXII.

—. 1998. 'Classical Theatre of Kerala During the Last 500 Years'. *International Conference on Europe and South Asia—500 years, Institute of Social Sciences*. New Delhi.

—. 2000. 'Traditional Theatre'. *National Seminar on Tradition and Contemporary Theatre*. Paper presented at Sahitya Akademi, New Delhi.

—. 2000. 'A Critical Approach to Some Kutiyattam Practices'. *Facets of Indian Culture*. New Delhi: Bharatiya Book Corporation.

Pisharoti, K.N. 'Kutiyattam'. *Kutiyattam Seminar Abstracts*.

Pisharadi, K.R. 1932. 'Kerala Theatre—I'. *Annamalai University Journal*, Madras, Vol. 1, No. 1, pp. 91-113.

—. 1932. 'Kerala Theatre—II'. *Annamalai University Journal*, Madras, Vol. 3, No. 2, pp. 142-160.

—. 1941. 'Ancient India Theatre'. *Rajah Sir Annanmalai Cettiar Commemoration*.

—. 1950. 'The Time of Staging a Sanskrit Drama'. *Indian Historical Quarterly*.

Raghavan. M.D. 1947. 'Folk Plays and Dances Of Kerala'. *Ramavarma Archaeological Society*. Thrissur.

Raghavan, V. 'Natyadharmi And Lokadharmi'. *Journal of Oriental Research*. Madras. Vol. 7 and Vol. 8.

—. 1957. 'Sanskrit Drama and Performance'. *Madras University Journal*. Vol. 29, No. 1, July.

—. 1963. 'Kutiyattam'. *Natya*, Vol. 6, No. 3.

—. 1966-1967. 'Kutiyattam: Its Form and Significance as Sanskrit Drama'. *Samskrita Ranga Annual 5*.

Rajagopalan, L.S. 1969. 'Music in Kootiyattam'. *Sangeet Natak* 10.

—. 1974. 'The Mizhav'. *Journal of the Music Academy of Madras*.

—. 1980-1987. 'Consecration of the Kuttambalam Temple Theatres of Kerala.' *Samskrita Ranga Annual* 8, pp. 22-40.

—. 1974. 'Eloquent Eyes—Bhava Abhinaya in Kutiyattam'. Madras. Journal of the Music Academy.

—. 1988-1990. 'Angika and Sattvika Abhinayas in Kutiyattam'. *Samskrita Ranga Annual* 9, pp. 46-54.

—. 1997. 'Comic Relief by Characters Other than Vidushaka in Kutiyattam'. *Purnatrayi, Ravivarma Samskrita Grandhavali*. Tripunithura, Vol. 23.

Rama Chakyar, Painkulam. 'Exposition of Present Stage Technique in *Kutiyattam*'. *Kutiyattam Seminar Abstracts*.

—. 'Musical Aspects of Kutiyattam'. *Kutiyattam Seminar Abstracts*.

Rama Pisharoti, R. 1934. 'Kerala Theatre'. *Journal of the Annamalai University*.

Richmond, Farley P. eds. Farley P. Richmond, Darius Swann, and Phillip B. Zarilli. 1990. *Kutiyattam in Indian Theatre: Traditions of Performance*. Honolulu: University of Hawaii Press.

—. 1978. 'The Rites of Passage in Kutiyattam'. *Sangeet Natak* 50.

—. 1989. 'The Bhasa Festival Trivandrum India'. *Asian Theatre Journal* (6).

—. 1971. 'Some Religious Aspects of Traditional Indian Theatre'. *The Drama Review (15)*.

Richmond Farley and Yasmin Richmond. 1985. 'The Multiple Dimensions of Time and Space in Kutiyattam, The Sanskrit Theatre of Kerala'. *Asian Theatre Journal* 2 No. 1.

—. 'Space in Kutiyattam—The Sanskrit Theatre of Kerala'. (Unpublished Paper).

Sreedharan Nambhoodiri, Kurumappilli. 'Mantrankam'. *Kutiyattam Seminar Abstracts*.

Sullivan, Bruce M. 1997. 'Temple Rites and Temple Servants: The Role of Religion in the Survival of Kerala's Kutiyattam Drama Tradition.' *International Journal of Hindu Studies* 1, pp. 97-115.

Sullivan, Bruce M. and N.P. Unni. 1996. 'Tapati-Samvaranam: A Kutiyattam Drama by Kulashekhara Varman.' *Asian Theatre Journal* 13:1, pp. 26-53.

Unni, N.P. 'Nagananda on the Kerala Stage'. *Purnatrayi* Vol. XVII No. 1.

—. 1977. 'Consecration of the Actor in Kerala'. *Journal of Kerala Studies*, Trivandrum, Vol. 4.

—. 1973. 'Mattavilasa on the Kerala Stage'. *Journal of Kerala Studies*, Vol. I, No. 1.

Varad Pande, M.L. 1979. ' Religion and Theatre'. *Sangeet Natak*, pp. 53-54.

Vatsyayan, Kapila. 1980. 'Kutiyattam', *Traditional Indian Theatre: Multiple Streams*. Kottayam: National Book Trust.

Venu, G. 1995. 'Recording Movement Through Dance Notation'. *RASA–The Indian Performing Arts in the Last 25 Years*. Vol 1. Calcutta: Anamika Kalasangam.

III. Unpublished Theses

Gilchriest Hatch, Emily. 1934. *The Kathakali: The Indigenous Drama of Malabar.* Cornell University.

Jones, Clifford R. 1967. *The Temple Theatre of Kerala: Its History and Description.* University of Pennsylvania.

Nambudripad, P.C. *Kutiyattam*. Madras University.

Sanalkumar Thampuran. *Natyadharmi and Lokadharmi in Kutiyattam.* Doctoral Thesis (unpublished). University of Calicut.

Sowle, John Steven. 1982. *The Traditions, Training and Performance of Kutiyattam: Sanskrit Drama in South India.* Doctoral Thesis (Unpublished). University of California, Berkeley.

Index